THE WIDOW ON DWYER COURT

BOOKS BY LISA KUSEL

STANDALONE NOVELS
Hat Trick
The Widow on Dwyer Court

SHORT STORY COLLECTIONS
Other Fish in the Sea

NONFICTION
Rash: A Memoir

THE WIDOW ON DWYER COURT

LISA KUSEL

BLACKSTONE
PUBLISHING

Printed in the United States of America

Paperback edition: 2024
ISBN 979-8-212-63291-1
Fiction / Thrillers / Suspense

Version 2

Blackstone Publishing
31 Mistletoe Rd.
Ashland, OR 97520

www.BlackstonePublishing.com

For MH

Sexuality is the lyricism of the masses.

—Charles Baudelaire

KATE

I am so amped up to start writing book two in my *Strong Lust* series that I jump out of bed before the alarm rings, brew a batch of coffee, then lock myself in my office. Other than the low hum of my computer powering on, the dark room is silent.

I open a new document and lean forward. All I need to do is figure out how to get Macon Strong and Lizzie Wilder to hook up. I want something fresh. Thrilling. After that, the rest of the story will flow.

Thirty minutes later I am still staring at a blinking cursor. And now it's time to wake Finley.

Darn.

I walk down the hall to Finley's room and open the door. Because the lilac-colored quilt covers her entire body, all I can see of my daughter is a patch of white hair. Between my dirty blond, straight hair and my husband Matt's thick dark brown hair, it's a wonder the two of us produced a child with curls the color of sun-kissed snow.

"Wakey-wakey, sleepy head," I say, giving my ten-year-old

a gentle nudge and a kiss on her head. "What do you want for lunch? Cream cheese and jelly sandwich or a frozen burrito?"

Finley springs up and throws her small body onto Munch, our rescued terrier who sleeps at her feet every night. "Um, can I just have mac and cheese?" she says, rubbing Munch's belly.

"Sure. Go wash up." Just as I am about to open the top dresser drawer Finley screams, "No, Mom, let me! I wanna choose what to wear today."

I drop my hand. "But I always lay out your clothes," I say, sounding whiny even to my own ears.

"Okay, but I'm ten years old. I don't need your help."

You don't need my help? I move toward the closet. "Can I at least—"

"No!" Finley jumps in front of the door, her arms stretched out sideways, blocking all access. "It'll be fine, Mom," she says with the assurance of someone twice her age.

Trying to act nonchalant I utter, "Have it your way," and walk out to the kitchen, Munch hot on my heels. After letting him outside, I scoop some leftover noodles into a Tupperware and pack it, along with a plastic spoon, a tangerine, a package of seaweed strips, and a juice box into Finley's pink polka-dotted Lands' End lunch box. Then I grab a red Sharpie and draw a big heart on a scrap of paper with "I Love You. Have a Great Day!" written inside it. *At least I can still do this for you*, I think, wondering when it is that mothers are supposed to allow their babies to drop out of the nest. Most of the women in our subdivision hover over their young so profusely, one would think their arms are propellers.

Just as I am zipping the lunch box closed, Finley comes in wearing a pair of dark blue jeans and a plain dark blue T-shirt. "See," she says, twirling in a circle. "I look good, right?"

"You look fabulous," I reply to the child-sized blueberry. "Go eat your cereal. I'll get dressed and walk you to school."

"You don't need to," Finley mumbles through a mouthful of Cheerios.

"I know I don't need to, but I thought you like it when I—"

"Nah. I'm going by myself today." Finley drinks down the milk, places the bowl into the sink and gives me a quick kiss on the cheek. "See ya later, Mommy."

It's only once the door to the mudroom slams that I realize how much her words sting. I know I should be proud of my child's growing independence, yet I can't shake the feeling that I've been rejected.

Sighing, I chastise myself for being too sensitive. Finley loves me. I'm the best mother in the world.

Ten minutes later, I'm back in my office gazing out the window at my backyard. I rub the scar on the side of my nose as I watch a crow land on the ground. It tucks in its wings and looks around with small quick snaps of its head. Five feet away Munch lies sleeping in a patch of sunlight.

"Macon, how are you going to meet Lizzie, the love of your life?" I ask the crow.

As though it actually hears me, the bird turns an eye toward me, caws, and flies off. I stand motionless, waiting for something more to happen. Other than Munch's back paw twitching, nothing does.

I close the curtains and sit down at my desk. Just for the heck of it I type:

Lizzie Wilder appeared on the crest of a mountain atop a white steed, her long diaphanous gown flowing across its bristling flanks. Macon Strong emerged from the barn, then looked up, whereupon his heart—

"That is so lame, Kate," I say, reaching into my pajama pants to scratch my upper thigh. Darn, but it's downy down there. When was the last time I got waxed? December? January? It isn't as if anyone is running their hands across my furry skin. But soccer season will be starting soon, which means I'll put on shorts—unless the weather stays cool, in which case I could keep wearing my sweat—

"Where was I?" I say, shaking my head.

I swivel in my chair and force my brain to focus on what I do best: contemporary erotic romance, with a bit of suspense thrown in for good measure. Why am I feeling the need to veer outside my skill set when I have a deadline to meet? "Think, Kate, think."

What if Lizzie's car breaks down while she's driving along the back roads to Canada? Or maybe she's the niece of the farm's owner. A herdsman's sister? A reporter doing a story on Vermont cheese? My mind leaps from one uninspired idea to another like a goat bounding its way up a rocky hill.

I look around my office searching for something to inspire me. Out of the corner of my eye I see the Stockwell Farms newsletter on top of the pile of mail on my desk. Stockwell Farms is a two-thousand-acre, working farm open to the public. People come from all over the world to hike the trails, pet the goats, take in the magical views of Lake Champlain, and taste the cheeses produced from the farm's Brown Swiss cows. Before Matt and I got married I worked there as an assistant marketing director and now Finley goes to their farm camp every summer. Stockwell Farms is the reason Macon Strong became a cheesemaker.

I flip through it. On page three there's a profile of Sasha, one of the farm's new interns who works with the dairy cows. She has long black hair and clear tanned skin. She is so gorgeous that I already know Sasha's fictional double will someday find herself moaning under some sexy hunk's body. But not in this book. This one is all about Lizzie and Macon.

I rip out the page and am just about to slip it into the CHARACTERS folder in my desk drawer when the answer hits me like a brick thrown through the window. "Duh! Lizzie's an intern!" I yell into the empty room.

Not entirely original, but good enough to get the story rolling.

I kick off my fuzzy slippers and lean back in my chair. "How's it going in your world these days, Macon Strong?" I ask.

Slowly, the story unravels like a ball of yarn tossed across the room: Macon's gotten over Phionna, his lover from book one, and now he's pining for his new conquest Lizzie, the intern who's run off. He's missing her. Maybe he's reminiscing about their too-short time together. I stop swiveling, close my eyes and visualize Macon on the farm. Then I sit forward and type:

Strong Lust: Book Two
by Daphne Moore

Macon Strong couldn't get Lizzie Wilder out of his head. Or his loins, for that matter. Ever since she went off to New York City to find her own place in the food world, he dragged through his days as Head Cheesemaker for Smiling Girl Farm. He'd been at it for close to a year now, and up until Lizzie took his heart, he relished his job, the sensual, almost arousing, aspects of turning cow milk into an artisan delicacy. Up at dawn to grab the first milking of the day—warm in the buckets; smelling of the sweet grass the herd eats. Then to the creamery where he'd Spotify sexy and soulful voices like Bèla Fleck or Alison Krauss as he filled the vats, added the cultures, then the rennet and salt. After that he'd grab a coffee break.

Or if Lizzie was on that day, it'd be a sex break—a quickie before they had to run from her cabin on the farm back to the vats where they'd drain the whey and knit the curds.

The first time they made love, it was to The Barr Brothers' "Half Crazy." She'd turned him on to plenty of good tunes in the short time she was an intern at Smiling Girl. *Turned him on* was more like it. Damn her for showing up that first day with her hair in pigtails and wearing a halter shirt that showed off her ample breasts and tightly muscled arms. She'd just graduated with a degree in Food Science and wanted to try her hand at cheese. Macon had taken on a few interns in his day, but not one that looked as hot in a hairnet, rubber boots, and white coat as Lizzie did. From the first day she stood next to him while they pressed the curds into the molds, Macon knew he had to have her.

And have her he did, four days into her three-week internship. Right after he asked her how she liked living in the "cheese shed," the one-room outbuilding where the rotating interns crashed.

"I like it just fine," Lizzie had replied with an impish grin. "Not sure I'd want to winter in it, but when I get the stove going, it's pretty cozy."

"Cozy, huh? Never heard anyone else describe it like that."

"It's all in the way you see what's in front of you, Macon," she'd said. "Hey, you want to come share a beer in my *cozy* cabin when we're done here?"

At the time, he'd wondered what Miles and Arthur—the couple who owned the farm in Holland, Vermont—might think about him fraternizing with the unpaid help, but he'd crammed the thought down one of the drains they were cleaning and said, "Indeed I do, Lizzie."

They'd walked together into the anteroom, where he removed his white coat and yanked the net from his head, sending his long black hair tumbling past his broad shoulders. As he bent to put on his cowboy boots, he sensed Lizzie's eyes roaming down his spine, checking out his butt.

Fifteen minutes later he had her up against the cabin wall. Lizzie was breathing fast. He took her hand and put it on his crotch so she would know what was coming. Something big and hard and far too inactive for such a good-looking twenty-nine-year-old man.

"I want you, Lizzie, I want you now," he whispered into her ear as he undid her flannel shirt. Before he got to the last button she pushed him away and dropped to her knees. While slowly unzipping his jeans, she peered up at him, her eyes—

The front door slams, and I jerk my head up. "Finley, is that you, kiddo?" I look at the clock and see that it's far too early for her to be home from school.

"No, Kate. It's me."

"Matt? What are you doing—" My husband bursts into the room and plants a hard kiss on my mouth.

"I thought you were coming home tomorrow?" I ask, the sweet vibration still on my lips.

He throws himself onto the couch. "I moderated three sessions yesterday that were so outstanding the beer folks canceled the rest of them. So, here I am," he says, aglow with self-satisfaction.

"Beer guys? I thought you were doing the new deodorant rollout."

"That's in Philly in two weeks," he says. Matthew Parsons—known in the business world as Proem Market Research—is one of the most sought-after focus group moderators on the planet. If a company needs to find out whether or not a new product it's developing is right for the market—from the name they pick to the color of the packaging—Matt's the man they call, especially if women are the target of the marketing campaign.

"Which beer company?" I ask.

"MillerCoors. They're trying to hitch a ride on the craft beer horse and wanted me to do some digging."

"I take it, therefore, that the groups were made up of only women?"

"Ladies only. Everyone knows men are willing to spend money on expensive specialty brews, but they're not so sure about women."

"And? Are we?"

He sits up and stretches his arms out along the top of the couch. "I'll let you read my report when I finish it," he says with a wink. "Now then, I gotta clear my head from all the beer chatter. Tell me what you're working on, *Daphne Moore.*"

"Macon Strong, book two."

"What's the title?"

"I'm not sure yet. Right now it's just *Strong Lust: Book Two.*"

"Got it." He sits up straighter. "What's my man Macon up to these days?"

"He's a cheesemaker on a farm in Holland, Vermont."

Matt laughs. "You're kidding, right?"

"No. Come on, cheese is sexy. It's totally hip. Plus I want to keep him in Vermont a little while longer."

"What happened to him quitting the cowherd job and going to vet school? Isn't that why Macon left the Canadian chick at the end of *Crossing Borders*? What was her name?"

Before I can answer he yells, "Phionna!"

"Yes, Phionna," I reply, impressed that Matt can recall both the cliffhanger *and* characters from my last book. "I love that you knew that."

He splays out his hands as if offering me the world. "Of course I knew that. These are *our* stories. We're a team, remember?"

"Yes. They are and we are," I say, agreeing. Not a single one of my books could have been written without Matt.

"Anyway," I continue on, "there's too many stories about veterinarians. Plus I want to set part of the story in New York City, and I think I found the perfect way. His lover, Lizzie, moves there to—" I stop talking when Matt starts digging around in his computer case. I guess I've lost him.

"I went to the High Museum of Art in Atlanta and got you this." Matt pulls out a wrapped box. He leans forward and tosses it onto my desk. "It's awesome. Go ahead, open it."

I dismiss my silly insecurity. Of course he was listening, but like the eternal child that he is, Matt doesn't know how to contain his enthusiasm. If he has something special to share, everything else will have to wait—including my plotline.

With Matt's grin focused like a laser on my face, I tear off the paper to find a miniature human figure shaped like a drawing mannequin, only made of wire. "What is it?" I ask.

Matt jumps up and yanks the box out of my hand, ripping at the packaging. "It's Adam the Doodles Man! Look," he says as he twists the figure's arm over its head. "See? He's like a doodle you can bend into any shape." I watch him pull Adam's legs straight and set him next to my penholder. Then he bends his arms around a pen. "You see? He's here to help you write." Matt falls back onto the couch, content. "He's cool, right? I got Rover the Doodles Dog for Finley. She's gonna love it."

"He's great. Thank you." I sip coffee from my MOMA coffee

mug and grin. No matter where he travels for business, Matt never misses a chance to visit art museums or their gift shops. "But you know, if he's going to help me write," I say as I spread Adam's legs and bend his body, forcing his face into his lap, "he should at least get into a more appropriate position. Macon was just about to get blown by his intern."

"Lucky him," Matt says, smiling.

"Yeah, well, Lizzie—she's the intern. She's about to leave him, which means I still need to find a new lover for Macon while he pines for her. Please tell me you can help," I say, praying he found what I need to make this new book my best yet.

"Ugh, Kate." His head falls forward onto his chest. "I'm so tired."

"But, you did, right?"

"I did—?"

"Meet someone?"

"Well, yeah, of course," he says with all the cockiness of a man who is unaccustomed to being doubted. "I just—I'm sort of talked out."

"Since when are you ever not in the mood to share?" Something is off. Matt is never hesitant. Plus, I don't like the idea of having to wait. For one thing, Matt's stories are always better when they're fresh. For another, I need a new face. A new body.

And I need her now.

"At least give me a taste," I say, pushing gently. I only have to get him to take those first few steps. Once he begins the climb, he won't stop until he's reached the summit. It's not in Matt's nature to do anything halfway.

Matt rubs his hands along the tops of his thighs, thinking. "I guess, sure, but do we have enough time?" he asks.

I glance at the clock. "We do. Get the door," I say, my toes curling in anticipation against the hardwood floor.

As he gets up and slams the door shut with the side of his foot, I grab a clean pad of paper from the desk drawer.

Matt relaxes his long body out along the teal-colored cushions, crosses his hands behind his head and says, "Okay. Are you ready?" He directs the question not at me but at the ceiling, distancing himself the way he always does.

And, like it does every time he's about to dive in, Matt's question feels like a punch in my gut. Am I ever really *ready* to hear his stories?

Not for the first time do I wonder if I am nothing more than a fool tempting fate. I might be stirring sandy cheese into a pot of bunny-shaped noodles for Finley or folding laundry or staring out at the backyard and the questions will suddenly leap from the darkness into my consciousness, like a vampire springing to life from an opened coffin.

Am I insane to allow him to do this?

What if this crazy arrangement ends up destroying us?

What if? The question hangs in the air between us.

I look over at Matt staring at the ceiling. My beautiful, devoted husband.

My best friend. My partner in crime.

The man I haven't made love with in years.

Okay, so we don't *make* love, but our love for one another is probably stronger than most married couples. We are certainly intimate. We constantly kiss one another and hold hands when walking anywhere. In bed, Matt usually falls asleep wrapped around me, his large strong body framing my back.

The difference is, we just don't have sex. And that makes me happy because I hate sex.

From the first time I had intercourse to the last time Matt and I made love, I've consistently despised the whole wet sloppy feel of it. The buildup, the kissing, the *do I smell okay* rigmarole

of it. Once the sex act began, I'd become an unwilling partici-
pant, going along for the ride as if removed from my own body,
praying for it to come to an end as quickly as possible.

Even as a teenager, I knew I was different. While my friends
were exploring tongues in mouths and hands on breasts or sharing animated whispers over seeing a boy's penis for the first time,
I couldn't have cared less. I sometimes felt physical stirrings, but
I didn't want to *do it*. Not even a little of it.

Then, while I was in college, I met Matt. After only one
date, we fell hard for one another. Emotionally, that is. Naturally, I assumed my body would follow my heart and I'd be into
having sex with him.

Nope. I hated it with Matt too.

Since I didn't want to lose him, I pretended to enjoy making
love every night. (Yes, every night.) Matt wasn't blind. He soon realized I was never going to be an eager lover, but he adored me enough
that he was willing to make it work. We were too much in love,
too connected, he said, to break up just because I didn't love sex.

Which was why it was easy to say yes when he asked me
to marry him.

And why, after two years of accommodating his needs, I
finally figured out what I had to do to stop us from getting divorced. I knew what would keep us both happy.

I gave my husband permission to have sex with other
women. Just as long as he followed the rules.

It was the best decision I ever made, both personally and
professionally.

I shake my head, loosening the grip the recurring doubts have
on my brain and redirect my thoughts to Macon Strong, who is
waiting for me to tell his story. I have a book to write and plenty
of readers anxiously waiting to read it. I square my shoulders, re-
assuring myself that I am ready, willing, and most certainly able.

"Ready," I state, snatching the pen from Adam. "How'd you meet her?"

Matt closes his eyes and takes a deep breath. "Okay, so her name was Audrey. She was older, but not old, you know? And, oh man, did she have the reddest hair ever. Like that actress—"

"Julianne Moore?"

"Yeah, she looked a lot like her. So anyway, I started by asking this one group how they decide which beer they're going to order when they're at a bar or restaurant. I wanted to know—well, the client wanted to know—do they order what their friends get, or do they talk to the bartender or waitperson? Maybe they just stick with their usual. I'm not leading them, I'm keeping it loose, you know? So we go around the room and everyone tells their story, yadda, yadda, and I get to Audrey and she says, 'I like to sample everything before I decide. I need to taste them all,' and she says it like she's asking me to come taste *her.*"

"Mm-hmm. I like that," I mumble to myself as I scribble: *older redhead . . . tasting . . . slowly sipping . . . sampling each part of her . . .*

"So, well, as you might have guessed, she was totally into me."

Matt presumes most straight women are totally into him. Funnily enough, he's usually not wrong. When we're out together in public, I often catch them staring at my husband. We can be waiting in line for a coffee or paying for groceries, and the barista or cashier will straighten up taller, poof her hair a little, or smile widely like a beauty contestant. I've gotten used to the way women react to Matthew Parsons.

"So she comes back to the hotel with me and right away before I even kiss her she pushes me onto the bed and hikes up her skirt like it's on fire and she has to get it off. Then she climbs on and straddles me and starts pulsating up and down like we're screwing."

"What color is her skirt?" I ask without looking up.

"Um. Black."

"Panties?"

"Red. Thong."

... on top ... red panties ... holding her skirt like it's burning her skin ... As he speaks I write, noting distinct phrases, detailing new positions. I zero in on the dialogue and images, divining fresh ideas from the onrush as quickly as I can transcribe them *... slowly up and down ... Zen-like ...*

"Did she talk?"

"Yeah, I mean she said *yes* like a million times."

I chuckle quietly. "What did her voice sound like?"

"Um. Okay, it was definitely sexy. Like silky and deep. Can I keep going or what?"

"Go."

I write furiously and fast, marveling at how adept he is at this. Matt can recite his memories so vividly it's as if I were there with them, smelling the sweat, hearing the moans.

"How does it feel?" I ask, driving into the story like high beams through a foggy night.

"Feel?"

"What does her mouth feel like? Did hers feel any different or was it just, you know, standard oral?" Occasionally I have to prod him a little, like one of Macon's cows.

"I guess, yeah. I'd say it was definitely one of the best blow-jobs I've ever had."

"Why was it so great? Tell me everything."

My wrist aches by the time he finishes. I flip through the pages, the dirty sticky words splashed across them; a new character already forming out of my husband's one-night stand. I look up from the notepad. Matt is staring at the ceiling, lost in the memory.

"Matt."

"What?" He hurriedly sits up, like he's forgotten I'm in the room with him.

"I guess you weren't as tired as you thought, huh?" I congratulate myself for once again knowing how to press his PLAY button.

"So? Did you get anything good or was it too much of the same old same old?"

"Well, I definitely found Macon's distraction."

"Nothing else?" he asks dejectedly.

"No, no, there's plenty of new stuff." I throw the pad on the desk and smile at him.

"Good. I'm glad. Otherwise this would be too weird."

"Nope. Still not weird," I reply emphatically, although I am well aware that what we have going on between us is far beyond *weird*.

"Awesome." Matt checks his watch. "Hey, school's almost out. I'm gonna make myself a quick smoothie and go meet Finley."

"Take Munch with you. He needs a walk. In fact, do me a favor and take them to the playground. I'd love to write a little while it's still fresh."

"A most excellent idea. See you later." He jumps up and runs out the door, because Matt can't just walk through a door, can he?

I scroll to the top of my document and change the book's title to *Strong Lust: The Taste of Her*. Then I look down at my notes.

"Welcome to Macon's world, Audrey," I say to no one.

Now then: How am I going to *insert* her into the storyline?

In keeping with the theme of the book, I decide it has to be about food. I have an idea and open the website for Sterling College, which is located near Holland. I search their list of food-related continuing education courses and when I read about the four-day

"Charcuterie: the Artisanal Preparation and Presentation of Meat,"
I yell, "Yes!" pumping my fist like I just won Wimbledon.

I lean over my keyboard and type:

> After butchering their pigs into various cuts, the instructor told
> everyone to grab one of their hind legs and follow him to the
> kitchen where they were going to learn how to cure it into pro-
> sciutto. The woman next to Macon was having trouble hoisting
> hers so Macon gripped her enormous ham in his other hand.
>
>   "Well, well, aren't you the gentleman," the woman said
> in a silky deep voice.
>
>   "No worries." Macon grinned. She was pretty for an
> older chick. She was tall, with long hair colored a shade of
> red that could only be bought in a fancy salon.

I type without stopping, my eyes darting between my notes
and the screen. When Audrey discovers that Macon makes Smiling Girl Farm cheeses—her favorite!—she invites him back to
her room so they can continue their conversation.

"This is good," I say. I am just about to move them over to
the bed-and-breakfast, but realize I've been at it for close to two
hours. I hit SAVE and push my feet into my slippers. I want to
keep typing, keep the flow going, but Matt and Finley should
be home any minute. If not for them, I would spend twenty
hours a day writing stories. There is nothing I enjoy more than
spinning gold out of Matt's straw.

I open the curtains to let the real world back in again
and stare out at the backyard, dappled under the slender
light of an early spring afternoon in Vermont. Two mud-
died soccer balls sit dormant in front of the net. A scatter of
Munch's chew toys and bones dot the lawn as if they rained
down from the sky.

I smile at the beautiful chaos of it all.

When I hear Munch barking, I go out front where I find him running around the lawn, his leash still attached. "Munch, why are you—?"

Panic rises up into my chest. Where are Matt and Finley? I rush to the sidewalk and peer down the street, where I see the two of them standing with a woman and a child at the corner of Monroe and Forest. I squint against the glare of the setting sun, trying to recognize them. I don't. Just as I am about to walk toward them, Matt leans in closer to the woman. He appears to whisper something in her ear, after which the woman and child walk away down Forest Road. Matt takes Finley's hand and they turn toward home.

When they finally notice me standing here, Finley lets go of Matt's hand, races up to me, and announces, "Mommy, there's a new girl in my class and we played together on the playground and her name is Terra and it means *earth* and she's from Colorado, and her mother's name is Belle, and Daddy, you said you'd give me a snack and practice soccer with me before it gets too dark, so come on," before running into the house.

I catch Matt's arm. "Is that who you were just talking to? A woman named Belle?"

"Her name is Annabelle, but she said to call her Annie."

"What's she like?"

"I don't know. She seems pretty laid-back, kind of groovy. They're renting the red colonial with the pool over on Dwyer."

"Is she married? What does her husband do?"

"No clue," he answers, looking toward the house. "Can I go play soccer now?"

"Of course," I say, letting go of his arm.

Before he makes it to the first step Finley appears and

knocks her fist against the doorjamb. "What's taking you so long, Daddy? Come on already!"

I laugh at how alike she and Matt are. When either of them wants something, they want it now, and if you know what's good for you, you'd be smart to get out of their way.

ANNIE

Fucking boxes. If I stub my toe or scrape my shin on one more flap of cardboard, I am going to haul them out to the backyard and start a bonfire. For someone who's prided herself on not being a mindless twenty-first-century consumer, someone who actually went a year without using a centimeter of plastic, you'd think I have nothing left to unpack. We've been in Rayburne three weeks already, and the only things I've managed to extricate were most of Terra's stuff; our clothing; a few art prints and family photographs to hang on the piss-yellow walls for the sake of aesthetics and familiarity; as well as all my cooking utensils. There's no way I'm going to survive this suburban hellhole without my kitchen accoutrements.

For the thrill of it, I slit open the box marked USELESS SHIT and peer in.

Ah, my husband's vast collection of mediocre nature photos. I finger through the countless suns setting behind mountain peaks in Switzerland, the achromatic river shots in Patagonia. For all the spectacular places Clayton traveled to over his lifetime, the man never took a single picture worth framing.

Whenever he returned from one of his trips, he'd upload his booty from his Canon to his MacBook, then insist Terra and I sit next to him on the couch so he could subject us to his agonizing display of dullness. He'd wait for us to *ooh* and *aah* appropriately, then, with me dying a slow death beside him, he'd continue staring at the screen for another five seconds before moving on to the next image.

Sure, the scenery was pretty enough, but it was the way Clayton had chosen to capture the particular moments that sucked. For instance, he always placed the thing that caught his eye dead center: the sun, the boulder in the river, the highest hill on the horizon. The man knew nothing from asymmetry. Or composition. Or lighting, for that matter.

What really annoyed me was that he had to have prints made as soon as possible so he'd get them done at *Walgreens*, that pestilent kingdom of plastic. Two years ago, when Terra was in second grade, her class went on a tour of the garbage dump, more sanitarily referred to as the Denver Arapahoe Disposal Site. Their teacher Darien wanted to open her students' eyes to the horrors of plastic pollution and imprint on their growing brains the ways in which the abundance of water bottles and grocery bags, etc., were destroying the planet. She showed them pictures (high quality, I assume) of rivers and streams and oceans teeming with plastic, but it was the photo of the seal pup being strangled by a slimy rope of plastic trash that really roused the kids. (Apparently a small covey of parents were outraged that Darien shared such disturbing images with their offspring. Personally, I think children are never too young to have reality shoved in their faces.)

Terra had come home fired up, blasting through the door like she was Rachel Carson personified, demanding that we STOP USING PLASTIC. I'd wanted nothing more than to honor my daughter's passion, so we three sat down—it was one of those rare occasions Clayton happened to have been home—and made a pact not to buy or use anything made of plastic, or which came packaged in plastic, for a year.

It was easy enough. We are of the alternative ilk anyway, so it wasn't as if I thought, *Bummer, I can't buy hummus*—because I've always made my own. We loaded carrots and beetroot into our hand-woven baskets at the farmers' market. I fished blocks of tofu from watery buckets and filled my mason jars with grains and shampoos and soap from the bulk bins at the local co-op. My yen for yogurt was problematic, but being that I possess a cerebrum, it took all of four nanoseconds to rectify.

So, we're maybe seven months into our blissful plastic-free existence, and Terra hadn't once whined about having to give up her beloved juice boxes or granola bars (polyethylene in the packaging). Then one night she and I were reading together on the couch and Clayton came home carrying a *plastic* Walgreens bag filled with his latest and greatest pics from his recent trek through France—or maybe it was Peru: I hadn't paid attention—and before anyone said a word, he threw the packs of plastic-coated prints, as well as a newly-purchased photo album replete with plastic photo sleeves, onto the coffee table like he was Moses bestowing the Torah onto his people. "Hey, Terra. Help me fill the album," he'd said innocently enough.

My small perfect daughter, looking as aghast as if she'd just witnessed a bunny getting decapitated, had jumped up and shrieked, "You broke the rules, Clayton! I hate you! I hate you!" before running out of the room.

I had reason enough to want to end the partnership before my husband's vulgar display of plastic worship, but that night became a turning point; the decisive moment when I knew our lives needed to be altered.

I pick up the carton of photos, carry it out to the curb, and drop it down next to the blue recycling bins. Then I head off toward Forest Road so I can go retrieve my daughter from her first day at her new school and see if maybe I can find myself a new friend.

KATE

While reclining in my chair, I stare at the couch and let Matt's story echo in my head until I visualize my next scene. I'm still not sure if Audrey should straddle Macon like the redhead straddled Matt in Atlanta or if they should do it doggy-style on the creaky single bed, making so much noise that the innkeeper has to knock on the door and ask them to keep it down.

I lean forward and am about to start typing when the doorbell rings. "Matt! Get the door!" I holler. A second later another loud DING slides across my keyboard. "Matt! Someone's at the door!"

Where is he?

I push back from the desk, stuff my feet into my slippers, and go out to the foyer, stopping abruptly. Maybe whoever is there will just go away. I tiptoe back toward my office, pausing when I hear a familiar voice.

"Kate, it's Heidi. Are you in there, Kate?"

I open the door and while hugging my friend Heidi, Munch races outside to the front yard to greet another dog. It's small and shaggy like Munch but with a black coat instead of a cream-colored one. And while Munch has about the most

darling terrier face in the world, the other dog's long narrow
snout seems to swallow up the rest of its features. Which, in a
sad way, is a blessing, since the dog has only one eye. Where the
other eye should be, there's only a red lump of skin. "Who's that?"

"I call her Ruby. Isn't she the cutest thing ever?"

"No. Actually, she's really ugly," I reply without thinking.

Heidi glances over her shoulder and takes in the dog as if
contemplating her looks for the first time. Heidi McGregor
runs Heidi's Haven, a dog rescue down south in Middleton.
We adopted Munch—formerly known as Buddy—from Heidi
after spending months clicking through photos on Petfinder,
searching for that perfect combination of looks and personal-
ity. Assuming it would take too much time from my writing, I
hadn't wanted a dog, but after a lot of begging, Finley and Matt
convinced me to hitch a fourth wheel to our family stagecoach.

The dog was every bit as cute and charming as Heidi described him. Within the first five minutes of playing with him,
we knew he was a keeper. As for Heidi, it took a little more
time, but she turned out to be a keeper as well. She's forty-six,
a decade older than me; divorced; her clothes are always covered
in dog hair; and she is usually flush with anger. But I like her,
and other than my family and fictional characters, she's pretty
much the only person I hang out with.

A few weeks after adopting Munch, Finley, and I volunteered at one of her adoption events. We got along so well she
called me two days later and asked me if I wanted to come
along with her and a pack of rescue dogs for an off-leash walk
in Geprags Park. To help socialize them, she'd said. It was one of
those rare mild winter days where you could almost feel the sun's
warmth through your down vest, and, besides which, I was stuck
in a bedroom with two highly aroused naked people, a rope,
and nothing to write. Ever since *Fifty Shades* was published, it

seemed as if every erotica writer on the planet wanted to jump onto the BDSM bandwagon. I also wanted to add a bondage scene, but since Matt had yet to tie anyone up, or be tied up himself, I'd hit a wall.

Plus, it'd been ages since I'd socialized with a real human being. Matt thought I was too much of a shut-in and kept harping on me to get out more. At his insistence, I'd agreed to have lunch with Christy Pell and Rebecca Mason, two women from our subdivision. Nothing much came of it. They mostly talked about their high-powered jobs and their remodeled kitchens. When we went for a run together a few weeks later, they chattered nonstop about their sex lives. Obviously, I had nothing to add to the conversation. I wasn't about to admit that my husband and I never made love, and I *certainly* couldn't tell them about my work. I needed them to think I was nothing more than a happy-to-stay-at-home mom, a girls' soccer volunteer, and a brownie maker for the PTA. If anyone ever found out I wrote sex-filled books as Daphne Moore, I'd be so embarrassed we'd have to move to another state.

Which was why when Heidi invited me along on the hike, I went. I figured she could use a companion who didn't shed. I also knew, given her impending divorce, the last thing I'd have to listen to were stories about Heidi's sex life.

I'd typed PLACEHOLDER in the document, made a note to ask Matt to find someone to *bond* with accordingly, and grabbed my hiking boots.

Before we'd walked more than a hundred yards into the park, Heidi started talking about her doomed marriage. "Mike and I, we created the rescue together, you know. He had a real job with the state, but he was there with me when I needed him." She stopped for a moment to scold two dogs who were wrestling in a pool of mud before continuing. "Anyway, he was at first. But after a while he began backing away little by little and then suddenly it was all me. I was a one-man band. I scooped the shit. I wrote the grants. I put down the ones who were too sick to adopt out. And I guess I started getting a little too, I don't know—compulsive?"

"What do you mean?" I asked, rushing to keep up.

"I couldn't stop rescuing. It was never enough. There's always one more about to get the needle and I'm standing there in a stinking high-kill shelter in Alabama trying to choose who to take, and it's the hardest thing ever. It's like *Sophie's Choice* all the time for me."

I'd twice wept through that movie where Meryl Streep has to decide whether to send her son or her daughter to a gas chamber, and I was about to tell Heidi that she was out of her gourd if she thought choosing between two children and choosing between two dogs was an equivalent analogy, but Heidi was on a rant.

"And then one night he says he wants me to shut down the rescue and maybe think about adopting a baby, and I'm like *what*? Where the hell did that come from?" She stopped short and I, still distracted by the idea of having to choose between two loves, almost tripped over Frankie, the Dachshund mix.

Just then a couple with two golden retrievers came around a bend toward us. "Oh, shit," Heidi said, and before she could yell, "No!" all eight dogs raced toward the leashed dogs, barking, jumping, sniffing. Although every tail was wagging happily and there was not an ounce of aggression in the air, the couple went ballistic.

"Get your goddamn mutts on leashes!" the man growled as he tried to yank his two well-coiffed purebreds away from the excited mess of fur.

"This park has a leash law," the woman screeched. "As soon as I have cell service, I'm calling the police."

"I'm really sorry, but it's not like they're hurting anybody. We're just going to keep walking, okay?" Heidi said, taking me by the arm. "You folks have a nice day." A few feet up the trail we turned around and began calling the dogs.

"Hank! Come."

"Come, Lulu, come here, good girl."

"Let's go, Elliott. Come boy!"

One by one the dogs quit playing with the goldens and ran to catch up with Heidi, their pack leader. All except Milo, a small muscular guy with two different ears. He wanted to stay with the couple, now heading back toward the parking lot. Heidi whistled for him and as Milo turned around, the man yelled, "Get the hell out of here you stupid mutt. Go!" kicking him hard enough to send Milo tumbling to the ground with a whimper.

Without thinking, I ran over to Milo and grabbed his collar. "Now who's going to call the police?" I screamed at the retreating couple's backs. "I am! I'm going to report you for animal cruelty, you stupid jerk! Yeah, that's right; you better walk fast!" My heart was pounding and my body burned with so much anger it was as if my veins had been injected with hot liquid. When I turned around I saw Heidi staring at me wide-eyed, like I had just committed a murder. "What?" I asked, dragging Milo along with me.

"Jesus, Kate. I didn't think you had it in you."

"Had what in me?" I asked, my heartbeat just now slowing.

She narrowed her eyes and smiled. "Fury," she said.

"Yeah, well, me neither," I said, suddenly embarrassed. What had gotten into me, roaring at strangers like a crazed lunatic? I had never in my life lost my temper to the point of blind rage.

I actually considered running after the couple to apologize, but when Heidi added, "Not everyone has the balls to fight the assholes of the world. You're my kind of people, Kate, and I'm glad you're my friend," I changed my mind. Her impression of me as someone who possessed courage was completely off the mark, but I still liked that she saw me that way.

Now, as she offers a biscuit to both Munch and the one-eyed dog, Heidi says, "So I was thinking maybe you and Matt could foster Ruby for me."

"What? No way, Heidi. We have our hands full with Munch." This was one hundred percent a lie because Munch is no trouble at all.

"I just transported ten more dogs up from South Carolina."

"Heidi!"

"You know I can't stop. Besides, Ruby is easy. I need to get a few of the easy ones out of the house and work with the hard ones. Please?"

"Hey, Heidi." Matt suddenly appears on the front lawn. He's wearing a pair of black running shorts and a faded green University of Vermont T-shirt. Sweat drips from his skin.

"Hi, Matt."

"You went running?" I ask.

"Yeah, why? Was I supposed to be doing something else?"

"No, but—why didn't you take Munch with you?"

Matt kneels down and pats Ruby. "I didn't want to. Who is this? Quasimodo?"

Heidi laughs. "Her name when I got her was One-Eyed Betty, but that was gross, so I renamed her Ruby."

"Hello, Ruby girl," Matt says, running his hand over the dog's most uncomely face. "Damn, you're ugly." He stands up to go into the house. "Nice seeing you, Heidi."

I call after him, "Matt, Heidi wants us to foster Ruby for a little while. What do you think?"

"Another dog? Actually, I think it's a really bad idea. Sorry, Heidi. I've got a long contract in Philly coming up, so I won't be around to help."

"And soccer season is starting soon," I add, frowning. As much as I want to help Heidi, I don't want another distraction in my life.

"No worries," Heidi says, shrugging. "I figured it couldn't hurt to ask."

After a dog-scented hug, I hurry back inside. I want to get back to Macon and Audrey, but when I hear Matt's booming voice reverberating off the shower walls I walk into the bathroom. "Thanks for that!" I yell through the steamy glass doors.

Matt stops singing. "Thanks for what?" He has his back to the door. I stare at his muscled buttocks clenching and unclenching as he reaches down to wash his ankles. Macon has that same butt.

"For helping me come up with a good excuse not to take Ruby."

"You know there's nothing I love more than helping you, Kaybee," he says, turning around, grinning.

"Nothing?" I say, raising a dubious eyebrow. Before I can stop myself, I glance down at his crotch, his thick whirls of pubic hair streaked through with soapy bubbles. Objectively-speaking, Matt's large smooth penis is magnificent. It's certainly satisfied a lot of women.

It's a shame I'm not one of them.

KATE

Even though my phone shows a number I don't recognize, I answer it anyway. "Hello?"

"Hi, Kate. This is Annie Meyers, Terra's mother. I got your number from the school directory. I'm assuming Finley mentioned us."

"Oh, hi, Annie. Gosh, I am so sorry I haven't called to welcome you to the neighborhood or invite you to dinner. I've been so—"

Annie laughs. "Please don't apologize, Kate. The last thing I need is for people to make a big deal about us being here."

"Oh, okay," I reply, thrown off a little by the remark.

"Anyway," Annie continues, "it seems the girls have fallen majorly in love and Terra wants to get together after school for a playdate. How's tomorrow?"

"Tomorrow sounds great." I have no intention of letting Finley go home to Terra's house—not until I've met Annie face-to-face and can be reassured that her family is this side of normal. "We'd love to have Terra here after school."

"Most excellent."

"Great. Do you want to come get her after, or should I walk her home? I mean, I'm happy to bring—"

"You should walk her home, Kate. That way you can decide if we're acceptable enough for Finley to come here sometime."

How does Annie know I won't allow Finley to go there until—? Well, come on: any responsible parent wants to be sure a new friend's house isn't bursting with guns or poisons or a husband who likes to fondle little girls. Any parent would want to—yet Annie doesn't seem to give a hoot about sending Terra off without first vetting *my* domain. Then again, she met Matt at the playground and then walked partway home with him. He obviously made a respectable enough impression.

"Why don't you bring her home around five? Gotta run," Annie says, hanging up.

Terra Meyers is small for a ten-year-old and remarkably quiet, yet her manners could use a little improvement. When she and Finley erupt into the mudroom, Terra kicks off her shoes against the wall, throws her pack on the floor, and piles her jacket on top of it—never once noticing the shoe cubbies or hooks. I hold my tongue because I don't want Terra to think I'm finicky. Certainly, I have my quibbles about chores and tidiness, but overall I consider myself a pretty relaxed mom.

"Hi, you must be Terra," I say to the little mop of a child. Terra's hair is dark, more black than brown, and long. Long and dirty and knotty.

"Yeah," she grunts, running past me into the house. I'm not surprised, given her mother's brash mannerisms on the phone yesterday. After arranging the shoes and hanging the coat, I find the two girls in the living room playing tug-of-war with one of Munch's pull-toys. Munch runs around in circles, barking while trying to snatch it from them.

"You guys hungry?" I ask.

"We'd like mac and cheese, please," Finley says with an ex-aggerated smile.

Terra stops pulling and looks at Finley. "Is it organic? I'm not allowed to eat the crappy Kraft kind."

I remember Matt describing Annie as *groovy*. He pegged her pretty well. "It's Annie's," I say, laughing at the coincidence. "Is that okay?"

"Uh-huh," Terra replies, still not addressing me.

As I watch the girls wolf down their bowls of cheesy noodles I wonder what it is that Finley likes about this kid. Terra holds her spoon like a shovel, doesn't use her napkin, and after she fin-ishes eating, she shoots up from the table without clearing her dish. Most oddly, the two of them say nothing to one another, eating in a sort of clairvoyant silence, giggling between bites.

Finley ignores Terra's bowl but puts her own into the sink. "Mom, we're gonna go play soccer, okay?"

"Sure. Have fun."

While I'm cleaning up, Matt phones. "Hi, babe. I'm be-tween groups so I thought I'd check in and see how my two favorite girls are doing."

"We're both doing very well. How's Philadelphia?"

"I have no idea," he says, laughing. "I've been inside a con-ference room since the plane touched down."

"I'm sorry. How's the deodorant thing? Pretty smelly, huh?"

"Very funny—What? Okay, thanks. Hey, Kate, I'm on again in five minutes. Let me say a quick hello to Finley."

"I would, but she's out back playing soccer with Terra."

"She's—who?"

I spot a few pieces of macaroni under Terra's chair. "Terra," I repeat as I wipe up the orangey mess with a paper towel. "The new kid Finley met at the playground?"

"They're together?"

"What do you mean? Of course they're together. I just said that."

"Sorry. I got distracted."

"I could tell. You get like that when you're in work mode."

"I gotta go, Kate. I love you. Say hi to Finley."

"Will do, I love—"

But Matt's already hung up.

I dump the macaroni into the compost bucket and go to my office. Before closing the curtains, I peer outside, observing the girls kicking the ball back and forth. Again, they aren't talking much, but even from behind the glass I can tell there's a genuine connection between them.

I flick off my slippers and sit down to reread the last section I was working on. After a week of scorchingly hot sex at the B&B, Macon falls hard for the mature, intelligent Audrey, but also knows he's probably seen the last of her. After all, she is married to Harland Mansfield, a wealthy entrepreneur who spoils her rotten. Which is why Macon is both surprised and thrilled when he sees her black BMW pull up at the farm. Audrey tells him she just happened to be in the neighborhood, but Macon isn't that naive. Ever the gentleman, he shows her around the creamery and the cheese cave, where the higher-priced cheeses are aged.

I am on the fence about whether or not they should have sex in the cheese cave. I haven't planned for it in the cursory outline I sketched, but there can never be too much screwing in an erotica book. I've learned enough about cheesemaking to know that the humidity in the cave has to be constantly maintained. Will their body heat disturb it? And what about the hairnets and smocks? Both are decidedly less than titillating, but they must be worn for sanitary reasons. Am I a nimble enough writer to be able to arouse Macon with a woman whose hair is tucked up under a dreary gauzy cap? I do so like the dirt floor, although the smell of pungent milk drying might be a turn-off to readers.

Hmmm.

I type *(Ask Matt if he thinks this is a good idea)* and move on to Macon introducing Audrey to Miles and Arthur, who take an instant liking to the classy woman. After sharing a bottle of bourbon, they hatch a plan to open a cheese and charcuterie shop in New York City and ask Macon if he's willing to move to Audrey's pied-à-terre in Greenwich Village to run it. As long as it means being able to find Lizzie again, Macon enthusiastically accepts.

I left off where Macon brings Audrey back to his cabin because she's too tipsy to drive back to the city. She has just stripped naked and falls face-first onto his bed. Macon sits down in his chair and opens a book, assuming she's passed out, but when her hips start rising and falling, he knows she wants him.

I start in again and get as far as having him bind her hands and legs to the bedposts with four of his bandanas before I lift my fingers. I have no idea how to aptly describe a man having sex with a woman who is tied-up *face-down*. Matt had come through for me when I needed another bondage scene, but he'd done it face-up. I can't write another face-up scene. I need to keep my sex fresh or my devoted readers will start to complain. The last thing I want is a bunch of whiny comments on Goodreads.

Of course, I check my reviews on Goodreads. Constantly. Other than my family, no one makes me feel as important or as appreciated as my fans. Matt once accused me of being addicted to the praise I get from readers around the world. I got a little defensive, but, if I had to be honest, he was spot on. I feel especially psyched when readers tell me my stories *helped* them. Just last week someone posted, "You saved my marriage; my sex life sucked until I read your books."

It's gratifying to be able to do for others that which I cannot do for myself.

I also read my competitors' reviews. Besides clumsy writing or lame characters, readers will pummel erotica books with one-star ratings if the sex isn't convincing enough. Or hot enough. Or if there isn't enough variety.

I can flip Audrey onto her back. No. Been there, done that. What about anal? Until now, I've resisted it, although I am well aware of its popularity.

I stare at the screen. Bend Adam's wire body in half. As long as Audrey is already on her stomach, I have the perfect setup for some good butt action. I would untie her, though. Skip the bondage aspect.

Matt had anal sex with a woman a while back, but I can't remember if she had been leaning over a table or flat on a bed. I unlock the bottom drawer of my desk and retrieve a stack of manila folders. "I think it was when you were in Minnesota, right Matt?" I say to no one.

I page through my notes and then notice the time. I have to bring Terra home soon. I lock the folder in the drawer, type *(PLACE-HOLDER: Macon and Audrey have anal sex)* and continue on.

Six months later Macon threw his duffel bag onto the white leather sofa in Audrey Mansfield's one-bedroom apartment in the modernist building known as One Kenmare Square. He looked around at the stark white walls, the enormous oil painting of Audrey, the stack of pretentious art books covering the glass coffee table. He grabbed a bottle from the glass-and-gold bar cart and poured three fingers of scotch into a crystal glass, downed it, and thought, as the warm liquid eased its way down his chest, how close he was to Lizzie.

KATE

Before she even greets me at the door, Annie grabs her daughter by her shirt and asks, "Did you pet their dog?" When Terra nods, Annie says, "Go change your clothes right now and wash your hands." Only then, when the girls go inside and run up the stairs, does Annie acknowledge me. "Hi. Sorry about that, but if I breathe in too much dander, I'm fucked. I'm Annie, by the way," she says, extending her hand. "You must be Kate."

I stand on the threshold wide-eyed, my hand in Annie's, wondering what to do next.

"Would you like to come in?"

"Um." I hesitate. "Finley and I—I'm probably covered in hair."

"It's fine. Look, if I wanted to completely avoid people who owned dogs, I'd become an eremite. I need to control it, that's all." She crosses her arms and smiles. "So are you staying or going?"

I have no idea what Annie is talking about but her smile makes me feel entirely welcome. "Staying," I say, stepping into the foyer of the large colonial and taking off my shoes. To the right of the stairs is a large living room with a dated brick fireplace. Instead of furniture there are countless moving boxes.

To my left, through closed French doors is the den, a smaller cozier room. Inside is a large comfy-looking green-fabric couch, a square pine coffee table, a few photographs and paintings on the walls, and still more opened but not empty moving boxes. I follow Annie into the kitchen, which, if not for the chaotic mess, would be a grand kitchen indeed. The countertops are dark gray granite, as is the huge kitchen bar with three unmatched bar-stools perched alongside it. The stainless steel sink overflows with pots and glasses, crusted-over dishes of all shapes and sizes. Covering almost every square inch of every surface are jars of beans and dried herbs, grains I don't recognize, and a half-sliced papaya around which a swarm of fruit flies circle. I sit up on one of the stools and slide aside a bowl of partially-eaten cereal. Annie spoons dried herbs from one of the jars into a large black teapot, then pours a kettle of hot water into it. "Tea okay?" she asks, settling the lid on.

"Tea would be great, thank you."

Annie Meyers is not an attractive woman in the typical sense, but her plainness, or maybe *earthiness* is the right word, imbues her with a kind of attractiveness I'm unaccustomed to. She's maybe five-foot-four—shorter than me by a few inches—and isn't what one would call slender. Because she has on sweatpants and a huge tan-colored cable-knit sweater that hangs past her wrists, I can't tell if what envelopes her bones is fat or muscle. She has long dark hair like her daughter's, tied in a messy braid. Her brown eyes are large, almost too large, for her small angular face. Her skin has an unhewn ruddy quality to it—something easily remedied with a translucent powder, although it's obvious Annie is the sort to shun makeup. Most women in the neighbor-hood have their hair done weekly with blow-outs or new cuts. God forbid they'd ever leave the house without a smear of lip-stick. I occasionally add caramel highlights to brighten up my hair's dullness and, sure, I wear lipstick, even when running to the store, but I like to believe I don't look like a stereotypical suburban housewife.

"Have you always been allergic to dogs?" I ask, starting up the conversation.

Annie stops pouring the tea through the strainer and glares at me. "We just met and already we're discussing my health issues?"

I suddenly want to yell for Finley and run home. I shift on my stool and look out to the pool in the backyard. I touch the scar on my nose, then put my hand back onto the dirty counter. "I'm sorry I brought it up."

Annie's scowl turns into a frown. "No. *I'm* sorry I just snapped at you like that. I don't know what set me off. Please forgive me."

I appreciate Annie being quick to apologize but still feel wary.

"Are we good? I'll kill myself if we're not good." Annie actually seems worried enough that I believe her.

"Of course. It was nothing. No big deal."

Annie stares at me. "Honestly?"

I raise my right hand. "Scout's Honor."

When Annie replies with, "Pedophile Scouts or Girl Scouts?" I laugh, and the tension between us disappears.

"Definitely Girl Scouts," I say, relaxing for the first time since knocking on Annie's door.

"Beautiful. So, do you really want to know about my fucked-up lungs or were you just making polite conversation?"

"No, I really want to know. Tell me."

"Alright, well, so I was fine growing up," she says as she finishes pouring the tea. "Not a rash or itch or allergy or hive, *ever*. Been a vegan slash vegetarian since I was eight. Then, this last winter, *bam*—" she slams the pot on the counter so hard I expect it to crack "—I'm diagnosed with AOA, Adult-Onset Asthma. Thirty-three years old, and out of the fucking blue I

start wheezing and having trouble breathing—like every day—
and it's getting worse, so I go see my naturopath and he gives me
herbs but nothing helps. I'm not sleeping at night and so I break
down—let's go into the den," she says, handing me one of the
mugs and walking out of the room—"and get tested and find
out it's asthma. Supposedly brought on by an allergic reaction
to our dog, Hester, which was too sad, because Hester, she . . .
anyway, we find Hess a good home. I vacuum the shit out of
the house. I get rid of all possible triggers—my essential oils,
candles, incense—because anything that smells good or could
potentially relax me could now kill me—and you'd think, I'm
good, right?—I won't have to use an inhaler filled with chemicals or take meds, but I'm breathing into my flow meter every
day because I'm still wheezing and for someone who's run two
marathons, now I can't run for shit, and . . ."

We sit on the couch in the den, Annie in lotus position at
one end. At the other end, I affix a look of concern and sympathy on my face while subtly checking out the photographs on
the walls and tabletops as Annie rages on about her condition.
". . . but every night I get into bed and every night the same
goddamn elephant follows me in and sits on my chest. What
the fuck, right?"

I nod.

"It was because of the ozone. Worst thing for an asthmatic."

"Ozone?"

"Yup. The American Lung Association gave Denver a D for
air quality, but who pays attention to that?"

"I don't know what—"

"Of course you don't because you know what? Vermont got
an A. No ozone."

"Is that why you moved here?"

Annie pulls her legs out from under her and drops them

onto the coffee table. "So, Miss Kate, mother of Finley, how the hell are you?"

Are we done talking about asthma? Flustered by the sudden shift, I reply, "I guess I'm great, thank you. What do you think of our little town of Rayburne?"

"It is most excellent. We are very glad to be here in sunny, clean-aired Vermont." She gestures out the window at the waning sun splashing its colors against a bright-blue sky.

"I feel bad I didn't bring cookies or a housewarming gift. I—"

"Nah, we're pretty much sugar-free over here on Dwyer Court. I would have fed 'em to the birds."

"Is that your husband?" I ask, pointing at a photograph of Annie, Terra, and a short but obviously athletic, bearded man; the three of them standing on top of a mountain.

Annie follows my gaze. "Yup, that's Clayton. *Il est mort.*"

"Excuse me?"

"Sorry—it sounds better in French. Clayton is dead. He died last spring."

I stiffen. "Oh my God, Annie, I am so sorry."

"Don't be. He was an asshole. Egomaniacal and selfish too, if you want to get descriptive."

"Oh." I am floored. As much as I don't want to be snapped at again, I want to know more. "Would you mind if I ask how he died?"

"Not at all," she says, taking a drink of her tea. "He drowned on the north fork of the South Platte. Well, technically he didn't drown. He was kayaking alone. Clay always had to go alone—I think he was born with an extra macho chromosome or something—and what we think happened was he was paddling through a radically hellacious set of class-five rapids at Bailey's Run and he flipped. Knowing Clay, he should have been able to roll up but he didn't. He must have gotten stuck so he went for a wet exit and I don't know, some river god must have been in a shitty mood that day because he didn't get laid or something because he hid a long sharp stick underwater. It went through Clay's thigh, slashing his femoral. He bled out in minutes."

I let go of the breath I've been holding. "That's horrible," I say, making a mental note. If I ever need to kill off a character, I'll be using that. It's sensational.

"Yeah."

"How is Terra—?"

"She's okay. Honestly, the guy was never around. Ever. When he wasn't climbing a mountain or racing a rapid, he was planning a trip. And the thing about Clayton was that he couldn't multitask worth shit, so something or someone had to get ignored and it was pretty much always us."

The tea in my mug tastes like mud mixed with oregano. I take another sip and wait for Annie to add something more. When the silence continues, I feel obliged to fill in the lingering space. "So you picked Vermont because the air is clean?"

"Yeah, well, I also have some ties here." A crash comes from above. Annie gestures her chin upward. "Terra's room."

"Uh-huh." I can only imagine what sort of war-zone it looks like. "But why Rayburne?"

"The Rayburne Waldorf school. Considered one of the best in the country. I figured if I had to tear Terra away from her friends in Denver, I'd at least keep her safe under Rudolf Steiner's blanket of goodness."

"But, wait, she's in Finley's class at Rayburne Community Sch—"

"It sucked," Annie says, interrupting me. She puts her mug down on the table and undoes her braid, running her fingers through the thick wavy locks. My hair is the polar opposite of hers: short, baby fine, and light. The same as it's been for as long as I can remember. "Worst teacher on the planet. He was new; took over for the teacher we thought we were getting when we paid the outrageous fee, but he left and they hired Mister Richard—Mister Moron, is more like it. So I pulled her out." She abruptly gets up and goes into the kitchen, returning with a bottle of agave syrup. She pours it into her tea and holds the bottle out to me. "You want a splash?"

"No, thank you. I like the taste of bitter."

Annie nods. "Good to know."

"Did you lose the tuition money? I heard they don't give it back if you—"

"So, what are you, Kate: a cop, a writer, or an aesthetician?"

"What?"

"Those are the three nosiest professions on the planet as far as I'm concerned."

I laugh. "Well, I'm definitely not a policeman. And I couldn't imagine giving someone a Brazilian." I flash on Audrey, one of the only female characters I've allowed to be hair-free down there. Pre-pubescent genitals are unquestionably less sexy in my opinion and I usually keep at least a "landing strip" of pubic hair. But, given her grooming standards and financial means, Audrey would definitely be waxed bare.

"So that leaves *writer*," Annie says.

I stop picturing Barbie-bald vaginas and answer vaguely, "Well, I guess you could say I do some writing here and there."

"Like as a hobby, or do you actually make money doing it?"

"Now who's being nosy?" I say, trying to be funny.

"Got me!" She stabs herself with an imaginary knife and flops backward.

I want Annie to stop playing dead and ask me more about my writing. Other than Matt and my editor, I don't talk to anyone about my stories. Sure, I chat with my fans in

Goodreads community discussions, but as Daphne Moore, an imaginary human being. More than a few times, I came close to telling Heidi about my work, but I worried that she'd lose respect for me. Other than the time I went wild on those idiots at the park, Heidi sees only the side of me that is decent and caring. Finding out I write *indecent* stories might change her opinion.

How amazing it would be to have a friend I could be totally open with? I've known this woman for less than an hour, but I can already tell that Annie, what with her dark, sarcastic attitude, would probably find my double-life cool. She'll see that I'm unlike all the other women in the neighborhood, and she'll want to be friends with me.

I want Annie to open her eyes and continue quizzing me. If only I hadn't accused her of being nosy. One more nudge is all I need to spill a bean or two. But when Annie opens her eyes and says nothing more, I figure it's time to go. I drain the rest of my tea and get up. "So, Annie, this was great, thanks. You want to get together this weekend?"

"I would, but we're busy," she says, not looking as disappointed as I hoped. "Finley should come here next time."

After Finley and I put on our shoes at the front door, Finley gives Terra a tight hug.

"You know girls' soccer starts next week," I announce. "Finley plays. You think maybe you want to join the team too, Terra?"

Terra looks up hopefully. "Can I, Annie?"

"She calls you Annie?" I ask, a bit stunned.

"It's not a good time," she says to Terra, ignoring my question. "Maybe in the fall."

"But I really want to."

"Sorry, love bug, but as the man in *The Princess Bride* says, 'Get used to disappointment.'"

Terra whines so loudly Finley covers her ears. The child clearly doesn't want to get used to disappointment.

"It's a great group of girls," I say, trying to push Annie into changing her mind. "Finley's father—Matt, you met him at the playground—he's one of the coaches, and I volunteer. You could—"

"Okay, I'll consider reconsidering, okay?"

Terra and Finley "yippee" into the air.

"You promise you'll think about it, Annie?" Terra asks hopefully.

Annie holds up her hand. "Girl Scout's honor."

ANNIE

I walk through the automatic door, the whoosh giving way to the sound of me groaning uninhibitedly at the smell of disinfectant coupled with the buzz of the high-beamed fluorescents. The checker closest to the exit looks startled by my not-so-subtle display of displeasure. I clear my throat, grab a red basket, and head to the produce section.

Grocery shopping in Rayburbia is about as much fun as taking a bath in a tub of raw chicken. I could have driven a few miles to one of the hip, warmly lit health food stores up in Burlington, but wishing to leave as small a carbon footprint on the planet as possible, I've chosen instead to walk to the neighborhood store. Not that I really believe this one small act is going to prevent Terra's children's children from having to apply SPF-9000 whenever they venture outdoors. Or that because I'm buying my broccoli a mile from my home, there will still be elephants roaming wild in fifty years. But I can at least try to be a role model for my daughter. After all, I am the one who moved us into a house large enough to accommodate an entire African village, with a water-wasting, chemical-fraught swimming pool, no less.

While picking through the subpar eggplant, hoping against hope I'll find one that borders on firm, I remind myself that our situation is temporary and I can survive anything for a few months. Even non-organic celery. Every bunch of kale looks as if they've been chastised by an angry nun, they are so wilted. The asparagus, very much in season, cost $5.99 a pound.

"Jesus. That's highway robbery," I say, noticing the checker staring at me again, her mouth curved into a sneer of distaste as if she's just suckled an overpriced kumquat. I assume she has super sensitive eardrums, but when the woman with the newborn *also* glares as she clatters past me, my curiosity meter surges. I sniff my underarms. Look down at my clothes. I have on a recently-cleaned pair of tie-dyed leggings with white wool socks. My hiking boots are a little rough around the edges, sure, but it isn't as if I—oh shit. I forgot I threw on my VEGAN AS FUCK T-shirt when I got out of bed this morning. Head slap.

I zip up my coat and move on to the fruit display, grimacing at the dearth of deliciousness on offer. I throw a few oranges and kiwis into the basket and steady myself as I approach the case of tofu and other assorted soy products. Shockingly, the selection is rather plentiful. Into my red basket go three containers of organic tofu, some locally produced tempeh—thank you, God—and a pack of tofu pups. I thought once our sans-plastic year ended, Terra might want to continue our pact, but the kid really missed those pups.

I toss in a second pack of pups and head for the checkout line furthest away from Evil-Eye, trying hard not to snicker as the anorexically thin housewife in front of me unloads three bottles of Chardonnay and box after frozen box of Lean Cuisines onto the conveyor belt. There is so much hairspray holding her follicles in place I fear it might trigger an asthma attack so I step back a few feet and continue watching her. She looks tense and undersexed. Sort of the way my new BFF Kate looks.

I like Kate even if she needs to learn to relax. Before I met her, I assumed she would be pretty straight and narrow, like a quintessential suburbanite shellacked in normalcy. Someone who eats frozen dinners and works out at the club. But no: she has a certain *je ne sais quoi* about her. A strength of character I find desirous in women. She's also funny and far more insightful than I anticipated. After I bit her head off—I really must learn to control my temper—I thought for sure she'd go scurrying out the door with her tail between her long legs. But she graciously accepted my sincere apology and stayed put.

I picture Kate sitting on a stool in my kitchen and as I watch the bright orange boxes of frozen lasagna and chicken teriyaki glide forward on the conveyor belt, I reach over and accidentally knock one of the bottles of white onto the tiled floor. The explosion of spraying glass and the chaos that ensues delight me.

Yeah, I'm glad I didn't scare Kate away.

KATE

Before they had sex on the conference room table, the woman in Philadelphia asked Matt to go into the other room and watch her strip through the two-way mirror.

"She did it slowly, moving like she could hear music. A total tease, I tell you," Matt pronounces from his usual position on the teal couch. "She's got these really hairy underarms, and at first I'm sort of turned off by it, but she gets on the table and spreads eagle and starts playing with herself and massaging her breasts and she says—she knows I can hear her—'Matt, I want you to . . . '"

As he speaks, I diligently transcribe . . . *Limber . . . like a pole dancer . . . wants to break through the mirror and take her now . . .*

The woman, a personal coach named Angela, was in one of the focus groups testing a company's collection of newly scented women's deodorants. She'd left her date planner at the session and when she returned, Matt was locking up for the night.

"Man, she had the moves. I was getting so hot watching her."

"What was her body like?"

"Her body? I don't know, medium build and her breasts were small but anyway, there she was fingering herself and her head is back, long hair flying around her shoulders and she says, 'Come in here now,' so I blast through the door and take her there on the table. I don't even take my clothes off; I just drop my pants down to my ankles and she lifts her legs . . ."

After I jot down *knees behind her neck,* I notice an erection arising under Matt's sweatpants. Given that the sex with Angela is pretty status quo, I don't understand why. Maybe it was voyeurism. It's a first for us: watching a woman strip behind a two-way mirror. I'll definitely figure out a way to use it.

"She really got to you, huh?" I say, getting up to open the curtains. We need to leave for soccer in ten minutes.

"I guess, yeah. It was great sex." He looks hurt.

"You don't have to get defensive. I just—hey, when's your next contract?"

"Seattle on the twelfth for a home security system. Why? Do you want me to stop—I mean, is it starting to get weird, Kate?"

"No, Matt, it's not getting weird. I need Macon to have a threesome and I was hoping maybe you could arrange one."

KATE

"Okay, open your legs wide and reach up," I say to the gaggle of girls assembled in front of me. "Now let's slowly stretch to our right. Don't forget to keep breathing." Behind me, Matt and the two coaches are unloading the bag of balls and setting the cones around the field for dribbling drills.

When Finley expressed interest in playing soccer last fall, Matt signed on to be an assistant coach. Since he missed too many practices because of his schedule, both of us just help out on an ad hoc basis. Not that I have any experience playing soccer. Other than leading warm-ups, supplying snacks, and cleaning up after the games, I mostly stand on the sidelines and cheer the kids on.

It's a beautiful Vermont day. Blue skies. Fluffy clouds. Over by the playground, seagulls and crows compete for crumbs left over from recess earlier in the day. As I balance on my left leg and hold onto my right ankle for a quadriceps stretch, my mind wanders to Macon.

Now that I've gotten him out of Vermont and into the big city, I'll finally be able to use the notes and photos from our many trips down to New York.

Matt loves Manhattan—or, well, he loves its museums. Over the years, whenever we visited the Big Apple, we'd leave Finley with my parents in New Jersey and Matt and I would train into the city. Matt would haul me from exhibit to exhibit until my eyes and feet got so tired I'd beg him to let me go sit in a café for an hour. As much as I appreciated Matt wanting to share his passions for cubism or surrealism or impressionism, I got much more enjoyment out of the hours I'd spend watching people and eavesdropping on conversations. I knew at some point I'd embed much of what I'd seen and heard into my stories.

I switch legs and visualize Macon working in the newly opened cheese shop. Who are his customers? What do they—?

Suddenly Terra flies into Finley, almost knocking her to the ground.

"Terra, what are you doing?" I look over to my left and see Annie striding across the field toward us.

"Hello, Kate," she says.

"Hi! What's going on?"

"As you can see, the kid wore me down with her whining and I acquiesced." Annie rolls her eyes, pretending to be exasperated. "Tell me it's not too late to sign up."

"Yay! I'm sure it's not too late. But you'll have to fill out the paperwork—you know, parental consent forms and—is that okay?" I say, the words coming out in excited bursts.

"Sure, whatever I need to do."

"Okay, give me a minute." I herd the team over to Coach Eric, who's chatting with other parents. "Hey, guys." I give everyone a perfunctory wave. "They're all stretched and ready to go, Coach."

"Thanks, Kate. All right, ladies, give me a lap around the field."

"Eric, could we take another player?" I ask after the girls take off running.

"Depends on if she can kick or not."

"Very funny, Eric." Christy Pell punches him in the shoulder.

"That hurt!" Eric wails, backing out of punching range. "Kate, have whoever it is fill out the form. There's one on the clipboard there. See you later!"

As Eric races to catch up with his team, Christy asks, "Who's the new kid?"

I pick up the clipboard. "Terra. She and her mom are over there talking to Matt."

"Oh, her. Yeah, I saw her last week—"

I don't wait for her to finish and run over to my husband and Annie. "So, you two met again."

"I was just telling Annie that it's awesome Terra's going to play," Matt says with a huge smile. "Anyway, it was nice to see you again." He raises his hand as if he is going to touch her shoulder, but stops, leans toward me, and gives me a lusty kiss on the mouth. "Come on, Terra, let's hit the field."

Feeling as awkward as I did back in high school whenever I witnessed other kids' PDA, I shuffle my feet and thrust the clipboard toward Annie. "Here's the form."

But Annie isn't paying attention to me. She's watching Matt run Terra over to the other girls. After an eruption of high-pitched cheers and giggles, the entire team swoops in for a group hug, folding Terra into their pack like a protective group of penguins.

"What?" she asks, turning toward me.

"Fill this out."

Annie takes the clipboard, drops it on the ground, then sits down, spreads open her legs, and leans forward. I feel silly standing, so I sit too.

Annie has on a pair of baggy white cotton shorts and a camouflage-patterned tank top. What was under the sweatpants and baggy sweater she wore is the opposite of fat; Annie's legs and arms are all muscle. And hair. Looking at the dark hair protruding from under her arms and covering her legs, I wonder how the woman can possibly go out in public.

"Hey, thanks for the playdate. I think the girls really like one another," I say, trying not to stare.

"They most definitely do," she says as she fills in the blanks on the form. "You know," she raises her head and glances over at the girls, "you're lucky you have a husband who volunteers for his kid's shit. I was the designated parent in my world."

I follow her gaze across the field to Matt. "Yeah. He's gone a lot, but when he's home, he's totally present."

"I won this award a couple years ago." Annie attaches the pen to the clipboard and flops back onto her elbows. "I'd done some volunteer work—pro bono stuff—for the local food bank. Their donations were way down; people weren't getting enough to eat and I'm there dropping off a load of veggies from my food share and I start talking to the folks who work there and I find out how bad the situation is and I say, 'Let me see what I can do to help,' because, well, I've got a lot of contacts in the city."

"What do you do for work?" For all the intimate talk we shared, I still know so little about the woman. But I know I really like her.

"At the moment, I'm on hiatus, but I, ah, let's just say I'm in procurement." Instead of looking at me, she speaks while watching the girls. I realize I've been staring at Annie's hairy legs again and abruptly turn to pay attention to Finley dribbling a ball down the field, her long blond ringlets flying out in all directions from her head. Matt runs alongside her, shouting encouragement.

"Anyway, I mess with their website and spread the word through various channels, blah blah, and things turn around, you know? In a few weeks they've got a surplus of food. It's all good. No big deal."

"Mm-hmm."

"And then I get a call that I've been nominated for this positive impact award. PIA. I have no idea what it is, so I look it up online. Every year they pick twelve women—Wait. Let me back up. So, years ago twelve uber rich women in Denver pooled their money and bought this totally ostentatious diamond bracelet— like half a million dollars ostentatious—and they all shared it, you know, like they each got to wear it for one month."

"Uh-huh."

"And after a few years I guess one of them climbed off her throne and said, 'I have a brilliant idea, darlings,'"—she lowers her voice into a fake upper-crust accent. She sounds exactly like Audrey does when she speaks in my head—"'What do you say we do something, you know, *benevolent*. Let's find twelve women who are making a positive difference in the community and allow *them* to wear it for a month!'"

I would love to wear a fancy diamond bracelet for a month, but nothing I do, I realize with a bit of guilt, makes much of a difference. Impact, maybe. Difference, definitely not.

"So the night of the awards ceremony rolls around and Clayton asks if he has to go, and I tell him, 'Nah, it's probably a lot of bullshit but I should go anyway,' and when I get there— it's at the Four Seasons—I see it wasn't bullshit at all. I mean it was totally black ties and gowns and I'm the most underdressed person in the room."

I have no trouble believing this.

"All the winners are given this huge Lucite trophy and people are congratulating each other like it's a big gushy altruism orgy and I'm bored out of my mind, but I figure it'd be the classy thing to do to stick it out until my name is called, right? So I suck down a few glasses of wine and listen to the speeches. One by one, these women go up to the podium and graciously accept their hunk of acrylic for helping the homeless or drugged-out teenagers or whatever the fuck they did to deserve this great honor, and then it suddenly dawns on me that they're all saying the same thing."

I freeze when Casey, the clumsiest ten-year-old I ever saw, trips over the ball she's dribbling and lands face-first. I almost get up to check on her but Matt beats me to it. I look back at Annie and ask, "What were they saying?"

But instead of answering, Annie jumps up and performs a cartwheel as if she were a five-year-old showing off to her parents, then lands in a split. "Every single one of those women, Kate, thanked their husbands or partners for supporting them. Every one of them," she says before cartwheeling back over to me again. "There was no way I was going to thank Clayton, and not because he was dead—not yet, anyway—but because *he* hadn't done a single thing to support me. So when it was my turn to speak, I thanked Terra for inspiring me to make the world a better place."

She reaches down and picks up the clipboard. "Next time I get an award for being Superwoman, it'd be nice to have Superman standing beside me," she announces before skipping off toward Coach Eric.

KATE

Macon wiped his hands on his apron and greeted the first customer of the day—a suited man in his twenties, wearing thick black glasses. "Good morning. Let me know if you want to sample something."

"Just browsing." The man put his right hand on the counter and bent to survey the cheese case. "You don't just sell Smiling Girl cheeses. Damn, you've got a lot to choose from."

Macon nodded. "Cheese has got to have friends too. It's like a brotherhood, you know?"

The man looked up. "No, I don't know," he said flatly, as if challenging Macon. Macon had been warned that New Yorkers could be rude, but being surly about the shop's selection of cheeses was ridiculous. But if Macon wanted to stay in the city so he could win back Lizzie, he had no choice but to take it up the ass for the owners. "Artisan cheesemakers are a small breed, but we're growing fast," he replied in a friendly tone, though what he really wanted to do was smash the guy's glasses into his face. "We try to support each other; spread the cheese love around."

Ignoring him, the man walked over to the display of aged cheeses on the wooden shelves in the corner of the tiny shop. "Looks like you've got mostly Vermont cheeses, no?"

"We're a Vermont company, so sure, we're pushing the local goods. But if you've got something against the Green Mountain state, we carry lots of others, like Rush Creek Reserve out of Wisconsin, Bay Blue from Point Reyes, California, and there's half a dozen from Washington—"

"Great. Thanks," the man said before walking out the door.

"And fuck you too," Macon said to his retreating back. Macon shook his head then dropped the anger onto the floor, kicked it under the cheese case, and went back to slicing up the salumi. He had two days to find Lizzie before Audrey flew down for the weekend and he needed to concentrate on his plan.

I save the document and lounge back in my chair, rubbing the side of my nose for a few seconds before sitting forward again to type Annie Meyers+Denver into Google. Nothing relevant shows up. Annabelle Meyers displays an obituary in *The Denver Post* about a woman with that name who, at ninety-two, died from Alzheimer's. The Positive Impact Award of Denver site lists this year's recipients but nothing about past winners.

I type in Clayton Meyers and find an article mentioning his death:

Law enforcement officials in Park County are continuing their investigation into the death of 37-year-old Clayton Meyers of Denver. Sheriff Dennis Brown says Meyers apparently got trapped by a branch and drowned, but first responders on the scene reported seeing a large wound on his leg. Brown says rescue crews recovered Meyers's body shortly after he was reported missing by his family early Wednesday morning. An autopsy is scheduled to be conducted this week.

Why perform an autopsy? Just for the heck of it, I open the website for the coroner's office and see that autopsy reports in Colorado are public records. I fill in the blanks and hit SEND. Easy enough. An automated message informs me that I will receive my record in two to four weeks.

I pick up Adam and twist his legs so they are behind his head. Then I set him down and go back to my book.

ANNIE

I rip the invoice out of the printer and scribble my name at the bottom. Bastards had better pay up this time or I'll sue on principle alone. It isn't as if we need the money: Clayton's death had proven to be quite the bounteous windfall. I had no idea he'd taken out an extra life insurance policy before his last trip to the Himalayas. I guess he thought it'd be risky. What a thoughtful man he was.

I go outside to put the letter in the mailbox and am just raising the red flag when I hear a car slowing down to a stop behind me. I have an inkling it's one of my neighbors and they are going to want to talk to me. For how long I can pretend to have trouble lifting the flag into place I have no clue, but here I am, with my hand on the rusty metal, my back turned, hoping they get impatient and drive off.

"Hi there. You must be the new people who moved in."

Maybe I can pretend to be deaf, or what if I don't speak English? I can turn around and say something in Swahili and walk away.

"I'm Steve Hodges, from the gray house at the end of the street."

I surmise from his aggressively friendly tone, Steve Hodges is a tenacious creature and he plans to stay fixed to the road until I fulfill my half of the neighborly transaction.

"Annie Meyers, from the red house right here," I say, giving him my full frontal. I am momentarily taken aback when I see that Steve Hodges is an exceptionally handsome man. A thick, unkempt mob of salt-and-pepper-colored hair swarms over his large head. He wears thin round silver glasses and has a tiny onyx stud in his left ear.

"Nice to meet you, Annie." He reaches through the window and extends his hand. I have no interest in touching him—yet—and offer him a friendly nod while stuffing my hands into my pockets.

"Where'd you folks move from?" he says, retracting the arm.

"Denver."

"And what brings you to Vermont?"

That's really none of your business, Steve. "Oh, you know, stuff. Change of scenery. That sort of thing."

"Well, welcome to the neighborhood."

"Thanks."

"Hey, if you or your, uh, husband ever need any help with anything . . ."

Knowing that ceding my widowhood will only extend the conversation, I reply, "No, we're good. Thanks."

I envision his brain trying to come up with another topic with which to continue our hollow chatter, and swiftly cut him off. "Nice to meet you, Steve. Have a good one," I say and walk back inside the house.

I consider unpacking another moving carton, but instead I go into the kitchen to make a cup of passionflower and lemon balm tea to help calm me. I am starting to regret inviting Kate's family over for dinner this coming Friday. I visualize the three of them and the two of us sitting around the table making talk small enough to squeeze through a mousehole.

"Do you miss Denver?"

"And what kind of work are you in, Matt?"

"How is Terra liking her teacher?"

"The dentist thinks Finley might need braces."

Before adding water, I throw in a spoonful of valerian root. It will make me sleepy, but my mind feels like a spiderweb with too many delectable flies pulling at its sticky strands, desperately trying to break free.

I have a lot riding on this relocation and need to stay focused.

I put the lid on the teapot and set the timer.

KATE

I'm sitting on the edge of the bed watching Matt unpack. "So, tell me. How was Seattle?"

"Hard," he says. "But, you know me. I was at the top of my game," he says, hanging up his suits.

"Why was it hard?"

He empties the hotel laundry bag from his suitcase into the basket on the floor. "It was kind of strange, you know? Before introducing the product, I had to get people to talk about their fears. I asked them if they were afraid of being robbed. If they thought it was likely to happen to them."

"Was it a mixed group?"

"Yeah, but all upper middle class. I guess poor people don't lie awake at night worrying about home invasions or their kids getting kidnapped."

"You mean there's no way they can *afford* the security system, which is why they weren't recruited in the first place."

"Exactly." He sighs. "Anyway, I collected a lot of data. It's going to take me hours to compile the reports."

Although my gut is telling me that odds are he didn't find

any sexually amenable women strewn in among the fearful, I ask anyway.

"I don't suppose you met anyone," I say hopefully.

Matt laughs. "No, I didn't. I am so sorry, Kaybee. I think maybe it was me. I wasn't putting out the vibes like I usually do." He shakes his head. "Not sure why."

"Oh, well," I say, and before I stand up Matt puts his hands on my shoulders and leans toward me.

"I really am sorry. I know how much you needed another chapter. Can you forgive me?" He kisses me softly. I taste mint on his lips. As he moves away, my right hand reaches out and clutches the front of his shirt, pulling him to me, opening my mouth and sticking my tongue deep into his. Matt pushes me back onto the bed and rubs my right breast through my shirt.

I have no idea what has gotten into me, but now I'm stuck. Stuck with Matt kneading me. Stuck with his tongue flicking around my mouth. I keep up the charade for a few seconds more, but when he gazes down at me with a Is-this-really-going-to-happen? look on his face, I roll away and get off the bed.

"I'm sorry, Matt," I say, vibrating with guilt. I can't meet his eyes. Starting something I knew I wouldn't finish was a clumsy move. What am I trying to prove? Matt knows I enjoy our intimacy. A kiss here. A warm hug there. Nothing's changed in ten years.

Matt jumps up. "Don't be. I thought maybe Macon was getting to you a little, but hey, no worries," he concedes before giving me a cold peck on my cheek. "Oh, wait, where is it?" He grabs a plastic bag from his suitcase. "I went to the Chihuly Garden and Glass Museum. I bought you this," he says, handing me a green marbled pen. "And I got this for Finley." He holds up a purple T-shirt with a childish line-drawn pink octopus covering the front. "It's pretty cool, isn't it?"

It is pretty cool, but more to the point, why on earth would he think I've suddenly changed? It isn't as if I don't want to be a "normal" wife, one who can't wait to make love to her husband the moment he gets home from a long business trip. But I'm not that person, and I am pretty certain I never will be that person. Why did I just kiss him like that? Why did I feel the need to mark my territory like a dog lifting its leg? Nothing between us has changed. Atypical though it is, we have a finely tuned satisfying partnership. Matt screws. I write. And, both of us are considerably accomplished in our respective fields, if I do say so myself.

"It is cool. Finley's going to love it," I reply, relieved that this small misstep of mine is already history.

After Matt slides the empty suitcase under the bed and walks out of the bedroom, I call after him, "By the way, Annie Meyers invited us to dinner tomorrow night."

Matt stops halfway down the hallway and then backs up, his hand grasping the doorjamb a second before his face appears. "Dinner at Annie's? Um. Sorry. Nope."

"Why? You should get to know her. She's really funny."

"I'm sure I will get to know her, but I need a couple days of not being around other people. Other than you and Finley, I mean." He smiles.

"I get it. You've got human overload."

"What I've got is sensory overload. Plus, I've got a huge report to write. Please send my regrets."

"Will do," I reply, more relieved than disappointed. If Matt joins us, he and Annie will dance the get-to-know-you waltz. And since they are both so at ease with themselves, so casual and talkative, I'll be left out. At least for a little while, I want to keep Annie to myself.

I pick up the basket and head to the laundry room in the basement. A lot of women complain about housework, but I like it. I've come up with some of my best ideas while sweeping the kitchen floor or scrubbing the toilet or separating the whites from the colors.

I start a hot wash and stuff Matt's dry-clean-only shirts into a Gadue's Dry Cleaning bag. After I drop the bag on the floor by the mudroom, I find Finley on the couch reading a book. On the rug below her, Munch twitches in his sleep.

"You're not in the bath yet? Where's Daddy?"

"Dunno," she answers without lifting her head.

"Did he show you the shirt he got you?"

"Yeah." She pulls it out from behind her, waves it once, and releases it onto Munch's head. Munch doesn't move.

"It's already eight-thirty. Come on. Bedtime."

"I'm finishing this chapter first," she replies defiantly.

"Put your bookmark in, and go brush your teeth now," I say, sounding more impatient than I should because there are probably a lot of other parents in our time zone who are instead uttering, "Turn off the television and go brush your teeth."

"Okay, fine." Finley slams the book closed with a bang and slowly slithers off the couch like a snake until she is draped over Munch. Only then does he wake up and start wagging his tail.

"Finley, please. Get off the dog."

"Mommy, can I go to Terra's tomorrow?" she asks as Munch licks hamburger grease from her cheeks. She's filthy and needs a bath, but it's too late for one. Normally, when Matt is home he takes over the bedtime routine, but tonight he only got as far as showing his daughter her present and then promptly forgot about her. What is he doing that is so important? "You are going to Terra's tomorrow. We're having dinner there."

"Yippee!" She walks off toward the bathroom, dragging one of her legs behind her like it's dead weight, moaning, "I don't know why I have to go to bed. I'm not even tired."

"Go!"

"Terra's lucky because she only has one parent to boss her around."

"Finley Parsons!" I say loudly, stunned that such a callous sentiment could erupt from my child. "That was a horrible thing to say."

"Why?" She is genuinely baffled.

"Terra's parents aren't divorced, sweetheart. Her father died."

"I know," she says, casually kicking her formally dead leg back and forth.

"She must be terribly sad, Finley." A larger lesson could be imparted here though I do not wish to overwhelm my daughter with thoughts of dead fathers before bedtime. "We'll discuss this tomorrow, okay? Go get into your PJs, and Daddy and I will come—"

"But that's what *she* said, Mommy." Her hands are on her hips. "Terra is the one who said she's lucky."

"She said that?" I don't buy it. Losing a parent, even a ragingly selfish one, has to be devastating. Terra was obviously hiding her emotions in front of her new friend. No ten-year-old wants to interrupt a playdate with a crying spell.

"Yes, she did," Finley stresses. "Terra said she and her mom are lucky because now they can be free like birds and fly whenever they want."

Annie claimed Clayton was an egomaniacal jerk and he didn't support her, sure, but come on—Terra feels lucky her daddy's dead? As I consider how twisted this is, Finley says, "I'm gonna go brush my teeth and read my book," and walks into the bathroom.

I march over to the guest room-*cum*-Matt's home office. Back when we moved into the four-bedroom house a decade ago, I worked there while Matt had my office at the back of the house, further away from the three main bedrooms. After I started writing erotica, I worried that one of our rare overnight guests would find pornographic notes I'd left on the desk by accident. I was also afraid that Finley, whose bedroom shares a wall, would overhear me muttering something unbecoming, given my penchant for talking out loud while I write.

The room is a study in organized chaos, thanks to IKEA. Against one wall is a gray Friheten couch that can fold out into a bed. White Ekby shelves line the entire top half of the opposite wall. They are piled high with so many papers and heavy binders I've often feared they will come crashing down onto the black Bekant desk beneath them. I pray that when and if that happens, Matt won't be sitting there.

At the moment he's hunched over his MacBook, typing so intently he doesn't register my presence. "Matt!" I say to his back.

He slaps the top down and spirals around. "What? God, you scared me."

"You didn't run a bath for Finley." It was just a few days ago when I gloated to Annie about how present my husband is when he's not traveling. Matt's behavior at the moment makes me feel like a liar.

"I'm sorry, Kate," he says, smoothing his large hands over his face. "I needed to get some shit out of the way. I'll go now." He looks angry.

"It's too late for a bath. Anything wrong?" I ask, sitting down on the couch.

"No," he says flatly.

"So, Finley just told me that Terra told her that she and Annie are—and I quote—*lucky* Clayton died."

"That makes sense. She told you he was an asshole, didn't she?"

"Matt!"

"What?" He is shaking his right leg impatiently and I can see it isn't worth fighting about. Besides, I am looking forward to dinner tomorrow night. Annie is peculiar, but she is not a monster. The more I think about it, the more I'm convinced Annie didn't really use the term *lucky*. Or if she did, it was to help Terra get over her father's tragic death. Not that I would ever say we were better off without him, but if, God forbid, Matt died, I'd say most anything to soothe Finley's sadness.

"Nothing," I reply, discarding my skepticism.

"Tell Finley I'll be there in a minute. I gotta finish this."

After kissing Finley goodnight, I go to the kitchen to boil water for tea. If Matt is working tonight, I will too. I've been away from Macon for too long and miss being in his head. I cross my arms, trying to form a clear picture of how he and Audrey are going to have sex in her apartment. I don't want them to do it on her bed since I'm saving that spot for the threesome. On the white couch? The kettle whistles, and I pour the water over the Earl Grey tea bag, watching it float to the top. As I pinch the label and pulse the string up and down, I think about Matt kissing me on the bed, squeezing my breasts. Before I have a chance to rebuke myself, I turn my attention toward any details I might be able to work into my book.

He tasted like mint. I've been meaning to add more sensory descriptions so that's good: Audrey will taste like mint when Macon kisses her. There was also something unfamiliar about Matt. I squeeze the tea bag and toss it into the compost bucket while trying unsuccessfully to pinpoint what was different.

I am just passing by the dry cleaner bag on the floor when it hits me. After I undo the drawstring I pull out a white Brooks Brothers dress shirt, and hold it against my face, breathing in deeply. Nothing. I remove another and sniff again, now realizing what was off.

"Mommy, why are you smelling Daddy's clothes?"

I whip around to see Finley staring at me. "What? Oh." I kneel down and stuff the pile of shirts back into the bag. "I was check-ing to see which ones were dirty. What are you doing out of bed?"

"I was wondering if maybe Daddy forgot about me."

"Of course not, sweetheart," I say, trying not to fixate on the fact that none of the shirts smell like aftershave. "He'll be in soon."

KATE

The house is in as much disarray as before. There are as many un-emptied boxes taking up floor space and as many unwashed dishes taking up sink space. As I sit up on the barstool with a glass of wine in my hand, I watch Annie grate a carrot while moving her hips to a Bob Marley song playing on a Bluetooth speaker. I take another gulp of wine and ease into the comfortable silence between us.

"You know," Annie says without looking up, "I'm actually glad it's just us girls tonight."

"Me too. What are you cooking?" I ask, only moderately curious. As long as there are vegetables involved, I'm happy.

"I am making for you, Miss Kate, mother of Finley, my *molto* famous Glory Bowl. More wine?"

"Yes, wow, I drained that pretty fast, didn't I?"

"Cheers." Annie clinks her glass against mine. "To new beginnings with new friends."

"I'll drink to that," I say, smiling. "So, Miss Annie, mother of Terra, what's a Glory Bowl?"

Annie starts grating a blood-red beet. "It's a majorly popular

Canadian dish I plagiarized. Lots of raw and cooked veggies, rice, and tofu, topped with a sauce so good you'll want to bathe in it. Believe me, sweetheart, eating this will add five years to your life."

She called me *sweetheart*. I am sure I am blushing. "But what makes it Canadian?" A few years ago, we spent spring break visiting the sights and sounds of Quebec for research I was doing for my third book. I never came across anything like a Glory Bowl.

Annie moves on to the block of tofu, slicing it into small cubes. "It's named for a famous ski resort in Nelson, British Columbia."

Ah, that's the *western* part of Canada. "Hey, Nelson! That old Steve Martin movie, *Roxanne*, was filmed there!" I shriek way too loudly. "I remember that because I'm one of those obsessive types who has to watch the credits," I say, snatching a carrot stick from the counter. "I like to see where a movie was filmed, or if it was based on a true story or, you know," I say, chewing. "Shoot. I forgot what I was saying."

"You'd just seen *Roxanne*."

"Oh yeah. It was filmed in Nelson!"

"Huh." Annie scoops a blob of coconut oil into a pan that has seen better days. "Never saw it."

"It was an updated version of *Cyrano de Bergerac*. It was actually a pretty lame movie, now that I think about it."

"Ah, *oui*. 'A kiss is a secret which takes the lips for the ear,'" Annie recites in the worst French accent imaginable.

"What is it with you and your quotes? The day I met you, you recited something from *The Princess Bride*."

"Dunno." She pushes the sizzling cubes of tofu around with a large roughed-up wooden spoon. "I guess I've got glue in here," she says, tapping the side of her head. "I forget nothing."

When I say, "I'll have to remember that," we both giggle.

I take my glass and wander over to the large picture window

that looks out at the backyard. A cement patio, bordered by a lush green lawn, surrounds their pool. Behind the lawn is a wall of thick tall trees. For suburbia, Annie has quite a secluded spot.

A wave of panic sloshes through my wine-filled stomach. If Finley is ever invited to swim here, I will make sure to come along. Or am I being too much of a helicopter mom? Annie wouldn't let the kids swim without supervision.

I turn and regard her as she cooks and hums, a satisfied smile on her face—a face I am starting to think is actually handsome. Annie is so carefree, so comfortable in her own skin. Nothing like other Rayburne women, the Type A supermoms with their sparkling kitchens and supposedly robust sex lives. I want to have a real girlfriend to hang out with. Someone who lives in my neighborhood. We would see each other all the time. Take tea breaks. Our children would be best friends. We'd have dinners together. Go on trips.

A pang of guilt thumps up against my heart. What about Heidi? Sure, she obsesses too much about her dogs and she lives way down in Middleton, but I really admire her spunk. I love that Heidi devotes her life to helping homeless animals. Annie's also altruistic. She won an award for her good deeds. Come to think of it, Annie and Heidi are a lot alike. They are both direct, funny, and smart. They both want to make a difference in the world. They'd love each other! In fact, I'll introduce them. All three of us could go on a pack walk. "Hey, you have to meet my friend Heidi. You would totally—" I slap my hand over my mouth.

Annie raises an eyebrow. "I would totally, what?"

"Oh my God. Please forget I mentioned her name," I say, shaking my head. "She runs a *dog* rescue." Heidi would have to be quarantined in a dog-free cell for a month before Annie could possibly get anywhere near her.

"Ah. Okay." She pops a piece of tofu into her mouth. "I

will strike the name *Heidi* from my memory bank. Thanks for looking out for me, girlfriend."

Okay, I can't share crazy Heidi with her, but I want to share *something* significant with my new GF. Maybe I'll tell her that I write erotica. I'll bring up the movie again and casually mention that, just like *Cyrano de Bergerac*, I write *my* characters' stories through someone else! Annie will get such a kick out of it; she'll think I'm oh-so-fascinating.

But what if she asks whose stories I use? I would have to admit—

Finley and Terra rush into the kitchen. "Not Glory Bowl again!" Terra whines when she sees the tofu browning in the pan.

"Come here, child." Annie pulls Terra close to her and wraps her un-stirring arm around her shoulder. "Look in this pan? Do you realize how many soybeans had to give up their lives so we could eat this beautiful food?" She says this with such seriousness Terra's lower lip quivers.

"Poor dead soybeans," Terra utters. She's on the verge of tears and I try to think of something funny to say to lighten the mood, but all of a sudden Terra high-fives Annie and they both begin laughing so hard Terra actually falls onto the floor.

Within seconds Annie starts coughing and wheezing so much she clutches at her chest and howls "Fuck!" before shoving an inhaler into her mouth.

We all freeze like figures in a diorama. Finley and Terra stare in shocked awe. Annie sags over the counter, gasping for air with slow tortured heaves.

The smell of burning oil propels me from my petrified state, and I instantly reach over and turn off the stove. I want to do more to help but am at a loss. Should I call 911? Rub her back? I do nothing. Two or three minutes pass before Annie's breathing calms. She turns toward the girls.

"Are you better now, Annie?" Terra asks anxiously.

"I am, darlin'. I'm almost there," Annie says, still winded but clearly more comfortable. "You girls go play. I'll call you when dinner's ready, okay?"

Terra hesitates as if anticipating another attack, but Finley squeezes her arm and pulls her from the kitchen. I am guessing that my daughter has to be as rattled as I am by what we just witnessed.

After the girls flee, Annie turns on the stove and looks at me. "Whoever it was that said laughter is the best medicine," she announces as she picks up the spoon, "obviously didn't have asthma."

"You mean you don't actually *know* who said it?" I say, pretending to look shocked.

"It's from the Bible," Annie answers with a grin. "'A merry heart doeth good like a medicine.' Proverbs 17:22."

"You, Annie Meyers," I say, shaking my head, "are killing me."

I offer to help clean up after dinner, but Annie insists I come sit with her on the couch. "Leave it. I'll get to it before the next century."

I am more than a little buzzed, so I pass when Annie tries to refill my glass and gratefully accept a mug of tea. "I think I might someday learn to like the taste of this." I sip the hot, strangely sensual liquid and relax back into the cushions, my feet up on the coffee table. "What's in it?"

Annie puts her feet up next to mine. "My own concoction. I call it my LayLow blend. It's good for mellowing out."

"It's what we had last time, no?"

"Nope. That was GoodTimes. I drink it during the day to give me a boost of energy."

They both taste like herbed mud. I close my eyes and breathe in the earthy steam.

"I have a mix for everything," says Annie. "It's the shaman in me. I must have been a healer in my past life."

"Well, I feel extremely mellow, so you must have had lots of satisfied clients in that past life."

Annie lets out a small cough. I tense, waiting for the ghastly wheezing to start up again and am relieved when it does not. "You know, I've actually thought about starting a tea business, but"—she gulps the rest of her wine and stretches her arms over her head, revealing an unexpectedly taut belly —"I've got other things I need to take care of first."

"You should, Annie! You should totally do that. People love alternative stuff," I say, instantly unfurling a fantasy about going into business together. It'd start out small and we would come up with cute packaging and Matt could hold a focus group to find out the best name and we'd expand to the internet and there'd be news stories about the two moms in small-town Vermont who started it all. How fun would it be to have a project with a friend? "You could call it Annie's Remedies. And you'd have teas for insomnia and infertility and—"

"Horniness. That'd be a bestseller. I call it GoodLove."

As if it'd reached the edge of a cliff, my business plan comes to a complete halt. "Horniness? You make tea for that?"

"I do. I have a girlfriend in Denver who used it and said it changed her marriage. She told me that she and her husband hardly ever made love because she wasn't into it, so I created this mix to boost her libido: some yohimbe bark, a bit of yin yang huo, a few other magical additions, and now they're screwing like bunnies."

I slide my feet off the coffee table and sit up. Dare I tell Annie about . . . ? "Hunh. Maybe I would like to . . . um." My mind cleaves in two. On one side is Kate the wife, who would love nothing more than to have a *traditional* relationship with her husband. On the other side is Daphne Moore, the successful author of erotica novels who needs her husband's sexual adventures to stoke her literary fire.

"Maybe you would like to what?"

I look up at the ceiling, wanting to escape Annie's fierce focus. I couldn't possibly tell Annie that Matt and I haven't made love in over a decade. I feel my hand on the door but I lack the nerve to open it. "Nothing. Hey, it's late. I should get Finley to bed."

"Come on, sister. It's obvious you're holding onto something that needs to be set free. Look around this house," she says, sweeping out her arms as if a game show hostess showing off the grand prize. "Ain't nothin' here gonna bite you."

When I unknowingly reach up to touch my scar, Annie edges closer to me and takes my hand away from my face. "Why do you do that?"

"Do what?"

"You rub that silly scar all the time like it's a touchstone." She runs her finger along the pink jagged line.

"I don't know, habit?" I say, inching back until I am pushed up against the end of the couch. "I feel like it's all people see when they look at me." I've never admitted this to anyone, not even Matt.

Annie maneuvers even closer and stares into my eyes. I want to look away but her gaze is intense, almost hypnotic. "You should stop. It's annoying. Plus, it detracts from your irrefutable beauty."

I scoff. "Please. Even I know—"

"As the very gay and very wise Somerset Maugham once said," Annie interjects before I can continue putting myself down, "'Perfection has one grave defect: it is apt to be dull.'"

"Point taken," I say, grinning. Her words couldn't have been more *perfect*. "Thank you."

"*De rien*." She scoots away toward the other end of the

couch. I'm thankful for the space between us. "Now that that's settled, let's get back to the topic at hand, shall we?"

I say nothing. The sparkly air from a moment before again darkens.

"You know you can trust me, Miss Kate, mother of Finley."

I do know I can trust her. "Okay." I breathe in a large breath. "The truth is I also have really low libido. No: strike that. I have zero libido," I say, certain my face is in full blush. Yes, I'm embarrassed, but now that it is out, I feel better than I expected. It's like when I dropped off three bags of books and clothing at Goodwill last week—I feel purged.

"You mean you and Matt don't have a lot of sex?"

I stare down into the mug. "No. We don't."

"But you do sometimes, right?"

I shake my head.

"Ah, so then Finley was adopted," she says facetiously.

"Ha-ha. No. We were intimate for a while. Then . . . " I don't want to get into the specifics. I know exactly what Annie is thinking right now. "You're wondering why he stays married to me, right?"

Annie releases a hard audible breath as if she's just run to the end of the street and back. "No, I'm wondering how to make you believe how sorry I am to hear this."

"Thanks." Now that my buzz is wearing off I almost regret sharing such a colossally personal secret. Instead of Miss Kate, mother of Finley, Annie might now think of me as Mrs. Kate, defective wife. So much for becoming best friends. "I shouldn't have told you," I say, moving to stand up.

"What?" Annie reaches out and grabs my arm, forcing me back down. "You are not going anywhere, my friend."

"I just . . . I'm . . . you're the first person I've ever shared this with and—"

"And, what, now I'm no longer going to like you?" Annie says as she folds her remarkably pliable legs across each other like a master meditator. "You do know, Kate, that there are countless women *and men* on this planet who, for a million different reasons, do not wish to take part in the mating ritual. Some people don't want anything to do with sex. There's even a term for it: sex-repulsed. It might be because of some past trauma, or because that's just who they are, meaning they're born that way. And you know what? I bet they're probably okay with it." She untangles her legs and pushes her big toe into my thigh. "Hey. You there, at the end of the couch with the sad face. Did I not just seventy-three seconds ago tell you about my friend in Colorado? Hmm?"

"But your friend *wasn't* born that way. You said she wasn't into sex because of her libido." My confusion about the subject is beginning to overshadow my curiosity.

"Yes. For her it was her libido. As well it might be yours. And"—she scoots close and takes my hand—"if it turns out your physiology is out of whack, I'd be happy to tender a solution or two."

This is all a bit much for my tired mind to take in. Admitting that I have faulty wiring is more than enough for one night. Perhaps if we get together again, I'll figure out a way to convince Annie that Matt isn't suffering. I hate the idea of Annie feeling sorry for him. "Sure. Hey, thank you for everything, Annie," I say, rising abruptly and going over to the stairs. "Finley! Time to go home!" I yell.

Annie walks up next to me and squeezes me into a hug. "Thank you for being here," she says, releasing me before I can hug her back. "Do you want to take home a bowl of food for Matt?"

Annie's affection takes me by surprise. I want a do-over. I want her to hug me again so this time I can hug her back because that small body of hers felt so good against my own. "Thank you, no,"

I say, disappointed by the lost moment. "He would have hated that meal. Finley isn't a huge fan of mushrooms, but Matt outright despises them." I flash back to our first date when a slice of mushroom pizza almost ended our relationship before it'd even begun.

"What kind of person hates mushrooms?" Annie asks skeptically.

"The Matt kind. Don't get me wrong; I thought it was delicious, but not Matt," I say, putting on my shoes and coat. "The man lives on meat, potatoes, pizza, and smoothies. Period. In fact, he refers to tofu as 'hippie cheese.'"

Annie rolls her eyes. "That's original. Not."

Finley and Terra bound down the stairs. "Seriously, if he was married to you, he'd starve."

"Nah. If he was married to me, I'd have him begging for tempeh."

KATE

We met at the University of Vermont when Matt, a business major, went looking for a tutor to help him pass biology. I had just finished a session with an annoying student named Colin, and was putting away my books when a tall, supremely gorgeous guy strolled into the Tutoring Center. He was wearing jeans, a red flannel shirt with the sleeves rolled up, and a red bandana tied around his shoulder-length dark hair. I watched him through the study room's large window as he scanned the sign-up sheets on the bulletin board, marked his name on one, then walked out. I immediately ran out of the room and wrote my name on the form. I had a class at the same time he scheduled his tutoring session, but I figured some things were worth skipping Vertebrate Anatomy for.

He showed up fifteen minutes late for the session and I'd spent those fifteen long minutes rechecking and reconcealing the pimple on my chin, smelling my underarms, pacing. I had on a pair of stonewashed jeans and a white blouse. A wide navy blue hairband kept my short cropped dirty blond hair pulled off my face. After walking in, he extended his hand. "Hi. I'm Matt Parsons."

"Kate Burke." I shook his hand for a second, letting go before he could squeeze mine. "So, you want to get started? We only have forty-five minutes left," I uttered crisply, pretending to be annoyed by his lateness. I wasn't about to let him see how anxious I was to be near him.

"Yup," he said, sitting down next to me. "Let's hit the books."

This time he wore loose khaki pants and a blue shirt, again with the sleeves rolled up to expose his muscled forearms. I was on the tall side, at five foot seven, but Matt towered over me. And he smelled good. I usually hated aftershave, but what he'd splashed on smelled earthy, manly. I squirmed a little, trying not to stare at the pink hairband holding his long dark hair in a ponytail, and got down to business.

It took no more than five minutes to realize Matt Parsons was no rocket scientist. He asked inane questions, couldn't completely grasp the difference between meiosis and mitosis, and doodled on his page as he took notes. He was never going to win the Nobel Prize in Physics, but he was seriously hot.

"So, let's move on to gametes."

"Gametes. Sure. Let's."

"You get that they're haploid cells, that they only contain half the chromosomes of a normal cell, right?"

"Half. Right." He twirled his pen and wrote nothing.

"And with meiosis you get—"

"So, you're like a bio major?"

"Uh, yeah. You?" I asked.

"Business. Marketing focus."

"Cool." *Cool?* Had I actually said that? He was sitting too close to me.

"Do you really want to be a scientist? You're too cute to be a nerd."

How deeply had I blushed? I was sure I looked like I'd just

spent an hour in the Caribbean sun. I wondered if maybe he hadn't yet noticed that because I'd been a competitive swimmer all through high school my shoulders were a little too broad for my small waist. I was pretty enough, but I'd always been self-conscious about the scar on the side of my nose—courtesy of the first time I went ice skating when I was nine years old. I was with my friend Gillian who turned out to be as clumsy as I was. When we both fell at the same time, I landed face-first onto the blade of her upturned skate. "No, actually I want to be a writer."

"And, what, learning about *gametogenesis* is giving you material for the next great novel?"

I reached up to touch my nose, then stopped myself. "Well, yes, actually. Writers should have all sorts of background knowledge, you know? I mean, if I majored in English, I'd only be able to write about writing. I'm not as good at pulling things out of thin air as I want to be," I admitted with a bit of self-consciousness. "When I was little, I wanted to be a veterinarian, so I thought I'd study bio to see what it was like, and maybe for one of my books I'd make a character a vet and . . . well, yeah."

He was staring intently into my eyes. "That is one of the smartest things I've ever heard a girl say. You're, like, trying to take in the world, make it your own, so you can tell better stories. I love that."

I blushed again. Looked down at the diagram of chromosomes in the book. Clicked my pen.

And then he said, "Hey, you wanna blow this off and go grab some food?"

We'd gone to Manhattan Pizza and Pub where I ordered a single slice of mushroom pizza and refused to let him pay for it. Matt ordered three slices of pepperoni and insisted on buying our Cokes. While eating, we filled one another in on our lives: he was from Laconia, New Hampshire. He had two younger brothers. His father, whom he hardly ever saw, was an airline pilot. After an ugly divorce caused by their father's infidelity, their mom, an RN, raised them.

"I'm sorry. That must have sucked," I said, nibbling on my food. I could hardly breathe around him, let alone eat.

"Yeah, I sorta hate the man for what he did to my mom. You make a commitment to someone, you stick to it, you know?"

I nodded.

"What about you?" he asked, picking up the third slice.

"I'm from Montclair, New Jersey. Only child. Dad owns a real estate company. Mom's a guidance counselor. End of story." I shrugged as if apologizing for not having any familial drama.

"And someday you're going to be a famous writer and your heroine will be a veterinarian who falls in love with the owner of a dog she saves after it gets hit by a car, right?"

"A love story? You think I want to write love stories?"

"For sure." He leaned closer. "I love love stories."

Of course he did.

"Maybe. But first I need to—" I didn't want to admit that I would actually need to *experience* love if I was ever going to write about it.

"First you need to, what?" he asked, genuinely interested.

"Like I said, I have to, um, you know, research a topic if I'm going to write a story about it."

He laughed. "You mean you need to research love?"

Why had I just admitted that to him? What a total dork. "Whatever. So, anyway, what do you want to be when you grow up?" I said, changing the subject.

"Nope. You first. You've never been in love?"

In love? I wasn't sure I'd ever been in *like*. When it came to the opposite sex, I wasn't sure about anything. "Not yet," seemed safe enough for the moment.

"Me neither."

"What? No way."

He grinned. "Don't get me wrong. It's not like I haven't been with lots of—shit. Never mind. Sorry."

"What? You were just about to say you've been with a lot of women, right?"

He nodded.

"How many? Like more than a hundred?" I tried to sound casual.

He cocked his head to the side and uttered a weak, "Um . . ."

"More than a thousand?" I knew I sounded panicky.

"I don't know, Kate. I mean, it's not like I ever counted." There was an edge to his voice. I was pushing too hard.

"So then shall we just stick with *a lot*?"

"Yeah, sure," he said, obviously relieved.

As if on cue, a cute young woman wearing a University of Vermont sweatshirt over enormous breasts appeared at our table. Strands of purple twine were wrapped around each of her red-colored pigtails. "Hi, Matt," she chirped.

"Lizzie! What's up?"

"Oh, you know." She sort of half-giggled.

"Lizzie. This is my good friend, Kate," he said, flicking his head toward me. I had no clue why he'd just referred to me as his good friend, or why he didn't introduce me to her, but it wasn't exactly the best time to start questioning his social skills. Lizzie glanced at me for half a second, tossed a small wave, and said, "Hey," before staring into Matt's eyes. "How have you been, Matt?" she asked.

"I've been great, thanks. Hey, did you dye your hair?"

"I did!" As Lizzie lifted one of her pigtails and looked at it as if she wasn't sure it belonged to her, I figured it was time to leave. Matt was probably out of my league, anyway. For all I knew he was just hungry and once we walked out of the pub, I'd never see him again. I reached around to grab my backpack off the chair, but when Lizzie uttered, "I totally wanted to thank you for helping me ace that art history exam," I twisted back around again.

Art history?

"Awesome." Matt high-fived her. "I told you—it's all in the context. You've gotta see the imagery through the eyes of the artist, right?"

"Yeah, for sure but those flashcards you made me memorize totally helped."

"Excellent."

"You, like, know more than the teacher does. I mean, you totally made me get it. I owe you one," she said with such a lusty edge I felt a burn of jealousy spread out across my body. I hardly knew this man and was already feeling territorial.

"You don't owe me a thing, Lizzie. I was happy to do it. Everyone needs a little help now and then, right?" He locked his eyes onto mine and winked. "Listen, Lizzie, Kate and I are having a pretty deep discussion here. Do you mind if we, ah—"

"Oh, sure. Sorry," she added with another awkward giggle. "See you around, Matt. Nice meeting you, Kate."

I shook my head in disbelief. "I don't get it. If you're so smart, why do you need a biology tutor?"

Matt locked his hands behind his head. "Because I'm only smart about things I'm passionate about. Stuff that, you know, stirs my insides."

"And what—cytokinesis doesn't get you hot?"

He threw his head back and laughed. "Definitely not. I don't give a shit about the difference between telophase and anaphase but ask me to write a ten-page essay about expressionism and I'll blow your mind."

He was already blowing my mind, for reasons I didn't totally comprehend. He was gorgeous, yes, and clearly there was depth there, but he was probably only looking for a one-night-stand. Something I would never be. No way. Still, I wasn't ready to ditch him. I leaned forward onto my elbows. "So, okay, back to what you were saying about being with *a lot* of women but not ever being in love."

"Nah. Let's move on to another subject, okay?"

"Oh, come on. Just tell me or . . . or I won't let you walk me home," I said before I could stop myself.

"Walk you home, huh? I'd like that."

"You would?" I asked, surprised. Why was I feeling so insecure around him? I was pretty. Smart. Funny. Okay, my breasts weren't luscious like Lizzie's, but I'd been holding my own in the dating world. Well, that wasn't entirely true, but I didn't need to dwell on it.

He put his hand over mine and gave it a small squeeze. "Yeah, Kate. You know I would."

There. He liked me. So much for believing he was out of my league. I squared my shoulders and said, "Then fess up, Parsons. Tell me more about the man I'm eating pizza with."

I watched his eyes wander around the pub, behind me, over toward the pool table, the bathrooms, before looking at me. "What can I say? I love the opposite sex. Actually, no. I love sex," he said as flatly as if he'd admitted he loved peanut-butter-and-jelly sandwiches.

"Did you sleep with her?" I asked, gesturing my chin toward the thankfully departed Lizzie.

"Yup," he said, rubbing his face with his large hands.

"Okaaaay."

"I mean, it's like, ever since I was, I don't know, fifteen, girls were way into me; like I didn't have to try."

No need for him to have stated the obvious. Hadn't I run out into the Tutoring Center hallway like a crazed woman after seeing his face? "But no real relationships? Ever?"

He tucked a loose strand of hair behind his ear and pulled his ponytail tighter. Then he sniffed and wiped his hand across his mouth. Finally he said, "Well, okay, I mean there was this one chick, Fiona. She was a lake girl."

"A lake girl?"

"Yeah, so in the summer a billion tourists come to Winnipesaukee. Girls who are always up for a good time, you know? Me and my buddies, we called them 'lake girls' because we'd, ah, jump in, get wet, then jump out, see?"

"That's disgusting." Why was I still sitting here?

"Calling them that was pretty gross, you're right, but sex isn't disgusting, Kate. Not if the two people doing it are into it."

He wanted me to agree so I did. I nodded even though I had yet to be one of those two people who happened to be into it.

"Anyway, then I met Fiona. She was different. She was real."

"Real?"

"Yeah. Like, well, she was selfish—no; not selfish—more like she knew what she wanted. She said she was going to be a famous chef, and no one was going to stand in her way. That really turned me on."

"Maybe because she was a lot like you?"

"What?" He thought about it for a few beats. "Yeah, maybe. How'd you figure that out?"

I pointed to my head. "Big brain," I said, grinning.

"Big heart too," he replied, placing a hand gently on my chest. When he touched me, I felt as if a dozen sparklers had ignited inside me.

"So what happened?" I asked through the burst of lights.

"Nothing," he said with a shrug. "We hung out all summer together. She made me stop seeing other people and I was cool with that. I mean I would have done anything for her. When summer ended, she and her family went back home to Connecticut. I thought we'd keep it going somehow, but nope. She let me slide like a big fish she'd caught and threw back."

As much as I wanted to point out the irony in that statement I kept silent. "But you said you've never been in love."

Matt moved his empty plate to the side of the table. "I guess it was more of an obsession than love, you know? But it really hurt."

I knew nothing from obsession or desire on that scale, though I definitely found it intriguing, if not a little frightening.

"You're done with me, right? I shouldn't have told you any of this," he said, concerned.

"So, what, am I just another *lake* girl?"

"You? Never!" he yelled. A few people stopped chewing and looked over at us. "I liked you the moment I saw you sitting behind that window in the Tutoring Center."

"You—?"

"You're also different."

"Like Fiona was different?" I was definitely not someone who knew what she wanted.

"God, no."

"Then how am I different?"

"It's like I can't put my finger on it exactly, although"—he touched the scar on the side of my nose—"I like this a lot. It gives you character."

I pushed his hand away. "Please. That is so—"

"No. I mean it. It's beautiful. You're incredibly beautiful. And smart. This is so gonna sound lame, but I feel like I can totally be myself when I'm with you. I mean I've never told a girl any of this. You make me feel, I don't know, *safe*."

The door of the pub slammed, and in walked a herd of loud frat boys. "I do?"

"Yeah, you do," he said in a voice so gentle I couldn't help but believe him. "You are, Kate Burke, one hundred percent *not* a lake girl."

"So I shouldn't listen to my gut and run?"

"No, you shouldn't. You should let me walk you home instead."

As we got up to leave I picked up the rest of my slice and held it out to him. "Wait, you want to finish this?"

"Are you kidding me?" Matt scrunched up his face like he'd just sucked on a lemon. "I almost puked watching you eat it. I despise mushrooms."

"Why didn't you say something? I wouldn't have ordered it!"

Matt grabbed the pizza out of my hand and tossed it back onto the table, wiping his hand on his pant leg as if he'd just touched something rotten. "Because I like you more than I hate them."

"This is an awesome spot," he remarked when I showed him around my small two-bedroom apartment in the back of one of the prettiest buildings on Clarke Street. Originally built in the 1920s as a single-family home, it was cut up in the late fifties by the Francis family who moved their Trophy and Engraving business into the front of the building and turned the rest of the rooms into student housing. What my apartment lacked in furniture, it made up for with character and I appreciated that Matt seemed to think so too. "Look at these floors. And what a cool old stove."

"Yeah. I like it here. I used to have a roommate, but she never paid her rent, so I kicked her out last year."

"Hey, you own this?" Matt said, sliding a book off one of the bookcases. "Why didn't you tell me you took art history?"

"Um, because I didn't? It must have been my roommate's. She left most of her books here."

Matt took the book—*1910: The Emancipation of Dissonance*—over to my small couch. "Come, sit."

I sat and watched as he checked the index then flipped to a page. "See? Here's what I'm talking about," he said, placing the book on my lap. "Too bad it's in black and white, but you can see what I was saying. This dude's stuff makes me glad God gave us eyeballs."

I stared at the image of a somewhat distorted couple lying on a blanket, arms wrapped around one another. They were both naked, the woman's pubic hair very much on display. I read the caption at the bottom: "Fig. 13. Egon Schiele, *Embrace (Lovers II)*, 1917, oil." I looked over and saw him staring intently at the page. "You just like it because she's naked."

Matt ignored me and turned the page to a painting of yet another couple, even more exaggeratingly abstract. In this one only the man, almost puppet-like, was naked, his uncircumcised penis resting against his thigh. The woman sat behind him, grasping him around his chest as if holding on for dear life. Why were her eyes so sad and his eyes so glaring? "This is *Seated Couple*," Matt said, interrupting my thoughts. "It's him—Schiele—and the woman is his wife, Edith. She died while she was pregnant."

My hand went to my chest. "That's awful."

"What really sucked was he died three days later."

"From what, a broken heart?" I asked, my hand brushing across the doomed couple's image as if I could feel their pain.

"Nope. Spanish flu. He was only twenty-eight."

"I can see why you like his work." I turned the page and once again another naked woman stared up at me. "He's intense."

"Intense, nothing. He painted himself masturbating and also lots of nudes, but he wasn't painting sex, you know? He was a student of his time, right? Expressionism. It's about *expressing* what's inside you—not just trying to capture what's on the outside—like painting a bowl of fruit or something. You get what I'm saying?"

"I think I do." Oddly, I *was* getting the passion; the rawness. Matt's appreciation of it. How was it that this guy, someone who couldn't wrap his head around the simple components of cell division, could be so deep?

"You have to see his art in real life; not just what you're seeing here. Then you'll really know why I love him." He took the book from me and dropped it onto the floor with a thud. He sat back and draped his arm behind me. Before I could say another word, he put his forefinger gently on my chin, pulled me close, and kissed me on the mouth. I knew before the kiss ended I was about to become one of his many conquests, lake girl or otherwise.

Twenty minutes later Matt looked up from between my legs and said, "You're not a virgin, are you? I mean, you're sort of not moving, and I thought maybe—"

"What? I'm sorry, no. It feels really good. Keep doing that, yes," I said, letting my head fall back to the pillow and feeling frustrated that once again I was unable to experience the supposed joys of sex.

Before Matt, I'd been physical with two other men. My first time was senior year of high school with a boy named Tommaso, our neighbor's Italian exchange student. He was small-boned and perspired a lot, but I'd found his accent charming. He knew I was a virgin and had graciously offered to be my first (and "best!" he'd proclaimed) lover, since, after all, I'd helped him hone his English language skills. It seemed like a good idea, but within five minutes of making out with him, his tongue deep inside my throat, I knew I was not going to be into it. Since I'd already agreed to all four bases, I'd let him go all the way. After he climaxed I felt nothing but relief the whole thing was over.

Last year I'd gotten really drunk at a frat party and allowed Boy Number Two to talk me into his bedroom. Although I'd since forgotten his name, I remembered hating every moment.

I figured this time, with a man I was fiercely attracted to, it'd be different. But it wasn't. Matt was perfect. Touching me perfectly. Using his tongue in a way that I assumed would give 99.9 percent of the women on the planet a fairly huge orgasm.

But not me.

So I faked it. Moved my hips and moaned. When he slowly pushed himself into me, and his gorgeous face stared down into mine, I gave him what he wanted.

From that night on, we were inseparable. Art exhibits, studying, campus parties, skiing on weekends: there was nothing we didn't do together. "I love you, Kaybee," he told me three weeks after our first date. "I never knew I could have so much fun hanging with a woman, like every day." Five weeks later he stuffed most of his clothes into the bottom two drawers of my dresser. A month after that, he moved everything else in. We made love every night and every night I pretended to enjoy it. While it was obvious to both of us I was never going to be a great lover, Matt was patient and encouraging.

Other than the fact that I didn't enjoy having sex with the most sexual man I knew, we were blissfully in love.

I graduated and got a job as a marketing assistant at Stockwell Farms. Matt graduated and went to work for Burton, the snowboard company. When Burton started their Learn To Ride program, designed to get novices hooked on boarding, they asked Matt if he'd be willing to travel around to ski resorts to promote it. "I'll be gone a lot, Kaybee. You okay with that?" he told me when he came home with the news.

"If you're happy, I'm happy." As much as I adored Matt, I was looking forward to a little time off from sex.

"You know what would make me even happier, Kate Burke?" he asked as he disappeared into the bedroom.

"What?" I yelled through the wall behind me. I was sitting on the couch drinking a glass of wine, my book open on my lap.

Matt came back into the living room and dropped to his knees. "If you'd marry me," he said, holding out a small blue velvet box.

Two years into the marriage, the sex was getting harder to take and Matt's patience was crumbling. We were down to having intercourse once a week. I would steel myself, as if going into battle. After we made love and he finally rolled off me, I could breathe again.

I knew he was miserable. Matt, the consummate optimist and life-lover who bounced rather than walked started to grow dark. We fought. He drank too much. "You know I love you, Kaybee, but you not being into sex is starting to kill me a little," he said to me one night. "Maybe we can get counseling, or—I don't know. We should try to figure this out, right?"

Thinking maybe there was something in my body that wasn't working correctly, I made an appointment to see a gynecologist up in Colchester. I told him about my issues and then he inserted his fingers into my nether parts in search of a physical deformity. He stood up and snapped the gloves off. As I waited for him to say something, I felt the damp jelly oozing onto the white crinkly paper. He said nothing for a few beats and I tried not to stare at his bad comb-over. Finally he suggested maybe it was all in my head.

"You know," he stated, as he tapped his own head to make certain I understood which part of my anatomy he was referring to, "it could be psychosomatic."

The next day I sat Matt down and said, "Look. The doctor can't find anything wrong with me and, I don't know why, but I just don't like sex and since you cannot live without it, you are going to start having sex with other women."

"I'm going to—what?"

"I know you love me and I love you more than myself, Matt. I don't want to get divorced."

"Divorced? No way!"

"Which is why you will have sex with other women. But you have to promise me four things," I said before listing my ground rules. "Rule number one: you have to be safe. Rule number two: you are not to get involved—emotionally, I mean. You cannot see anyone more than once. Number three: don't ever let me find out what you're doing or who you're doing it with—not through mail or emails or phone calls, anything. And rule number four: you must swear you will stay one hundred percent invested in this marriage and that you will never leave me."

Our arrangement worked beautifully. Matt was sexually satisfied, and I was no longer afraid of losing him. One night, under the drunken blur of too many wine spritzers, I thought it'd be entertaining to jump my husband's bones. I was wrong. There was nothing fun about it. Though, we made Finley that night.

It was also the last time we had sex.

Soon after I got pregnant, we bought a white ranch house in the quiet suburban neighborhood of Rayburne. Matt left Burton for Prime Marketing, a small PR firm in Essex, where he went knee-deep into qualitative research, training in focus group techniques. Then, as a high-grade contractor for The

Harris Poll in Rochester, New York, he rose to the top and found his true calling.

When Finley started school, I started to write. First I wrote a murder mystery set in the world of real estate. After that, a novel about a cluster of lonely housewives living in a small Vermont town who have to solve a murder. Neither novel went beyond my hard drive.

"Why are you stuck on murder?" Matt asked after I showed him my latest rejection letter.

"I don't know. I don't know what else to write about. For some reason, murder seems sexy."

Matt laughed. "Sex is sexy, Kate. Go write about sex. It's what's selling, right?"

"Matt, I want to write about what I know," I said, pouting.

"And you know about murder how?"

He had a point. The next day I went to the supermarket and bought a pile of paperbacks with the steamiest covers I could find. I read those, as well as a few dozen downloaded e-books. I sifted through a staggering number of sub-genres (including sci-fi, vampires, BDSM, gay, straight, romance, cowboys, military, paranormal, historical, and fantasy), and figured I should probably start with some basic straight erotica.

I failed miserably. No way could I write about sex. I might as well have tried to write about open-heart surgery.

Then one night I had an epiphany. I woke Matt up and repeated what was bouncing around in my head. "I want you to tell me about the sex you have with other women."

"What the heck?" He forced himself up against the wall and turned on the light.

"I want to write sexy books. Come on," I said when I saw the look of disbelief on his face. "You were the one who suggested it."

"I get it but you made it clear you never wanted to hear about it. That's rule number three, remember?"

I was fired up. "Okay, so for now I'm jettisoning rule number three. But the other rules still stand. One time only; you can't get involved emotionally; and you can never leave me."

"You know I would never leave you, but—" He ran his hand through his sleep-strewn hair. "This is really out there, Kate."

"Oh come on. I'm only asking you to share some of the, uh, the *details*. The, you know, the nitty gritty."

He rubbed his hands over his face, and I knew I had to strike harder.

"Matt, please. So many people are reading erotica. And please, you're like the sexiest man in the world. You will be my model. My muse."

"Why don't you watch porn? There's plenty of it on the internet. I can show you the best—"

I sat up onto my ankles and gave him a playful punch on his chest. "Gross. I'd rather carve my eyes out with a grapefruit spoon."

"Seriously, you don't think it'll be weird?"

"If it gets weird, we'll stop. How's that sound?"

Matt closed his eyes. I could tell he was struggling with the idea of sharing the details of his sexual encounters with me, but I was determined to squeeze his stories out of him like he was a tube of toothpaste. "Please, Matt. I can do this, but I need your help. We're a team, aren't we?"

"Yeah, but this is like the craziest game plan ever."

"Nice one," I said, admiring his apt comeback. "See? Already you're out on the field with me! Let's hit this one out of the ballpark together!"

"Ugh," he said, shaking his head. "You gotta stop with the sports."

Not until I was over the finish line would I stop. I jumped off the bed and raised my arms into the air like a referee. "He shoots! She scores!" I yelled, my eyes wide.

"Jesus, fine. Okay." He slumped down and pulled the covers up under his chin. "If you promise never to use football, baseball, *or* basketball in any of your stories, I'll do it."

"Really?"

"Sure. I'm *game*," he said, turning off the light. "But if you want me to take one for the team, you're gonna have to let me get some sleep. Good night, Kaybee, you crazy woman."

"Good night, Matt."

Three weeks later I listened with my eyes shut tight while he unleashed his story about Maeve, a tall brunette with a yen for having hard sex up against walls. During the first couple minutes he spoke, a tiny flicker of jealousy simmered in my belly. He must have seen it on my face because in the midst of licking one of Maeve's nipples he said, "This is too weird, isn't it?"

Desperately needing my cockeyed idea to work, I doused the burn. I wanted to write erotica and the only way I was going to be successful was if I toughened up. Believed that what he was doing to Maeve had no bearing on our marriage. I had but one objective: suck out every detail.

"Nope," I insisted. "Keep talking."

Eight months after that night I published *Opening Doors: A Firm Offer*, my first book in a two-book series featuring Ashton Blake, a hunky real estate agent in New Jersey who gives more than just home tours. The books ended up being so popular, I was offered a hefty advance to write another series.

Next came *Strong Lust: Crossing Borders*, starring Macon Strong, the soul-searching, sex-hungry hunk who was never going to settle down with one woman. I'd made him a herdsman on a farm in Vermont's Northeast Kingdom, way up north where you could hear the Canadians whisper if you listened hard enough. On his days off, Macon often crossed over the border to explore Canada's gustatory offerings, and there, in the small town of North Hatley, on the northern tip of Lake Massawippi, he'd met his match: a woman named Phionna Bouchard. Phionna ran a patisserie on Rue Principale, and when she wasn't kneading dough, she was screwing men. After the first time they had sex, she told Macon that her favorite time of year was when the tourists came to summer on the lake. That was when she got to pick and choose among *les mecs du lac*—the lake boys.

Macon fell hard for Phionna, but, in the end, she gave him an ultimatum: she was tired of the monthly visits and demanded he move to Canada permanently. As much as he lusted after her, Macon chose to leave Phionna, *after* they had unbridled sex in a canoe in the middle of the lake.

Strong Lust: Crossing Borders blasted its way up the erotica book charts and Daphne Moore—my nom de plume—became a top-ranked author on Goodreads and Amazon. All due to Matt's exploits, and because I listened, focusing on the details of his affairs like a scientist counting blood cells under a microscope. It got to where I could hardly wait for him to return home from one of his focus group gigs so I could hear his stories—each one with a new plot or face or body. Like an addict, I craved hearing him describe climbing on top of an untried woman, undoing her shirt, letting loose her breasts. I made him tell me what they felt like, tasted like. What did his penis feel like inside this one as opposed to the last one, I'd ask, writing in my mind, typing the story on my keyboard after he finished and went off to work or play ball with Finley.

I had finally become a writer. A happily married writer.

KATE

On Tuesday I am walking out of Rayburne Market when I see
Annie opening the door to Kevin's Koffee across the square. As
much as I want to get home to Macon, I throw my groceries in
the trunk of my Subaru and head over. I pause before touching
the handle, and peer in the window. If Annie is meeting someone, I don't want to interrupt them. I watch Annie look around
the mostly empty café, choosing a table in the back corner. She
pulls a MacBook and a few papers from a canvas satchel and
sits down. As long as Annie is alone . . .

I put my hand on the door, then stop, remembering Friday's dinner conversation. The more I think about it, the more
I regret letting Annie know Matt and I are in a sexless marriage. But Annie has another friend with the same issue and
she doesn't appear to be the least bit fazed by it. In fact, she in-
vented a special tea for her.

Still, I don't want to talk about my libido anymore. Other
than last week, when I stupidly threw myself at Matt, I can't
remember the last time we even acknowledged the fact of our
nonphysical relationship. It took a while, but we adapted to it,

making the best out of a bad biological situation. I would just as soon let sleeping dogs lie.

As I turn around to leave, a young guy appears next to me. "You going in or what?" he says, rudely pushing past. I recognize him as one of the twentysomethings who hangs around with Eli, Suzanne Madden's son. I've gotten to know Suzanne over the years and we are friendly. Ish. We both volunteer for the Rayburne Winter Toy and Food Drive and have gone on a few runs together. When her husband left her for another woman three years ago, I made a point of giving Suzanne a firm hug when I ran into her. I insisted Suzanne call me if she needed anything, but I never heard from her.

Eli works at the deli counter at Rayburne Market. Suzanne wanted him to go to college, but he chose instead to take a "gap year" which has, apparently, evolved into gap *years*. This past fall, during a run through Mekins Cove, the large farm which borders our development, I came upon Eli and two of his friends—this one included—passing a pipe around. I considered reporting what I saw to Suzanne, but Matt wouldn't let me. He didn't think smoking pot was such a big deal. "Besides that," he said, "it's not up to you to tell the woman what her son does when he's not slicing bologna. You don't need people calling you the neighborhood narc."

Eli's friend has on a pair of paint-splattered jeans that hang down low enough to expose his white boxer shorts. As he pushes open the door, I cannot help but stare at his arms, which are be-strewn with colorful tattoos. I am still taking in the green serpent winding up his biceps when I hear my name being shouted. I look up to see Annie waving at me.

"Annie!" I say, approaching her table. "Hi."

"Hi yourself."

"What are you doing?"

"I was having trouble breathing in my house so I thought I'd come check this place out." Her hair is coiled in a messy bun on top of her head. She's wearing the same sweatpants and oversized sweater she had on the day I first met her.

"What? You mean because of your asthma?"

"No, because of the suburbs," she says, slamming the laptop closed. "Why don't you sit down and tell me what's going on in your small corner of the universe, Miss Kate, mother of Finley?"

"You want something to drink? I think I want a latte."

"Make it two. Soy, double shot for me please."

When I come back to the table holding our drinks, I catch Annie staring at the tattooed pot-smoker, who is gazing fixedly into his phone while sucking a pink fruit smoothie through a green straw.

"Are you seriously checking him out?" I whisper as I sit down.

"He is rather appetizing," she says, grinning.

I glance behind me and subtly look him over, trying to suspend judgment and take him in objectively. He's quite model-esque. Unruly blond hair falling across an angular Nordic face. Smooth skin. Thin, but with a buff upper body. With my mind's camera I snap a photograph. I'll use him for one of my next books. Perhaps I'll let him keep his tattoos. He'll be a bad boy named—what will I name him? Liam? I could make him European. Uncircumcised. I've never written an uncircumcised penis into any of my stories, but I should, given how many of my readers live overseas. Tommaso's penis was the only uncut one I knew of *firsthand*, but I barely saw it, let alone touched it, before he'd inserted it inside me.

I shiver at the memory. God, I hate sex.

"He's a child, Mrs. Robinson," I utter, blasting the scene into oblivion. "I'll help you find someone in your own age bracket."

Annie seems so content; it never occurred to me she might be searching for someone to love again.

Annie clinks her mug against mine and nods approvingly at my comment. "Touché, sweetheart."

"Thanks again for dinner, by the way."

"*Ya pas de quoi.*"

"And that means?"

"It was nothing. I loved having you."

"I loved being had," I say, taking a gulp of my latte.

"Hey, so speaking of sex—"

Oh no. She's going to bring it up again. I don't want—

"What do you know about Steve Hodges?"

"Steve Hodges?" I repeat, brimming with relief. Steve Hodges? I have to think about who he is for a second. "Oh, you mean Steve Hodges who lives on Dwyer?"

"No, I mean Steve Hodges who lives in Rhode Island." She cocks her head.

I raise my eyebrows. "Why do you ask? Hmm?"

"Just wondering. I met him the other day in front of my house."

"Ooh. The plot thickens. And?"

"Shut up. Tell me what you know or I'm going to take yonder child home with me and make a man out of him."

"You have a crush on Steve Hodges! Ohmigod!" I shriek like a teenager, but when Annie shoots me a look of contempt, I wipe the smile off my face.

"Never mind. Forget I asked."

"No, wait. I'll tell you what I know." I take in a deep breath, trying not to smirk. "He owns Computer Works. That place," I say, gesturing out the window at the store next door to the market.

"Mm-hmm."

"He only moved here like, I don't know, maybe two years

ago? It was his parents' house and they both died and I guess he decided to live in it. I have no idea where he came from. Honestly, I don't have much more to give you."

"Married? Kids?"

"I have no idea."

Annie nods.

"Yeah, but don't get too excited. I mean, I kind of get the impression he's a little, I don't know, *off*?" I never actually spoke to Steve. I think back to the one time I saw him in the market. He didn't make eye contact with me, so I didn't bother to say hello. I remember checking out his basket and seeing five cans of black pitted olives and a canister of Reddi-wip in it. What had he been planning to do with so many black olives? Fill them with the cream? Actually, that sounds kind of erotic. Maybe I'll have Macon fill figs or dates with whipped cream and feed them to Audrey. Or Lizzie. No, Audrey would definitely enjoy them. But, shoot—I already used whipped cream on Phionna in my last book.

"I like *off*," Annie replies, pulling me back to the moment.

I smirk while checking my watch. Macon beckoned. Plus, I have to get the yogurt and milk home before they spoil. I drain the last of my cup and say, "This was nice. Thanks."

"You're going? School's not out for another two hours. Tell me more about—"

About Steve? I have nothing more. About my nonsex-life? No, thank you. About the highly regarded erotica books I write? I desperately want to tell Annie more, but first I need to be sure I can trust my friend Miss Annie, mother of Terra. Can I? *Are you good at keeping secrets, my new friend?* I ask silently.

"I need to get some writing done," I let slide, testing the water.

But when Annie replies, "Okay, I've got plenty of work of my own to do," I realize there is no way I am diving in.

KATE

With his heart slamming against his chest, Macon excitedly clicked on Lizzie's email.

"Hey, Macon. Sorry I haven't written in a really long time, but guess what? I'm into cheese these days. You must have rubbed off on me," she wrote, adding a smiley face.

Yesterday he'd gone to Café D'Alsace, where he thought she worked, only to find out she'd quit a month ago. She hadn't given him her new phone number so now he was lost.

"Where are you, Lizzie?" he emailed back, hoping she wouldn't sense the desperation in those four small words.

While he waited for her to write back, Macon put his feet up on the glass coffee table in Audrey's apartment, four inches from a half-drained glass of scotch. She was into cheese. Selling it? Serving it? Eating it? Making it? Is it possible she had gone back to Vermont? If it turned out Lizzie had moved north at the same time he shifted south—that they'd passed in the night like two trains heading in opposite directions—he'd have to break something. No way could he leave the cheese shop.

He'd already invested too much energy into making it happen and to drop it now and go running back to Vermont was out of the question.

Macon closed his laptop, and a second after he drained the glass Audrey let herself into her apartment, tossing the keys into the crystal bowl on the table. He watched her unbutton her trench coat and drop it to the floor next to her suitcase. She wore nothing but a red lace push-up bra and matching thong undies.

"You flew like that?" he asked.

"I did," she said with a sexy smile, "and I was wet the entire flight. I almost came when we hit turbulence." She clicked her red high heels over to the couch and shook her red hair out of its tight bun. It fell like silky water around her shoulders and he noted the new hue, a richer red than before. When he reached up to touch it, she smacked his hand away.

"Don't. I just had it done."

"Oh, okay." For a moment Macon wanted to smack her back, but when she unhooked her bra, he changed his mind.

"Are you hungry?" she asked, taking off her shoes.

"Always."

"Good." She stepped up onto the couch and planted a leg on either side of Macon's body. "How about we begin with a little amuse-bouche?" she purred.

I lift my fingers off the keyboard and stretch my arms up over my head until my upper spine cracks and the muscles in my shoulders relax. Turning away from the screen, I flip through the notes I jotted down from when Matt had sex with one of his focus groupies in Houston a while back. The woman straddled his face as he sat on the couch. After she finished, she sat on his lap with her back to him, leaning over the hotel room's coffee table while they had sex. Audrey will do the same, but first she'll use her mouth on Macon. Does she need to? I try to remember how many fellatio scenes I put in *Strong Lust: Crossing Borders*. I don't want to be redundant. Readers devour my books because I give them sexual variety. That, plus darn good writing. Careful plotting, as well as meticulous character development and believable motivations, are why I think my readers keep coming back for more. Though when my first royalty check arrived, I said as much to Matt, and he burst out laughing.

"You're out of your mind if you honestly believe thousands of people read your books because they think you write well. Don't get me wrong, Kaybee—you are a great writer. But your sex scenes rock. Shit, they even give *me* hard-ons and my hard-ons are *in* the book!"

But I read the reviews readers submit, and plenty of fans care about more than just the sex. I liked one of the reviews of my second book so much I keep the screenshot of it on my desktop:

> There's all kinds of sex and it's hot sex. But Daphne Moore is also a great writer. She knows how to tell a story. If you're looking for a good erotic romance that actually has a plot, this book is it!

I should stop thinking about what other people think of me and get back to Macon. I sigh and rub my nose. I have to concentrate. I lean back, close my eyes and picture Macon and Audrey going at it on the white couch.

I remember Annie's expression as she lusted after that boy in the coffee shop. And her arch response when I told her I thought Steve Hodges was a bit "off." That evil lusty grin of

hers flashes behind my lids and before I can stop my brain
from pulling back, I picture Steve and Annie making out on
her green couch.

Steve's rubbing his crotch against hers.

His hand is thrust under her large sweater.

Annie's small strong body writhes with pleasure.

When I open my eyes, the scene disintegrates like an old
movie melting in an old-fashioned projector but I can't shake
an uncomfortable feeling that lingers. I was stupid to share my
personal impotency. Annie is clearly a highly sexual woman.
With few obvious boundaries. And now I suppose I need to
worry about her going after Matt. I can imagine the two of
them finding one another desirable enough that—

"Stop it, Kate!" I say loudly. Annie's my friend. She likes
me. She's trying to help me.

I need to get back to my writing.

I left off just as Audrey and Macon are about to have sex.
Since I'm no longer in the mood to write anything bordering
on erotic I type *PLACEHOLDER (Macon and Audrey have sex
in her apartment)* and insert a page break before the next scene.
I close my eyes and conjure up my post-coital couple.

They will, naturally, be famished, so I seat them at Café
Select next door to Audrey's apartment. While waiting for
their food, Macon notices Audrey's dazzling diamond bracelet. Back when Annie told me that story about the bracelet
those twelve Denver women bought together, I knew I had
to use it.

"Wow. Those are some huge rocks on your wrist. Did Harland
give you that?" Because the two men shared Audrey's body
Macon sometimes felt an odd kinship to Harland Mansfield.
He knew that Harland owned a real estate development firm;

that at one point in his life, he'd been a competitive downhill skier; that he was significantly older than Audrey; and that he worshipped her enough to allow her to go for walks on a long leash. Macon figured if he ever met the guy, he'd like him, want to shake his hand and drink the scotch he was pouring.

"No. I bought it myself. Well, actually"—she dangled the extravagant bauble around her slim wrist, its sparkle reflecting the lights above their table—"last fall I hosted a jewelry trunk show: estate pieces from Lippa's Jewelers, just for a few ladies from one of the boards I sit on."

"Mmm-hmm."

"And well, we all fell in love with this piece. They say it was owned by Zelda Fitzgerald, though there's no real proof."

"And you had to have it."

"No, we all had to have it! Oh, hello—" The waitress appeared by the table. Audrey ordered a half dozen oysters, a rocket salad, and a vodka martini. Macon had his usual: a burger with horseradish sauce and a side of their famed rösti. Dogfish Head on draught. After the waitress left, she continued. "Heavens no, we're talking six figures, darling, and even I'm not that extravagant. But the girls and I, well we thought it'd be a hoot to buy it together and take turns wearing it!"

"And now it's your turn."

"It is. But"—she ran her fingers over the bracelet with her left hand—"now that I have it on, I sort of never want to give it back. I suppose I'm not as good at sharing as I thought I was."

When the drinks arrived, Macon downed half his beer and twisted in his chair to take in the crowd. Usually he sat where Audrey sat, with his back to the wall so he could check out the scene while he ate. At times he felt like the consummate sore-thumb tourist; the people around him speaking a language he couldn't interpret. Other days, he blended into the space like a local would—feeling relaxed and almost cool enough to gab with the stranger at the table next to him. Now, sitting with Audrey, he felt as if a line had been drawn down the center of his body—half of him a sophisticated New Yorker; half of him a hick from Vermont missing the sweet woody smell of hay drying in the fields.

Which side would Lizzie rather be holding right now?

He turned back around and watched Audrey squeeze a lemon over a freshly shucked oyster then hold it out to him. "No. Not my thing," he said, starved but not desperate enough to chew on what looked like it'd been gagged up from the throat of a coyote.

Audrey slurped it down. "You know, swallowing this is a little like swallowing your cum," she said taking a sip of her martini.

"I wouldn't know." Where was his burger?

Audrey wiped her mouth with a dainty pat of the napkin and sat back. "So listen. Two things. One is Harland is flying down tomorrow night to check out the shop—see where his money is going. Which means you need to get out of the apartment for the night. Do you have someplace you can go or shall I find you a hotel?"

"I'm good." He had no idea where he would sleep but there was no way he'd let Audrey pay for a hotel room. "What's the other thing?"

"Well, I've been thinking." The food arrived and Macon bit into the juicy burger, spiced just right by the tangy horse-radish. Audrey waited for the waitress to grind black pepper on her salad before going on. "I know how hard you've worked all these months to help open a shop that's not even yours. I mean, Miles and Arthur and I, we're all impressed, not surprisingly."

"Thank you," Macon said after swallowing.

"Well," she said as she picked up an arugula sprig with her fingers, "I'd like to get you a present."

Macon downed the rest of his beer and shrugged. He didn't need to be rewarded for his work. He'd come to New York to find Lizzie Wilder, but even if that turned out to be a bust—not that he'd let that happen—he had no regrets. Sure, he didn't have a financial stake in Smiling Girl Cheese Shop, but he loved the shop. Being around cheese all day, turning people on—most people—to the taste of aged-just-right Vermont milk, pleased him in a way he might not have imagined before. "You don't have to get me anything—"

"I'm not suggesting any*thing*, Macon, darling. I'm suggesting any*one*. If you're up for it, and my foot is telling me you are indeed up for it"—beneath the table she had her toes pressed against his crotch—"let's finish up here and go find some dessert."

I sit back, relieved to have gotten part of the scene out of the way. Now, though, I need to run to the market to buy snacks for this afternoon's soccer practice. Maybe I can ask Matt to do it.

"Matt?" I call through the closed door. "Matt, are you home?" When he doesn't answer, I get up from my desk. He isn't in the house so I go out back. Munch is busily digging a hole in the far corner by the fence. "Munch, no!" I yell, admonishing him for destroying the yard. When we bought the house, the lawn had been in pristine condition, but with a child who runs around in cleats and a dog who buries then digs up every treasure he owns, our backyard now looks more like a neglected city park.

Where is Matt? I dial his phone.

"Hey," he says, instantly picking up. He sounds winded.

"Where are you?"

"Out for a run on the Turner Trail. You were writing and I didn't want to disturb you."

"You're funny. Why'd you answer the phone if you're on a run?"

"I don't know. Thought it might be important. Is it?" he asks, his breath slowing.

"No."

"I'll see you in about ten minutes." He hangs up.

Again, he didn't take Munch with him. "Sorry your dad forgot you," I say, patting the dog's head. I pick up a muddy ball and throw it across the yard. Munch chases it down, but instead of retrieving it, he goes back to digging.

"Oh well," I say before running inside to get my keys. As I'm backing out of the driveway and twisting the steering wheel to the right, Matt appears around the corner, coming from the opposite direction of the Turner Trail, the five-mile gravel path that runs along Rayburne Bay. I brake and lower the window.

"Good run?"

"It was almost too hot," he says, lunging his right leg out next to the car. "Where are you going?"

"Soccer snacks."

"Great." He wipes off a line of sweat above his lips. "I'd kiss you but I stink. I'm gonna go shower."

"Okay. I'll be back in a jiff." I take my foot off the brake, then tap it again. "Matt," I yell to him, "I thought you said you were on the Turner Trail. That's that way," I say, pointing north. "You came around the corner from the south."

He stops midway across the front lawn. "What? No, I went running in Mekins Cove."

Which explains why he didn't take Munch along: dogs are not permitted on the privately owned land.

"Oh, I thought you said—never mind. See you later."

ANNIE

I don't love playgrounds, particularly ones with tire swings, but if my child wants to spend a few minutes defying gravity on equipment composed of petroleum products, I will just have to suck it up.

The offerings next to Rayburne Community School are state-of-the-art crap compared to the whimsical wooden structures Terra played on back in Denver. It's like comparing desiccated cans of Play-Doh to freshly-picked apples. Besides the tires, there's a row of plastic-seated swings; a rusty metal slide that, in the heat of the summer, probably charred many a delicate thigh; and monkey bars, across which my daughter is currently climbing. As I watch her cautiously crawl from one bar to the next, I reach into my pants and pull at my moist underwear so it isn't all bunched up against my crotch.

I retract my hand and give it a quick sniff and am about to lick my fingers when I become aware of a brood of motherlings eyeing me from the other side of the field. I shouldn't have glanced over because now one of them is gliding toward me.

"Hi," she says, through an immobile smile. "I'm Allison

Conway." She extends her hand and I hesitate before taking it. If she puts it anywhere near her face she is going to get a nose-full of piquant vaginal juice amalgamated with fresh musky semen.

"Annie," I reply.

"You're new here, right? That's your daughter, hanging upside down?"

"Fruit of my loins, yes."

"Oh." She laughs uncomfortably and pushes her highlight-streaked hair off her face. I wait for her expression to change when she catches a whiff of the bouquet of cum which has finally stopped oozing out of me, but she appears not to notice. "That's my Isabel over there in the pink pants," she says proudly.

"Nice pants," I say.

"Thank you. I got them at that new children's boutique, the one over on—"

"Terra! We're leaving," I yell. "Hey, nice to make your acquaintance, Allison Conway, but we've got to get home," I say, not wanting to wait around for her mind to regroup. I've had enough banality tossed in my general direction for one afternoon.

"Come on, Terra. You're done," I say to my child's down-turned face.

"Aw, okay." I hold her as she slides her legs through the bars and touches down.

While walking together down Forest Road, Terra says, "Clayton would have hated this place."

"Yup," I reply to my astute child. "Your father would have thought it the opposite of wild." I think back to the last morning I saw him alive: he was on his way out to go kayaking; I was handing him a thermos of tea.

"Yeah."

"You miss him?" I ask Terra.

I, in fact, never miss him. After Clayton died, someone slipped me a pamphlet describing all the supposed stages of grief: denial, anger, bargaining, something, something. The only stage I experienced was relief. No. Okay, there was also the pleasure stage.

I nudge Terra to the side of the road as a massive SUV zooms by. She looks up at me. "Sometimes, like when I see Finley with her dad playing soccer, I sort of wish Clayton—"

"Your father would never have volunteered for soccer."

"He was always too busy, wasn't he? I mean, like to do stuff with us."

"That he was." I take ahold of her hand and kiss it. "But we're doing pretty okay on our own, aren't we?"

She yanks her hand out of mine and jumps up onto the curb, balancing with her arms stretched out, her heavy backpack bouncing behind her. After a few steps, she turns and faces me. "You think maybe you'll get married again?"

"Is that what you want? To have another father?"

She hops off the curb and takes my hand again. "It'd be fun to be three people again, don't you think, Annie?"

"I do," I say as we turn the corner onto Dwyer Court. "I think it's a most excellent idea."

KATE

I'm cinching a bag of discarded juice boxes and granola bar wrappers when I see Annie walking barefooted across the field carrying a large mason jar filled with dark liquid sloshing around.

"Hello, Miss Kate, mother of Finley. Thanks for the coffee klatch the other day."

"You are very welcome, Miss Annie, mother of Terra," I say, delighted by the names we call one another, as if these monikers are passwords into a secret club only we belong to. "How's it going?" I ask.

"Going, going. Just riding the momentum of life."

I laugh and make a mental note to use that line.

"I want to watch practice. Let's go sit closer," she says.

We sit down together near the sidelines and when Annie pulls a blade from the warm grass and sticks it in her mouth, I cry, "Annie! Do you have any idea how much crap is on this field? Seagulls poop on it all day. Spit it out!"

Annie laughs loudly while tucking her hands under her knees and rocking back and forth. "Kate. You have so got to calm the fuck down. Dirt is our friend. I just read an article that said kids raised on farms have far better immune systems than kids who wash their hands in antibacterial soap a hundred times a day."

I remember reading something along those lines too. Still, the thought of so many pairs of gum-coated sneakers and peeing dogs . . . "It's your life. If you want to suck on bird guano, I won't stop you."

"Excellent word choice. *Guano.*"

"Yeah, it's a good one." In front of us the girls are racing around the field screaming bloody murder, half of them kicking balls; the other half trying not to get hit by one. "They love this drill."

"What is it?"

"It's called Hunter and Lion." I watch Terra, a designated hunter, chase down Casey, a lion, before shooting the ball into her shin, causing Casey to yelp. I tense, expecting Casey to crumple down to the ground and sob like she usually does whenever she gets hit, and am relieved when she takes her position with the hunters. "So, what have you got in the jar?" I ask hesitantly.

"I hope you don't mind. I made you a couple of quarts of my special GoodLove tea, the one I gave my friend."

I'm touched. "Thank you, Annie."

"Before I hand it over though, I need to know if you take anything for your thyroid or blood pressure? If so," she says with a raised eyebrow, "you can't drink it."

Matt was recently put on a beta blocker because his blood pressure is so high, but all I take is a multivitamin—when I remember to. "No. Nothing," I say.

"Excellent. Obviously you don't have to drink it if you don't want to, but here it is."

"I'm not saying I will, but if I were to try it, is there anything special I need to do?"

"Heat up a cup at a time. Please do not put it in the microwave."

"Why not? What would it do to it?"

"It might change the chemistry, so do me a favor and use a saucepan, okay?"

"Yes, ma'am," I say with a silly drawl.

"You might want to add honey or agave to cut the bitterness." She rolls the jar between her hands as if bestowing it with magic. "When you first start drinking it, it might make you feel a little nauseated or dizzy. And it could raise your heartbeat a little, but that's just at first. Keep drinking it so your body gets used to it. But only one or two cups a day. And try not to drink it too close to bedtime because it's got some kick."

"That sounds a little scary. Is it safe?"

"How about you pretend I'm wearing a long white coat and have a stethoscope around my neck. Now do you trust me?"

I laugh. "How long before it—?" I keep my eyes on the girls—not on Annie.

"How long before it gets you horny?" Annie places her hand on my shoulder and gives it a squeeze. "Everyone's different. It could take a day, a week, or maybe a lifetime. Remember, that which does not kill you will only make you stronger, so why don't you start drinking and see what happens?"

"We'll see. Thank you, Annie. That was really sweet. Can I pay you for it?" I'm guessing she won't take my money but feel I should offer something in return. Maybe I'll introduce her to a neighbor or two, although for selfish reasons I don't want Annie making new friends. Besides, I doubt anyone is as open-minded as I am. I glance over at the other parents standing around watching the practice and decide against it. None of them will be able to see beyond Annie's contrariness to the funny and clever person she is.

"Please, Kate. 'Do good to them, and lend to them without expecting to get anything back. Then your reward will be great.' Luke 6:35."

"Ah, but you left out the beginning part: 'But love your *enemies*, do good to them . . . ' et cetera, et cetera. Honestly, you're like the last person on the planet I'd expect to quote scripture. Do you even own a Bible?"

"Of course. I keep a copy in the bathroom."

I flop back onto the grass and scream up into the sky, "Annie Meyers, you are so weird!"

"Hey, don't knock it till you try it."

I sit up and turn my attention back to soccer. Matt is on his knees, retying Casey's sneakers. I'm not convinced a bunch of herbs can miraculously transform me into a sexual being, but I'll give GoodLove a try. If the tea works, if it sparks even a dram of sexual excitement, if I can give Matt what he wants, we'll win the prize for the happiest married couple on the planet. But, if Matt and I become lovers, he'll stop sleeping with other women. He'll only want to be with me.

It's not as if I can use myself as a character in my novels. Even when we used to make love, we never experimented with crazy positions, let alone ropes. Matt tries new things during his business trips that he'd never try on me. I won't want to be tied up. I can't imagine begging Matt to take me on the kitchen table. Tea or no tea, there's no way I'll agree to a threesome.

This could kill my writing, destroy my livelihood. If Matt doesn't supply me with new ideas, new characters, my stories will dry up and die like an unwatered plant in an abandoned house.

I consider the unused notes from Matt's affairs stowed away in my desk drawer—not nearly enough to fill another series. How many more business trips does he have planned? I should outline the next series before the horny tea takes effect—*if* it takes effect, that is. Get Matt to have sex with as many new women as—

"Actually, you *can* do something for me," Annie says, sticking a screwdriver into the panicked thoughts spinning around my mind. "I've got to fly to Denver this weekend to deal with the house and some bullshit with Clayton's estate, and Terra really doesn't want to miss her first soccer game on Saturday. Would it be cool if she stayed with you guys for three nights?"

"Absolutely." Of course the house will need to be professionally dry-cleaned after that whirling dervish of a child eats and plays her way through the weekend. "Finley will love it."

"Excellent. I'll be home in time to get her from school Monday. And hey, I'll make you a spare key. If the weather stays like this, you should totally use our pool."

"That's a great idea."

"Plenty more where that came from, sister."

KATE

The threat of my writing career possibly coming to an end is sucking up all my creativity. "You know you're not going to work," I say to the mug of Annie's GoodLove tea on my desk.

I make a deal with myself. If or when I become filled with desire for my husband, I will hide it until finishing the series. Matt doesn't need to be in on the fact that I'm drinking libido-boosting tea. There's no harm in leaving him in the dark.

I slouch back in my chair, staring at the office's teal couch. Touch my nose. Sit forward. I get up and open the curtains. Look out the window. Close the curtains. Sit back down.

I know what needs to happen next but cannot concentrate. It's during unsettling times like these that I wish I belonged to a writers' group so I could share my frustrations with people who can relate. But I can't very well log on as Kate Burke, and I already spend too much of my time slipping into Daphne Moore's persona while answering questions and chatting online with my Goodreads fans. As entertaining as it is to impersonate a spectacularly rich author who lives in Hawaii with her sculptor husband and their five cats, it takes a lot of effort to come across authentically.

I want to reveal my alt-life to Annie. I'm certain she'll find it mind-blowing. Maybe next time we're together I'll—I suddenly push the thought away.

"Focus, Kate," I say to the room, suddenly feeling sick to my stomach and a little dizzy. It might be a reaction to the tea. I've managed to drink five cups of the brew over the last few days and have actually started to like the taste of it. Annie warned me it might make me feel a little sick. She also said it might take a while for it to work. So far there hasn't been so much as a tingle down there. Not that I mind. Writing erotica gives me more pleasure than I ever felt being intimate with another human. Composing a perfect sentence, crawling into Macon's body, transcribing Matt's lust onto a blank page: these are the moments I feel most sated, satisfied, complete.

I don't want to give any of that up.

"My God, girl, you have a book to finish!" I'm wasting precious writing time worrying about my future, my would-be friends. My libido. I get up and go into the kitchen to make another cup of tea. As I wait for it to heat up, I visualize the next scene. I need someone hot for the threesome Audrey wants to have with Macon. I already know where they'll meet her: The Anchor, a hip club I scouted out last year during a visit to see my parents. The woman will be twentysomething. Blond—a visual contrast to Macon's black hair and Audrey's red mane. I don't yet know her name.

I take a sip of the tea as Munch races through the dog door.

"Hi, Munchie," I say, bending down to scratch him on his lower back, instantly setting off his back leg. I smile, picturing how Finley gets hysterical anytime one of us makes the dog do his "phantom kick." I give him a few more jolts and as soon as I remove my hand he barks, reminding me why he bothered coming inside in the first place. "Sorry, Munch. Is it lunchtime already?" I add kibble to his bowl and as I give his head another pat, I remember Heidi's one-eyed dog.

"Ruby," I whisper to the empty house. "It's a perfect name."

Back in my office, I grab an old fashion magazine from my desk and flip through it. No one Matt ever slept with fits the Ruby I have in mind. Neither, unfortunately, does the old *Vogue* in front of me. What about using Sasha, the intern at Stockwell Farms? No. Ruby will be tall. Angular. Scandinavian.

And then it comes to me. The young guy Annie coveted in the café. I named him Liam and committed him and his un-circumcised penis to another book. But a bird in the hand . . . Once I finish transitioning Liam into Ruby, I start back in.

Two blocks further on they saw a small group of people smoking outside of The Anchor, a hip-hop beat spilling out onto the street from within.

"I read something about this place. It's supposed to be pretty happening," Macon said.

"Shall we give it a try?" Audrey asks with a raised eyebrow.

"Sure." Relieved it was still early enough in the evening not to have to plow through the typical packed-sardine crowd of a New York City club, Macon steered Audrey to the bar. After ordering drinks, he turned and surveyed the scene. Beside him, with her martini in hand, Audrey scanned the room like a deer hunter staring intently into a thick forest glade.

By the time they got their second round of drinks, more people crammed the room. The DJ lifted the music up a few levels. When Macon turned around to the bar, a woman brushed against his shoulder.

"Oh, sorry." She was in her twenties and had a flower tat on the side of the neck he could only see half of—the stem of it hidden by the collar of her black striped shirt. Her blond hair was short and spiky, with dark black roots showing through. She had a long sharp nose. He dropped his eyes and saw she had on sexy black leather pants tucked into high black boots.

"No worries," he said.

"I'm Ruby."

"The Rolling Stones Ruby or the red rock Ruby?" He liked that she was tall and could meet his eyes dead on.

"The Stones."

After he said, "Do you change with every new day?" she rolled those eyes. "Yeah, as if you're the first person to ever say that," she said, laughing, then shoving her shoulder against his shoulder—on purpose this time. "What's your name?"

He felt Audrey's hand squeezing his left hip. "Macon."

"Fuck. I've got no comeback for that."

"Too bad." He liked her energy. And he could tell she had a smoking body. He'd love to screw her, with or without Audrey, but remembering their objective, he stepped back from the bar to let Audrey have a look.

She gracefully extended her braceleted hand and said, "Hi there. I'm Macon's friend, Audrey."

"Oh, hi." Macon could see Ruby was a little embarrassed not to have realized he was with someone, and for a second he thought Audrey had scared her off, but no, she put her hand in Audrey's and grinned. "Ruby."

"Nice to meet you. Can we buy you a drink?"

"Definitely. Thank you. I'll have a Maker's Mark, neat," she said to the bartender. "So," she asked after downing the shot and ordering another one, "what are you two up to tonight?"

Audrey slid closer to Ruby just as the music bordered on deafening. Macon could almost smell the heat coming off her. "Just out for a few drinks. What about you?"

Ruby emptied the second drink and licked her lips. "I was supposed to meet up with friends from work, but I'm tired of them." She shrugged. "You know how it is: sometimes the same old same old just isn't good enough."

"I do know, yes. If you'll excuse me a moment. Macon, get Ruby another drink, would you?"

Macon could see Ruby watching Audrey walk away. "Is she your girlfriend?"

"Nope. I work for her."

"Is that all you do for her?"

He remembered Audrey's tight ass slapping down against him a few hours ago. "Nope," he said with a straight face.

"She looks like a movie star. If I were into chicks, I'd totally do her."

"Are you not into chicks?"

Ruby traced the rim of her glass with her fingertip then looked into his face. "I'm into you, if you want to know the truth. But if you only come in a package set, I'm open to suggestion."

An hour later I have them settled in Audrey's apartment. Audrey and Ruby are kissing on the white couch while Macon sits in a chair, watching. After Ruby unbuttons Audrey's blouse, Audrey stops kissing Ruby and peers at Macon.

"We'll be more comfortable in the bedroom." She stood and pulled Ruby up with her. "Won't you join us, Macon?" she said, leading Ruby by the hand.

"Arrrggh," I groan into the air. Talk about hitting a road-block! Kimberlee, my editor at Amatory Press, insisted that I include at least one M/F/F or one M/M/F liaison in this book. How am I supposed to write a steamy *ménage a trois* scene without Matt supplying the juicy details? Not only did he not manage to get a threesome going in Seattle, he didn't have sex with anyone!

I hate having to type *PLACEHOLDER*. I lean back. Give the yellow legal pad a few taps. Look at the clock. Lean forward and take another sip of Annie's tea. Read the last sentence I wrote. Throw my pen at Adam the bendable Doodles Man.

I suppose if I have to, I could cobble together a sex scene out of my limited imagination. I should be able to swing through the machinations of a threesome. But how will Audrey lick Ruby while Macon takes her from behind? Will Ruby be under Audrey? Or . . . ?

I need Matt's body and Matt's moves to drive the scene, but Matt has given me nothing new since . . . wait a minute: if Matt didn't have sex while he was in Seattle, that means—I look at my calendar and count—he hasn't been with another women since the end of April when he was with that hairy woman in Philadelphia.

I stare at the paper, thinking it's a good thing, for both of us, that Matt's leaving tomorrow for Denver to conduct eth-nographic research on . . . what is it again? Dog owners. Dog owners! How on earth is he going to meet two women who will want to have sex with him while doing fieldwork in dog parks and pet stores? How will he—?

Annie is also headed to Denver this weekend.

A pebble of paranoia ricochets through me like a pinball.

"No way," I say aloud. It's a coincidence. Besides, Annie cooked up an herbal aphrodisiac to help me be closer to Matt. *Move on, Kate, move on.* Annie is my friend.

I drop my chin down to my chest and sigh.

Clicking open Google, I type VINTAGE PORN+THREESOME. I do not wish to see any of the modern porn sites filled with skinny girls getting their pink hairless vaginas slammed on someone's bathroom floor. The men's sagging bellies, poor posture, and shaved crotches diminish any traces of natural masculinity. The one time I opened *youporn.com* and scanned a few of the amateur scenes, I almost threw up. Vintage porn should probably be more realistic. At least the women used to be more full-bodied. Never shaved. And the men were more attractive.

I open *vintageXXX.com*. Browsing through the tiny square screenshots of the videos, I click on one showing two women performing oral sex on a hair-ringed penis. I hit PLAY and watch the women—both with long hair and too much eye makeup—lick and moan.

"Okay. Okay. Do something else," I coax, as if I were the director standing next to the camera. After another minute, one of the women climbs on top and eases herself down onto the man's erection.

"Good. Yes. Now, bachelorette number two? What are you going to do?" The second woman straddles the man's face, sinking down far enough for his tongue to reach her. The women paw each other's breasts while moving up and down, one on the penis, one on the mouth. The video abruptly stops.

"What?" I click the arrow to make it continue and another, smaller screen flicks open, telling me that Brandy in Rayburne, Vermont wants me to come *fuck* her.

"Hunh? Ewww." I close that screen and click back to the home page. Instead of what was there before, a stark white official-looking web page is headlined by Interpol, Department of Cybercrime.

ATTENTION

scrolls across the top. Beneath, in red letters:

YOUR PC IS BLOCKED DUE TO AT LEAST ONE OF THE REASONS SPECIFIED BELOW.

My heart slams against my breastbone. "Please, no. Oh my God." With increasing panic I read the words RAYBURNE and VERMONT and "You have been viewing or distributing prohibited pornographic content, thus violating—" I try x-ing out of the page, but it won't go away. I jab my finger on the power button and wait, holding my breath, until the blue light circling it goes dark.

I drop my head onto the desk and whimper, "Fuuuudge."

I grab my phone. Who can I call?

Matt left early this morning to bike the thirty-four-mile Lincoln Gap route in the Green Mountains. I dial him anyway and get his voicemail. No way can I haul my tainted hard drive over to Computer Works. Either Annie's new friend Steve Hodges or one of his techie employees will have a field-day with me, chuckling behind my back as I pay the bill.

I have no other choice. I yank the power plug out of the wall and run across the street.

KATE

Widower Bob—Robert Miravalle—seems pleased as punch to find me standing on his stoop. "Hello, Kate! Are you selling Girl Scout cookies?" He looks past me, as if Finley might be hiding there.

"Hi, Bob. No cookies. I, ah, you used to work at IBM, right?"

"Yup. Thirty-five years. It's a wonder I have any brain cells left." He grins at his joke, then, noticing the laptop in my arms, puts two and two together and says, "Something the matter with your computer?"

"Yes. I was on a website and this scary Interpol screen flashed and it said my computer was locked, and I think I'm in trouble."

"Well, I doubt that very much. Come on in. Let's see if Doctor Bob can fix you."

I step inside and when I bend to remove my shoes, Bob stops me. "Please, keep 'em on. I don't know what it is with all you young people and your need to have cold feet all the time."

To the right of the entryway is an extremely tidy living room. Against the far wall sits a large pink-and-green chintz couch with a precisely folded pink knitted afghan resting across one

of the arms. On the side table are gold-framed photographs surrounding a crystal vase filled with a bouquet of pink silk tulips.
A neatly fanned stack of *Good Housekeeping* magazines arches
across the center of the oak coffee table. When Bob closes the
door behind me, the air in the room shifts and I catch an odd
stagnant smell.

Muffling my guilt, I follow Bob through the kitchen to
a small closed-in porch overlooking a large expanse of green
manicured lawn. We've been living across the street from him
for ten years and, other than cooking him a few meals after his
wife Margaret died two years ago, I've never called or come by.
He is nice enough, but as far as I'm concerned, he has too many
power tools and too much time on his hands. In the summer
he weed-whacks. In the fall he drags out his leaf blower three
times a week. When gray December skies unload even a few
scant inches of snow, Bob's sure to be outside first thing in the
morning, snow-blowing a path from his door to his driveway.

I always ask how he's doing if I run into him in the neighborhood or at the market, but in truth I've been less than neighborly.
Now here I am asking him for a favor. In the future I'll go out
of my way to be more cordial, maybe invite him to dinner.

Bob sits at a desk littered with scraps of paper and mail,
unframed photos of grandkids perhaps, newspaper clippings,
a mass of gold screws. Piles of thick manila folders spill from a
file cabinet next to the desk. Atop that is a paper plate with a
half-eaten ham-and-cheese sandwich.

"Let me see what you got there," Bob says. "A Dell, huh?
You must be one of the last holdouts not to bite the Apple."

"What?"

"You still use Windows," he says, opening the laptop. "You
outlier, you."

"Matt says I should switch to a Mac, but I don't want to."

"Good thing we live in a democratic society and still get to choose which megacorp we want to support."

Apple. Microsoft. Who cares! I am freaking out that I may have lost my documents, or the computer is totally broken, or— My phone rings. It's Heidi so I send it to voicemail. Five seconds later, she calls again.

"You want to take that?"

"No." I set the phone to vibrate, stuff it in my back pocket, and cross my arms.

Bob presses the power button and I almost cry out with relief when the satisfying blue light glows. Okay, the computer isn't *dead*. Maybe just dying. My back pocket vibrates and I check to make sure it isn't school calling, or Matt, but no—it's Heidi again.

What can be so urgent?

"I'm going to need your password," says Bob.

"Munch68. Capital M. No space."

"That's your dog's name and house number, isn't it?" Bob says, adding a *tsk-tsk*. "You should think about changing it to something more secure."

"Sure. Fine," I say. This comes out sounding curt, and I am about to apologize to the man hunched over the keeper of my hidden identity when my phone vibrates yet again.

Bob glances up. "Why don't you take that call outside and give me a few minutes alone with this thing?"

I would prefer to stay staring over Bob the same way I prefer to stare at the seat in front of me when I fly: if I concentrate hard enough, I can make the plane land safely. But Bob obviously wants me gone. Reluctantly, I step onto the back deck, and, turning my face up into the warm May sun, I wait for Heidi to answer.

"Kate! Ruby's dead. Jesus, I'm so angry I could—AHH-HH—I could kill someone!"

For a split second, I envision Ruby slumped over dead on Audrey's white couch, her shirt still unbuttoned. "Oh my God. What happened?" I say, snapping back to reality.

"Those assholes next door to me, with all their broken-down cars and tractors and half-empty containers of shit they leave lying around—GODDAMMIT!—it had to be antifreeze. I'm gonna go over there with my gun and kill the motherfuckers."

"No you're not." I didn't know Heidi owns a gun.

"But Kate, I've gotta do something. I've gotta—"

"Heidi, take a deep breath and calm down. Tell me what happened."

"Shit. I don't really know because the vet can't tell for sure with antifreeze, but yesterday morning Ruby hopped the fence, and I found her rooting around in their field where they've got all their machinery lying around. Fucking half-wit dairy farmers. Why is it the only cheap land around here has to be next to a goddamn farm? I'd move if I could, but where am I going to find two acres for the dogs to run for what I'm paying? Where?"

A squirrel scurries across the neat yard, pauses midstride to scratch its belly, notices me, then runs off. "Antifreeze? What are you talking about?"

"Antifreeze is poison, Kate! Poison! And it's also sweet—sweet enough to want to lick, if you're a dog, that is. I just know Ruby got into it. She had all the classic signs but I missed them—drinking a lot, panting—but it was hot, you know, and she seemed kind of shaky, and I've got so many dogs right now, Kate, I didn't think anything about it. This morning she seemed totally fine so I took the pack on a walk and she could hardly keep up, and by the time I pulled into the driveway she was vomiting and having seizures." Heidi blows her nose. "I rushed her to the hospital, but the vet said if it was ethylene glycol she would've needed the antidote within twelve hours of ingestion. I was too late, Kate. I'm going to go kill them."

"Heidi!" I scream into the phone. "You're being irrational. You just said the vet isn't even sure it was antifreeze."

"Yeah, but—"

"Why don't they know for sure?" I ask, never one to leave an interesting stone unturned.

"The body breaks it down really fast, it's almost impossible to detect, and it's not like I have an extra two hundred dollars sitting around to pay for lab tests."

Behind me in his office, Bob's talking to someone. Himself? My computer?

"Maybe she was already sick when you got her from the shelter," I say.

"Other than missing an eye, Ruby was fine. Jeez, Kate, I'm so sad. I thought for sure I had a family in Williston who was going to take her. They saw her picture on Petfinder and I was going to bring her to meet them tomorrow."

I feel awful for Heidi. Every dog is like a child to her. This has to be breaking her heart.

"Kate!" Bob calls through the sliding door. "You can come back in now."

"Tell me how I can help, Heidi," I say, ignoring him. I consider offering to pay for the lab test, but that seems futile. It would only prolong her pain. "What can I do?"

After a great intake of air and a long slow release, Heidi replies, "No. I just . . . I just needed to vent. I really appreciate you listening to me, Kate."

"Of course."

"No really. You're like the only friend I've got."

"That's not true, Heidi."

"It is true, Kate. You don't care that I'm insane."

"Heidi, you are the best kind of insane." Why *am* I attracted to odd people?

"You know I'd do anything for you, don't you? Like, seriously, Kate. *Anything.*"

"I do know that, Heidi. Same here," I answer with a smile Heidi cannot see.

"Thanks, my friend. I've gotta go feed the gang. Talk to you later."

I rush into the office and see a small window open on the computer screen. "What's that?"

"I'm running a scan. That Interpol warning was a fake, a trojan ransomware virus. It locks you out, then tries to extort money from you to unlock it."

I feel like a patient in a doctor's office waiting to find out if the shadow he just saw on my X-ray means nothing or I'll be dead in six months.

"I did a System Restore in safe mode."

I have no idea what he's talking about but I like that he used the word *safe*. "And?"

"Well, I got your computer to go back to where it was before you got attacked. Now I need to find the buggers that bit you, and you'll be good as new."

Not a death sentence but I may have lost some writing. I didn't save the make-out scene before opening that dangerous video. As I lurk behind him, watching the blue scanning line slowly fill in, I expect Bob to ask me why I was rummaging around porn sites—not that I will ever do that again.

But he offers nothing more accusatory than, "If you're going to surf the web, you've got to have protection, Kate." Grabbing the stale sandwich off the plate and taking a bite, he adds, "Just because something looks safe doesn't mean you should trust it."

ANNIE

I have an hour to kill before my meeting and I've chosen to garrote that hour at the Clyfford Still Museum. I lived in Denver from the time I graduated from college until my move to Vermont, and had always planned to visit the museum, but never got around to it. Given the russet-colored haze covering the city today, I figured it was as good a time as any to sequester myself inside a concrete and steel cube, comfortably breathing potable piped-in air.

As I stroll through hall after hall, staring, mulling, squinting, I try in vain to grasp why the seepage that dripped from the man's brain earned him not only a wing but an entire building in his honor. All I see are a lot of red, yellow, blue, and black splashes. No objects. No subjects.

I make my way over to the room where Still's famous "Big Blue" hangs. There are about ten other folks in the gallery and we all stand—a few with their phones outstretched, others with our hands in our pockets—ogling the enormous painting which really is nothing more than a whole lot of blue paint. I have no idea what it means.

Tiring from listening to the art speak to me with a deaf ear, I turn my attention to Still's writings scattered around and stumble across one of his observations that, hallelujah, helps me comprehend the disequilibrium that, IMHO, raged through the man's psyche.

These are not paintings in the usual sense; they are life and death merging in fearful union. As for me, they kindle a fire; through them I breathe again, hold a golden cord, find my own revelation.

Ah. I like that. I sit down on a singularly uncomfortable bench and stare anew at a mostly yellow canvas streaked with red and gray, contemplating Still's artistic revelation. What he is saying is very yin-yang: when two opposing forces collide, they give off sparks, like sticks being rubbed together to make a fire. For Still, life plus death equaled a new vision. A new expression of his emotions.

I, too, need to merge life and death into a union, but not a fearful one. A joyful one. One that will provide my daughter and me with a new beginning. One which is real. Not abstract.

I pull out my phone and swipe through Tinder until a guard asks me to please remove my feet from the furniture. I sit up and walk out into the brown-streaked day.

KATE

PLACEHOLDER (*ménage `a trois* scene)

Early the next morning Macon gently removed Audrey's arm from his chest and slipped out of bed. After showering, he tiptoed back into the bedroom and when he bent to grab his clothes off the floor he saw a black bra peeking out from under the bed. His brain blazed anew with images from last night's threesome with Ruby and Audrey.

He picked up the bra and placed it on the end of the bed. When Audrey woke up, she'd toss the forgotten lingerie in the trash. They'd never see Ruby again, they both knew that. For Audrey, last night's trine fuck was a one-off.

Audrey stirred and opened her eyes. "You want to see her again, don't you?"

Macon took her hand. Knowing he couldn't afford to piss off his benefactor, he said, "Audrey, you're the only woman I want to see again."

Audrey slipped her hand from his and admired her nails. "I'm thinking of telling Harland about us tonight."

Macon felt as if she'd slapped him. "Why?"

"My husband should know there's another man in my life." She sat up in the bed, holding the silk sheet over her naked breasts. "Maybe I'll ask him for a divorce."

"But, Audrey, I, we—"

"What? You think I'm only in this for the sex?"

All this time he'd assumed she *was* only in it for the sex. Now what? His heart beat rapidly in his chest, each pulse pulling his emotions in different directions. "I have to get to the store, Audrey. Can we discuss this later?"

"Of course, darling. Although I'm disappointed you're not as thrilled as I expected you to be," she said, pouting dramatically.

"Audrey, you know I'm wild about you. It's just that—"

"It's just what, Macon?"

He leaned over her and kissed her, tasting the lipstick lingering on her red lips. "I gotta go, Audrey."

I get up and look out to the backyard. Finley and Terra are sitting on the muddy ground, legs crossed, playing a clapping game. I slide open the window and hear the "Miss Mary Mack Mack Mack" song I taught Finley when she was four. We played it so many times, our palms turned red.

I close the curtains, sit back down, and hook my big toe into my fleece-lined mule, dangling it. I let it drop. Pick it up. Let it drop. I do this a few more times.

Why am I so committed to Macon and Lizzie getting their Happily Ever After? Why not let Audrey get a second chance at love? Sure, Lizzie is young and they can have children together, but Audrey is smart and rich. If Macon falls in love with her, it'll be a twist my readers won't see coming—and readers love a good twist. Of course, I'll need to go back to the beginning of the book and change part of what Macon's thinking when he's with Audrey.

He will see something unexpected in her. She will be a bit gentler and—

"Really, Kate?" I say as if I'm speaking to someone sitting on the couch. I am being dumb. I have to get this thing written already. I can't go back.

I cut off a hunk from one of the Vermont cheeses arranged on a cutting board next to my computer and plop it in my mouth. I let it melt slowly, sucking its flavor onto my tongue before swallowing. Gouda is my favorite among the samples I bought. While not the best choice for a palate cleanser, I take a swig of tea. When Annie dropped Terra's clothes off at the house on Friday, she also lugged along a satchel holding three more 64-ounce mason jars of GoodLove tea. I let her know I was still feeling a bit dizzy and slightly sick to my stomach whenever I drank it, but Annie assured me that it can take a while for the body to get used to metabolizing herbs.

I take another sip, realizing that I've started to crave the bitter taste.

Too bad it isn't working.

Macon flipped the wooden sign hanging in the window of Smiling Girl Cheese Shop in Greenwich Village from SHUT to OPEN and went back to the cutting board. Four more Vermont cheesemakers had agreed to let him carry their product. Before cutting the wheels into a few salable portions and wrapping them in Formaticum Cheese Paper, he'd be sure to taste each newly arrived cheese to be sure they met his high standards.

He sliced off a piece of Glebe Mountain Swiss, a buttery natural rind cheese from West River Creamery and let it melt on his tongue, its nutty undertones forming a pleasant finish. Because it was far too early in the day for wine, the perfect palate cleanser, Macon reached for a baguette delivered by Amy's Bread in The Village. He topped it with a thick slice of Taylor Farm Gouda, the only farmstead gouda Macon considered rich and flavorful enough to sell. He was just cutting into Parish Hill Creamery's excellent mold-streaked West West Blue when an older couple came through the door. "Good morning," he said.

"Good morning," they both replied, politely enough.

Macon wondered if they were tourists, and hoped not. Despite their generally surly attitudes, most locals who knew food were willing to pay top dollar for the best cheese, which was why the business was flourishing.

"Could we try something? Is that okay?"

Definitely tourists. New Yorkers assumed the world owed them a taste or trial or sip or swatch of whatever it was they were in the market for. "Absolutely! Do you folks like blue cheese, because I just got in the most—"

"Not particularly," the woman, dressed in dated jeans and a loud flowered blouse, replied. "We're more cheddar people."

"If you like cheddar, I expect you're going to like this Cobb Hill Four Corners," he said, handing them each a good-sized piece across the counter. "It's from Hartland, Vermont," he added, knowing how much sway the word *Vermont* could have on people's minds. Mention Vermont to someone with a morsel of aged milk in their mouth and what instantly springs to mind were gently rolling green pastures and cows with curly eyelashes, sun-dappled dirt roads and covered bridges.

"This is delicious," the man said.

"I'm glad to hear that," Macon replied, suddenly aware of this change in him; this affability he never would have believed he could possess. He liked this new man. He knew Lizzie would too. She'd been put off by his emotional detachment. "Sure I like you, Macon. You're an amazing lover," she'd said before leaving Smiling Girl Farm, "but no woman's ever going to hand over her heart to you if you've got your arms crossed in front of it all the time. I need to know what you're feeling in here," she'd said, jabbing a finger into his chest, "not just here," she said, cradling his crotch with enough pressure to give him a hard-on.

He'd blamed it on his seventh-generation Vermonter stoicism. "The silent type runs deep in my bloodline, Lizzie," he'd tried. "Give me more time. You know I want you."

But Lizzie had the patience of a hummingbird, moving on from the farm for something she felt she had to attain somewhere else. She wanted to feel the embrace of the big city, she'd said.

Now that he was here, he got it. He hoped he'd be able to keep it.

When the door opened a few seconds later, Macon looked up expectedly, ready to talk cheese, but it was Audrey strolling in, holding two Starbucks cups—

"Mom, can we go swimming in Terra's pool?" Finley hollers through the door.

"What?" I swivel away from Macon and shut the laptop. Finley knows my office is off-limits and is never to enter it without permission. "You can come in, honey."

Finley opens the door. "It's hot and we're bored. Can you— hey, how come it smells like poop in here?"

"It's the cheese I'm snacking on," I say, laughing.

"Gross. Will you take us swimming? Please?"

Yesterday's soccer game was played in a downpour, and the rain continued on through the night, finally clearing out early this morning, leaving behind a gloriously sunny if not muddy Sunday. Having Terra here allowed me to sneak in a little writing, and as much as I want to finish the scene, I can't sit the girls down in front of a video: Annie made it clear that Terra is being raised television-free.

"That sounds like a great idea," I say. "Go put on your bathing suit. I'll grab towels."

Our neighborhood is laid out like a four-armed stick figure. Forest Road, the main artery—or body—runs north to south, with Hawick and Jennings Streets projecting off to the west, Warner and Monroe to the east. Beyond where Forest dead-ends at Dwyer Court and Linden Drive—the two legs that branch off—is a huge track of straggly third-growth forest. In the winter, a few neighborhood volunteers, Matt included, groom the forest's network of crisscrossing paths into flat, superbly fast cross-country ski trails.

Under the bright high sun, the three of us walk down Monroe to Forest, and turn left. The girls run ahead of me, kicking a rock down the street.

"Stay out of the middle of the road!" I warn when they get too far from the curb.

None of the streets have sidewalks, a civic slight common in most of the housing tracts in Rayburne. While we neighborhood parents don't much love having to watch our children walk to school alongside a curb, most residents drive more slowly than the posted 25 mph, and for as long as we've lived at 68 Monroe Street, there has never been an accident. Not even a close call.

Still, I shout again when they veer too far into the street the moment a car comes careening from behind us and turns down Dwyer Court.

It's Suzanne Madden's son, Eli. As I watch him slam the car door and go into the house next door to Annie's, I wonder if the two women have met. If not, I'll introduce them. After all, they are both single parents. They are both—I stop myself from going any further. Suzanne is far too straight. God forbid she tell Annie about her duteous involvement in the local church. I can only imagine what sort of irreverent comeback Annie would offer. If Annie tells her that she keeps her Bible in the bathroom, Suzanne would probably faint.

I unlock Annie's front door and Terra runs upstairs to get a bathing suit, Finley hot on her heels. I slip the keys back into my pocket and wander into the kitchen, not surprised to find it as dirty and disorderly as the last time I was here.

"Oh, Annie, Annie, what are we going to do with you?" I utter aloud before opening the dishwasher and starting to fill it with the contents from the sink and countertops. Minutes later the girls come crashing down the stairs. I follow them outside and make Finley stand still long enough to allow me to smear a layer of sunblock on her skin.

When I ask Terra if I can spread some on her as well, Terra replies, "Annie says, 'If God intended people not to have sun on their skin, He would have made us all turtles.'"

"So, no sunscreen then," I remark to the pale child.

"No, thanks."

"Mom, can we jump in already?"

"Go. Swim." I spread a towel out on the grass, flip down my sunglasses, and lie with my head propped on my hand, keeping a watchful eye on the girls while also thinking about what is going to happen with Macon.

Two hours later the girls are sprawled out on the grass wrapped in damp towels. "I'm going to do a little cleanup," I say, standing up.

"Do not *think* about going in that pool until I come back, do you understand?"

Finley gives me a thumbs-up and returns to giggling in Terra's face.

Once inside, I change my mind about loading the dishwasher and instead wander around downstairs, peeking into the living room's still-unpacked boxes, which are mostly filled with books. A few contain sheets of Terra's artwork, the childish crayon and pastel images smeared with tiny fingerprints. I slap my hand a few times against the top of a cardboard box, its hinge flipping down, then up.

At the bottom of the stairs, I hesitate, then with my heart beating nervously, I climb to the top. I peer into the blur of blue that is the bathroom. Blue tiles. Blue shower curtain. Blue toilet. I can't imagine Annie putting up with such ugliness.

As if trying not to wake a sleeping baby, I walk softly to the end of the hall and give Terra's room a quick sweeping glance. As expected: bedlam. Across from Terra's room is the master bedroom. I pause at the threshold. It's wrong, rude really, to snoop around Annie's private space. What kind of friend does that?

I step in.

A large platform bed is neatly covered with a thick white duvet. On the bedside table next to a pile of books and *Vegetarian Times* magazines is a framed photograph of Terra and Annie standing side by side on a ski slope. I stare at the large print hanging above the bed. A naked woman with muscular legs and buttocks is lying on her stomach, her long dark wavy hair tumbling over her back and chest, her chin resting on her hand. She looks deep in thought, almost sad.

A tickle of suspicion crawls like an inchworm across my skin. It's a Schiele.

I remind myself that lots of people own Schiele prints. He was an incredibly well-known artist. After Matt turned me on to his art, it seemed like I saw Schiele paintings everywhere. So what if Annie admires Schiele too.

Instead of heading back downstairs, I walk to the other end of the hall to the third and fourth bedrooms. I glance into a small, empty room on the right. If I lived here, I would also leave this room empty. Dark brown carpeting on the floor. Cowboy wallpaper. I give a dramatic shudder. "Who are these people?" I ask the room. I never met the owners of the house and know only that they are old and relocated to Florida. Annie was lucky to have found a rental in this neighborhood—they are scarcer than a giraffe in Maine—even one with a hideous blue bathroom.

I turn. The door to the last room is closed, but, hey, I've come this far, right? I twist the knob and enter Annie's office. An enormous ornately carved wooden table with a glass top takes up most of the small space. On top of it is a hefty book with lots of yellow sticky notes jutting out from the pages. The title is in French—*L'herbier Des Plantes Médicinales*—but it isn't too difficult to figure out what it is. I love knowing I'm friends with such an intellectual, worldly woman, even if that woman can't keep a clean kitchen to save herself.

I slide the book aside so I can marvel at the intricate detail in the wood, then gasp at the rows of copulating figures. Their smiles are as large as the erect penises being inserted into the backsides of other figures. Dominating the center of the desk are four people engaged in a contorted sex act: two women hold up the legs of another woman who is being impaled by a man who is upside down!

"Holy cow!" What kind of person uses a Kama Sutra desk? I will definitely *not* be introducing Annie to Suzanne next door. Remembering the girls, I shift to the window and look down into the backyard. They are taking turns with a jump rope. I should be down there with them instead of up here spying on my friend. I am about to walk out when I regard a white shabby-chic filing cabinet in the corner next to a floor lamp. That would look so much better than the ugly gray cabinet I have in my office. I'll ask Annie where she bought it.

No, I won't. I won't ever let Annie know I've violated her trust.

The cabinet has a lock on it. Just for the heck of it, I pull on the top drawer.

Again, I glance out the window and consider running downstairs to slather more sunscreen on Finley. What was that funny thing Terra said about turtles? I picture the two girls as jumping turtles. And then I think about Annie having a sort of turtle-tough carapace over her. If it cracked open, what would I find?

I pluck two paper clips from the ceramic bowl on the corner of the desk and choose a pen with a cap from the round metal pen holder. One of the perks of being the daughter of a real estate agent is that I know how to pick a lock. Growing up, I used to tag along with my father to this open house or that showing, and he'd growl in frustration when the lockbox didn't open, or when the owners stupidly locked the door to the basement boiler room or storage cubby, impeding him from being able to hype the updated furnace or the nifty air-tight spot for storing precious memories. Sometimes he'd take matters into his own hands.

I straighten one clip into a long pick. Using the pointy part of the pen cap as leverage, I bend the tip into a tiny hook. After sticking the hooked one into the lock's opening, I apply tension in the direction the lock turns and rake the pins with the pick until the first one clicks up and away. Then the second one clicks. Then—

"Mom! Where are you? We're starving!"

I bolt upright. "I'm coming!" I yell, shoving the twisted paper clips into my pocket. I am so flustered that when I jam the pen back into the holder I knock it over, sending the pens and pencils rattling loudly across the glass. Panicked that the girls will come upstairs, I hurriedly corral them together and am about to drop the bundle back into the silver cup when the bright turquoise color of a pen I am oh so familiar with catches my eye.

A piece of my heart cracks off and falls to the floor.

I leave it there and run downstairs, making sure to close the door tightly behind me.

KATE

"I couldn't believe my luck, Kaybee. I mean, a freakin' dog park?"

Matt is seated in his usual spot in front of my desk, his arms draped along the back of the teal couch. "Only you, the infamous Matt Parsons. Who'd you do this for again?" I don't know why I want to know: it's as if I am stalling. Pushing the inevitable off for as long as possible.

"It was a Needs and Motivators study for my pals at Heads Up Marketing. They landed a big flea and tick account, and then hired me to go out into the field and talk to dog people."

"Ah," I say, sitting back and admiring the turquoise pen in my hand.

Click-click.

Click-click.

"They wanted to, you know, get a handle on how the end customer chooses a product, or more like they wanted me to focus on who dog owners consider experts. Who they get their information from," Matt explains with his typical enthusiasm. "Like do they trust their fellow dog owners? Or the people they meet at dog parks because they're part of their social unit. Or do they only rely on the advice of their vets? That kind of thing."

"I get it." I also get that I am nuts allowing him to continue innocently on. Any sane person in my extremely furious state of mind would instantly go in for the kill. But I have a book deadline to meet, and I need to finish the Ruby scene.

"So, *anyway*, I'm wandering the park, watching people interact, listening in—"

"Didn't anyone think it was bizarre you were there without a dog?"

"Huh? No. I'm one thousand percent up front with everyone. I tell 'em what I'm doing, what kind of information I'm looking for, and it's great. I mean, everyone is happy to talk about their dogs. I'm hearing everything from what kind of toothbrush they use on their teeth to how many times a day their dog shits." He laughs. "You'd think I was asking them about their kids, but whatever, so these two women walk into the park and I'm standing by the water fountain talking to an old man about his pug and I think, 'Oh man, if I can score with these two, Kate is gonna buy me a Rolex,' so I go over and they're throwing a ball to this dog. It's a big dog, a golden lab named Murphy, and I give them my spiel. I'm outside so they can't sense my *tell*—"

"Your what?"

"My tell. Like in a poker game where you know when someone's bluffing. But right away I set them at ease. I don't want them to think I'm just there to score some sex, ha-ha."

"Ha-ha," I repeat. He does not detect the venom in my voice.

"At first I'm talking about ticks and flea collars, taking notes, but I start picking up a vibe from the blond one, Abby."

Audrey. Angela. Abby.

Annie.

"What did they look like?"

"Well," he says, reclining back on the couch to face the ceiling instead of me. "Abby had long dirty blond hair. It was in a ponytail. She was, oh, I don't know, late twenties, thirty. Super cute. Her friend—Rory—she was also really cute but less, you know, toned. Not my type, but I knew how badly you wanted me to find a threesome so I laid it on pretty thick." He pauses, waiting for me to acknowledge that I pushed him into the hookup he's about to tell me about. He wants me to assuage any lingering guilt before proceeding. It's become a ritual, checking to make sure I'm still okay that he's been with another woman.

I give him the customary slap on the back he longs for. "This is good, Matt. Keep going."

Click-click.

Click-click.

"So we're talking and throwing the ball, and I wander off to talk to other dog people a little bit. Then Abby comes over and asks if I'm done for the day and I say, 'Yeah, more or less, why?' and she says I should come back to their house for tea. Perfect, right? And talk about being convenient, they're just down the street from the park."

"Lucky you."

Click-click.

Click-click.

"Anyway, they live in this tiny house but they've got it furnished pretty nice. Fireplace in the living room. A few prints; no real art. Big couch taking up the living room. With the three of us in there I'm feeling a little claustrophobic and I'm hoping maybe the bedrooms are big enough to spread out in, but Rory turns on some tunes and throws herself on the couch and Abby goes into the kitchen and brings out three beers. So much for tea, right? And they both start grilling me about my life and job and trivial shit. You know, verbal foreplay."

I sit up straight, press the metal nib on the pen down, and write.

Verbal foreplay . . .

"We finish our beers. Abby grabs three more while Rory gets up and pours three shots of tequila and we shoot those. And now everyone's relaxed and they're telling stories and laughing at in-jokes. I'm laughing with them like I get it, even though I don't. Then Rory starts the whole thing, which sort of surprised me because she's the quieter one. She scoots over and puts her hand on my thigh and rubs my pants and asks me if it's okay she's doing this, and I'm like, 'I haven't had a woman touch me in a really long time,' and she says, 'Isn't it sad, Abby?' and Abby stands up and says, 'So sad, yes,' and whips her T-shirt off . . .'"

As if he just handed me a photograph, I transfer their bodies onto the page. As he talks, I write. It's all good.

". . . and at this point I think maybe we're gonna go upstairs because I'm jonesing to lay back and have them both go down on me, but it's not my place, and you know me, ever the polite guest."

Dammit. I want it to be in the bedroom as well.

". . . and then Abby sits up on the corner of the couch and spreads her legs wide open."

"I don't get it. How is Abby sitting?"

"She's got one leg out across the top of the couch and the other one on the arm. You want me to show you?"

"I think I've got it." *Audrey's legs spread open across the couch as Macon . . .* I try to draw the positions the three of them are in, but then return to writing: *Ruby on her knees . . .*

"And now I'm feeling a little pain in my back because I'm all twisted. My upper body is one way and my lower body is facing forward and I can't move my legs at all because of the coffee table in front of the couch. Rory jumps up and drags the coffee table over to the sliding door that goes out to the little yard."

"Is that where the dog is?"

"The dog?"

"Yeah, Murphy?"

"Oh yeah. That's where Murphy is. Anyway, Abby lays down on the couch . . ."

An angry shadow hovers behind me, breathing its dark breath against my neck. I ignore it. If I am going to construct one of the best threesomes ever, I will have to stay present, tuned in. Clinically detached.

I need this scene.

Deeper now, a flurry of body parts twisting, touching, tasting.

"Is Ruby facing you at this point?" I ask when they move into another position, remembering the abbreviated scene I watched before my computer got hacked.

"No, I'm looking at her butt."

. . . straddling . . . licking . . . so much movement . . . moaning . . . Abby says she wants—

"Wait, what?" I look up from my notes. "You just said Abby got on the couch, but isn't Abby already sitting on your penis?"

"What? Oh yeah, sorry. It's kind of a blur at this point, but yeah, Rory climbs up and bends over."

"No kidding," I mumble. None of Matt's liaisons have ever been this complicated, and I'm having doubts that I'll be able to capture it.

Macon slouches down lower . . . his hands on Audrey's breasts . . . Audrey leans forward toward Ruby . . . I try to get a clear picture in my head how that position might work on a bed, but cross it out. No way will Audrey have her face in Ruby's behind. Or maybe she would think that's kind of wicked. I place a question mark next to the sentence and keep writing. . . .*Both women sitting side by side . . . Macon watches, masturbating . . . Ruby orders him to drop to his knees . . .* After all that licking, it's a wonder he's still able to talk.

". . . and then Abby tells me to stand up and they both drop down off the couch and, you know, it's every man's dream to get a double blowjob, right? It was like nothing I've ever . . ."

Macon wraps his hands into their hair . . . has no idea who is doing what . . . he's lost; on another planet . . .

"Man," he says, letting out a deservedly big exhale after coming to the end of his tale.

"'Man' is right." I say. "That was good, Matt. Thank you."

Rather than sit up, he stays prone. He turns to face me, and, smiling proudly, says, "You are so welcome, Kaybee."

"I mean it sounds like the best sex you've ever had."

"Fucking amazing."

"Good." I throw the pen across the pad and cross my arms. "Because you're done."

"What?"

"You're done, Matt. No more sex."

"What are you talking about?" He sits up, stunned.

"Tell me, which one of those women was Annie? Rory or Abby?"

"Kate. What the hell are you—"

"Which one was Annie, Matt!" I scream. At last I can let it out.

"What on earth has gotten into you, Kate?"

"This has gotten into me!" I grip the turquoise pen—the one with PROEM MARKETING: TELL US WHAT YOU KNOW printed on the side. "I found this in Annie's house! You already knew her, didn't you?" I hurl it at him, barely missing his head.

Matt squints at the pen on the couch next to him and blinks. He looks both puzzled and amused. "A pen? Really,

Kate? You found a pen? Jesus. I had hundreds of these pens made. They're everywhere. I can't turn around in this house without tripping over one. Look at your pen holder. How many you got in there, Kate? How many?" His eyes narrow in challenge.

"Yeah, but how did it—?"

"Maybe Finley gave one to Terra. Or maybe the kid grabbed one and took it home with her. Who the fuck knows!"

I have a few more aces up my sleeve. "You were in Denver together, weren't you? It's too much of a coincidence she happened to be there at the same time as you."

"Annie was in Denver? So were half a million other people! I had no idea she was there. Something funny's going on in your head, Kate. Maybe you spend too much time in a fictional world. Your writing is making you delusional."

"What about the fact that she's got hairy armpits like that woman you had sex with on the conference room table, and how come you didn't take Munch with you when you went running? Is that delusional?"

"Finley's friend's mother doesn't shave her underarms and that means I'm screwing her?" He stares at me as if I'm a stranger.

I look down at my hands and see that they're shaking. My stomach feels as if there's a flock of fighting birds inside it, their wings whipping against my heart. My lungs. My breastbone. I showed him my hand and I have nothing, not even a pair of twos. I get up and go over to the window and open the curtains. Munch is lying on his side, panting heavily in a splotch of sunshine. If he got up and moved over three feet, he'd be in shade. Why are animals so thick?

And why am I so intent on proving that my husband is having an affair with my new friend?

Matt comes over and reaches his arms around me. "I love

you, Kaybee, and I love what we've got here." He turns me around and brings his face close to mine. "You and I both know I am the luckiest man on the planet."

"This is true."

"So why would I want to fuck up a good thing?"

"You wouldn't." How many wives out there are okay with their husbands having sex with other women? Very few, is my guess.

"Damn right I wouldn't."

He would have to be a fool to mess up our arrangement. An outright idiot.

I press my cheek against his chest and hug him close, eyeing the MOMA mug bulging with turquoise pens on my desk. He's right. The few signs I assumed were flashing indicators now look more like trivial coincidences.

"You think maybe it's time to stop?" Matt whispers into my hair.

I pull away. "Stop what?"

He gestures to the teal couch with his chin then points to the computer with his right hand. "This, Kate. Our secret world. Maybe it's gotten too weird and it's messing with your brain."

I think about the reviews I have on Goodreads. And the fact that *Strong Lust: Crossing Borders* is still being added to plenty of Want To Read lists. I have no doubt *Strong Lust: The Taste of Her* will be just as popular—if I finish it. I need to stop worrying.

"No, sweetheart," I say emphatically, "my brain is perfectly fine, thank you. Now, if you don't mind, I've got writing to do."

KATE

I want to go to the show tonight but not by myself. No way Heidi will drive up. I could call Christy, but she is probably unavailable. Between her full-time job selling laser equipment to dermatologists, and her troubled kid, she's always busy. I place my empty mug into the sink and dial Annie.

"Hello, Miss Kate, mother of Finley," she says. "Nice to hear your voice."

"What are you up to tonight?"

"Reveling in domestic bliss, I guess. Why?"

"I've got two tickets to see the Mark Morris Dance Group at the Flynn, and Matt doesn't want to go." I glance angrily over at Matt and Finley playing with Legos on the living room floor. I planned this outing ages ago. I booked a babysitter and made reservations at Bistro de Margot. We haven't gone on a real date in a long time, and I was really looking forward to spending an evening out in a fancy restaurant followed by a theater performance. It would give us something new to talk about, something other than Finley or Matt's lovers. I wanted to sit across a candlelit table from my husband and reconnect while sharing a bowl of steamed mussels. I even planned to apologize again for accusing him of having an affair with Annie. But, when I walked into Matt's office an hour ago to remind him, he had completely forgotten about it.

"Sorry, Kaybee," he said, not nearly apologetically enough. "Denver wiped me out. And you know, dance isn't my thing."

"Would you like to go with me?" I ask Annie.

"Hell, yeah!" Annie screams into the phone. "But only if I can get a last-minute babysitter. Do you know any teenagers who aren't serial killers?"

"Don't be silly. Terra can come here. Unless you're nervous about Matt babysitting her," I add with a laugh.

"If you don't think he'd mind another kid, sure."

"He won't mind. Bring her over around seven thirty. I'll drive."

"Your wish is my command, Kate Burke."

After I hang up, I join my family on the floor. "Hey, Terra's coming over, okay?"

"Yippee!" Finley throws a pile of red, yellow, and green rectangles into the air. A few land on Munch, waking him out of a dog dream.

"What? Why?" Matt asks.

"Annie needs someone to watch her because *she* is going to the dance with me."

"You asked Annie?" He connects a yellow piece to the top of a tower he's constructing. "Why?"

A splinter of mistrust pokes at the edge of my brain. "Why shouldn't I ask her?"

"Don't make a big deal out of it. I just figured you were gonna bag it, and stay home with us."

"Well, you figured wrong."

It was a mistake to offer to drive because after only three minutes in our Subaru's passenger seat, Annie started wheezing. I barely got as far as the school at the top of Forest Road when I realized the car was laden with Munch's hair. We turned around and switched to Annie's Prius.

"Sorry about that," I remark while subtly reclining back in the seat and brushing crumbs out from under my butt. Her car is as filthy as her house, strewn with used tissues, balled-up gas receipts, half-eaten packages of organic crackers, books, pens, empty mason jars, as well as a scattering of indeterminate dried-up food particles.

"Please don't apologize. But if you ever did want to kill me"—she flashes me a grin—"all you'd have to do is lock me inside that car of yours."

"I'll keep that in mind." I laugh. "I feel like I should apologize for Matt's behavior back there," I utter, moving from murder to bad manners.

"What do you mean?"

"I mean him not coming out to say hello or anything. I think he's burned out from working so much." Or he's dealing with some other stress he's not telling me about. I should have insisted we go out together. Just last night in bed, when I tried to discuss my book with him, I could hardly keep his attention. This, from the man who usually cannot wait to find out how I render his one-night stands. It thrills Matt, a man with an ego as large as the moon, to see his own sex immortalized through my words. I felt pretty dejected.

"Hey, if God had wanted men to be as thoughtful and

considerate as women, He would have given them vaginas," says Annie. She has on a pair of black baggy trousers, a long-sleeved black shirt, and flat black ankle boots. Around her neck hangs a silver necklace with a purple and white pendant.

"I've never seen the yin-yang symbol in anything but black and white," I say, referring to the stone's design.

Annie fingers it. "As long as one of the colors represents yin and the other yang, it doesn't really matter."

Not wanting Annie to know I have no idea what the symbol means, I'm relieved when she adds, "Walk into any yoga studio and you'll see yin-yang art plastered all over the walls. I used to think it was simply about the duality of life." She bangs the knob on the radio, silencing NPR's Meghna Chakrabarti. "But it's about opposing forces needing one another. Yin, the feminine—yay, us—is considered the negative force. Yang is the masculine, the positive force. But—here's the part that's so wondrously wise—the two sides: the dark/light, moon/sun, cold/hot, you get it—they cannot exist without the other. You can't have death without life, which is why"—she raises the charm toward me while keeping her eyes on the road—"there's a purple dot inside the white side and a white dot inside the purple. Neither exists on its own. So they're always dancing; at the same time, opposing one another. This, my friend, is how the world stays in balance."

"That's cool." I stare at the Victorian houses we pass along Union Street and think about creating more balance in the relationship between Macon and Audrey. I have the attraction down, but I'm not yet sure how the opposition will play out. "You want to make a left on Maple," I say, forcing my fictional characters into a closet and promising I will be back for them later. "There's always free parking there."

"Aye-aye, captain."

After Annie puts the car in park, I reach for my purse but Annie stops me. "Hold up a minute, darlin'," she says, sliding what looks like a thick black magic marker out of her pants pocket. I watch as she depresses a button on the top and a mouthpiece pops up. A light on the side of it glows purple.

"Is that for your asthma?" I ask.

"No. It's for my head. It's marijuana."

"What? Annie! How could you—?"

"Come on, Kate. Do you honestly expect me to watch modern dance without being stoned?" The light color changes to green and Annie puts her mouth on the tip and inhales. "This is a vaporizer," she says, exhaling a barely detectable yet identifiable mist smelling of marijuana. "It heats the herb at a low temp but it doesn't combust, so I'm not inhaling smoke."

"I'd think pot would make your asthma worse," I say, bewildered.

"You know some experts"—she makes quote marks around the last word—"actually say smoking cannabis expands bronchial passageways, but the last time I took a hit of a joint it was bad news, so instead I vape. Here," she says, passing the contraption to me. "Have a go."

I hold it in my hand and run my thumb over its smooth sleek surface "I don't know."

"You've smoked pot, right?"

"A few times in college, but it's been a long time. I'm not sure I—"

Annie grabs it out of my hand and sticks it in my mouth. "Just suck lightly. There you go. Wasn't that easy?"

I exhale a small amount of vapor and roll my tongue around my mouth and lips. "It tastes different than I remember. Sweeter."

"You're actually tasting the plant, not the smoke. You want another?"

"No. I'm good." I have no idea if one puff is enough to get me high, but oh how wicked I feel! What would the Rayburne ladies think if they knew I smoked pot?

Annie takes another hit, then pushes the top down with a click. "Okay, doll face. Let's go watch us some dance."

Walking up Church Street toward Main, I realize I am definitely high. I cannot wipe the stupid grin off my face. *Please don't let me run into anyone who knows me at the theater.* And why have I never before noticed how pretty Nectar's sign is, with its orange neon blazing against the black sky? "Hey, Annie. This is where Matt and I had our first date!" I squeal as we pass Manhattan Pizza and Pub.

"Right on," Annie replies, bouncing along beside me. "You were his biology tutor, right?"

"I was!"

A few minutes later the theater lights are half-dimmed and the artistic director is making his requisite speech about cell phones and flash photography when Annie and I find our seats in the balcony. I recline into the red velvet chair and leaf through the playbill to the benefactor section.

"Here, look," I say, shoving the program in front of Annie's face and pointing to *Proem Marketing*. "That's Matt's company." The image of a turquoise pen flashes in front of me, and I laugh at the absurdity of my paranoia.

"What's so funny about Matt's company?" Annie asks.

"No, I'm laughing because—" I want to tell Annie about how I confronted Matt after finding his pen in her house and how it made me mistakenly think they were having an affair. For sure, it'd make Annie laugh. We'd laugh about it together.

Or Annie will think I'm nuts. And she'll be angry I was snooping.

Matt and Annie are not having an affair. She would not have come out with me tonight if they were. She would not have made me that tea. Matt has never lied to me.

"Nothing," I whisper as the lights go out and dancers take the stage.

I lose myself in the first piece called "A Wooden Tree." Eight sinewy dancers dressed in old-fashioned Scottish garb mime and jump and cavort to humorous recorded songs. But during the "Italian Concerto," a balletic dance set to piano music, my interest wanes.

I look over at Annie. She's staring at the ceiling instead of the stage.

At intermission, she jumps up to go to the restroom. I am so high I get lost in the ornate art deco designs covering the walls of the theater before moving on to marveling at the variety of colors of the clothing people around me are wearing. The guy at the end of my row has on a bright yellow tie. And wow, everyone is so dressed up! I look down at my khaki slacks and white turtleneck and now feel embarrassingly underdressed. I look like a suburban housewife, not like a sophisticated woman out on the town. I should have worn the sexy dress I planned to wear, but when Matt canceled, I—Annie appears next to me and drops clumsily into her seat. She bends over and picks up the playbill from the floor.

I push aside my clothing paranoia and ask, "Are you enjoying this?"

"It's like a million variations on falling down and getting up again," she says. "What's your take?"

Smart educated people are supposed to enjoy modern dance, aren't they? "I'm bored," I admit.

"Thank God, girlfriend. Let's get a drink. I've got cotton mouth."

By *drink* I assumed Annie meant juice or tea, but once out the Flynn's front doors, she steers me down the street and pushes me into Jake's Pub. Since moving to Vermont, I'd probably passed by Jake's two thousand times without ever stepping inside. Now that we're at the bar, I get why.

"It smells like bleach and barf in here, Annie. There's a much nicer—"

"Relax, Kate. What are you having?" She gestures at the bartender, a woman in her forties with light brown frizzy shoulder-length hair and a pale pleasant face mottled by rosacea. She looks like a less muscular version of Heidi.

"Earth to Kate."

"What? Oh, sorry," I say. Heidi's look-alike is waiting for me to order. "I'll have, um . . . " I focus on the rows of shiny bottles. So many pretty labels and colors. "Um."

"Just make it two," Annie says to the woman while rolling her eyes.

After the bartender moves off to concoct two of something, I give the place the once-over. A solitary old man sits at the other end of the bar, keeping his body propped up by his elbow. In the back corner, playing a game of foosball, are four college-aged guys, all holding a Heady Topper in one hand, and using their free hands to twirl the black vinyl handles. "This is a dive bar," I observe, turning back around.

"Brilliant deduction, Sherlock," Annie says.

"Our first real date and you take me to a dive bar?"

She wiggles her eyebrows at me. "Just you wait and see what I've got planned for our next one."

"A vegan picnic at a garbage dump?"

She pouts. "And now you've completely spoiled my surprise."

The bartender puts two martini glasses down in front of us.

"Whoa," I say, after swallowing the cold pandemonium of sweet, sour, bitter, and something else, something mysterious. "What the heck is this?"

"Corpse Reviver Number Two. Good enough to wake the dead."

I drink more. "It's shockingly delicious."

"Yeah. It's like a taste bud gangbang."

That is such a good line I have to use it. I reach into my purse and retrieve my notebook. After I zip it closed and drain my glass, Annie asks, "What did you just write?"

"I wrote what you said, for my new book," I say, feeling loose as a goose. "May I have another one of these, please?"

After she orders another round, Annie says, "Tell me about your book."

Finally! "In a minute, but first I want to know: Did you ever hook up with Steve Hodges?"

"Did you really just say 'hook up'?"

"Yeah. Why? Isn't that what people say?"

"Maybe if you're seventeen."

"Oh?" Have I used that term in any of my books? If it isn't age-appropriate, my editor would have caught it. "Whatever. Have you *seen* Steve again?"

"As a matter of fact I have seen, as well as touched, tasted, and smelled my neighbor Steve again," she says with a provocative grin. "You weren't wrong when you said he was a bit *off.* He's warped but in a good way."

"You mean he's into, um—"

"You don't really want to hear about my depraved sex life."

"Why would you say that?"

"You know." She pauses while a group of clearly drunk college kids burst in and make for the back by the foosball and pool tables. "Because—"

"Because I have no libido, you think I have no interest in sex?" I take a swig of the newly arrived cocktail and leer at her. "Annie, Annie, Annie, if only you knew."

"Knew what, darling?" She wants it, and I am alive and open to giving it to her.

I shout, "I write erotica books!" after which I fall over laughing.

"You're fucking with me."

"Nope." I sit up as straight as my tipsy body will allow, put my shoulders back, and let her have it. Or, part of it, anyway. I tell her I've published three popular erotica books, but no matter how hard Annie pushes, I refuse to give her the titles or my nom de plume.

When Annie calls the bartender back, I put my hand up. "No more for me. We should get going." Another Corpse and who knows what I might give up.

"Should we get a taxi?" I ask.

"No. You should tell me the titles of your books so I can read them."

I shake my head as demurely as Princess Grace. "Nope."

"But . . ." She slaps her hands on the bar, confounded. "You're stressing me out here, Kate! How do you—Really? Erotica? Why on earth do you write erotica?"

"I'll tell you in the taxi."

Our driver is a New American from Somalia. Ali understands enough English to get us to Rayburne, but not, I hope, the meaning of our backseat conversation. "When I first started writing I wrote regular fiction. You know, mysteries. Chick lit. That sort of thing," I say, once Ali turns right onto South Winooski Avenue. "But I wasn't very successful at it. I mean," I readjust the seatbelt and face Annie, "I was at Price Chopper a few years ago and for no reason I bought one of those, you know, sexy books, and I actually enjoyed reading it, so I thought maybe I could write one. I mean, it's what's selling, right?" I say, echoing Matt's exact words all those years ago. Annie didn't need to know that Matt was the one who suggested I write erotica; nor that he stars in all my books. "And it turned out I was pretty good at it."

Annie slumps down in the seat and crosses her arms over her chest. "Jesus, Mary, and Joseph, Kate. I'm blown away. Are you—I mean, your fake name—is she famous?"

"Kind of."

"And you make money at it?"

When Ali puts on his blinker and pulls into the right lane, I think maybe he didn't understand the address I gave him, but a few seconds later a fire engine careens by, followed by an ambulance, their chilling sirens filling the car.

Once he's back on the road, heading toward Rayburne, I answer her. "I do."

"But where do you get your material? Do you watch porn?"

"No, you idiot. I make it up! Don't all fiction writers make up their stories? Think about it. Crime writers aren't necessarily cops or murderers."

"I guess. But if you're not turned on by sex, how do you turn your readers on?"

"Same answer. A good writer can describe anything," I say, lying through my teeth. Without Matt's details at my disposal, I'd never be able to so much as turn on a faucet, let alone a reader.

Annie nods as if it makes perfect sense. She believes me. I'm hoping I've impressed her. It's what I wanted to happen since that first day drinking tea with her on her couch.

I'm the cool friend.

As the taxi makes a left onto Forest Road, I say, "Annie, you must swear on Terra's life you'll never tell anyone."

"No one knows? Not even Matt?"

"Of course Matt knows! He's the only person, other than my editor, I mean."

"And it doesn't suck for him that you write about sex but don't *have* sex?"

It isn't the reaction I hoped for. Annie doesn't exactly sound as if she's accusing me of being a less-than-perfect wife, but the question kills my high, awakening a vulnerability and self-loathing I thought I buried long ago.

Thank you very much for the Corpse Reviver, Annie.

"Matt loves my books," I tell her. "And he loves me the way I am," I state defensively. "We're really tight."

She gazes at me as if I were a sad child who needs perking up. "I don't doubt that. You're amazing." After Ali pulls into the driveway and puts the car in park, Annie unclips her seatbelt and pulls me into a tight hug. She smells like a gangbang of gin and pot and lavender. In the rearview mirror, Ali stares at us, the meter on his dash continuing its ascent.

"Seriously, Miss Kate, mother of Finley," Annie says, letting go to look into my face. "I, too, love you just the way you are."

"I'll go get Terra," I tell Annie after Ali pulls away. "Then you don't have to breathe in dog dander."

Inside, I find Matt on the living room floor playing UNO with the girls. "Hi. How was babysitting?"

"So fun," he says. "I have close to a thousand points already."

"Mommy. Daddy cheats!"

"What? Are you trying to tarnish my stellar reputation as the world champion UNO player? Just for that I'm going to have to punish you, little girl!" Matt snatches Finley and holds her upside down by her ankles.

Finley screams, "Put me down!" then laughs when Matt—gently enough—drops her to the floor with a thud.

"Hey, Terra, your mom's waiting outside." Without a word of thanks to Matt, Terra gives Finley a quick hug and runs from the house.

I take Matt by the arm and pull him to the front door. "Come say hello," I demand.

Standing on the top step Matt says, "Hello, Annie," with a small nod.

"Hi, Matt," Annie replies. "Did Terra give you any trouble? Do I need to put her in stocks for the night?"

"Nope. Good as gold. Nice to see you," he says and walks back into the house.

"You want me to drive you home?" I ask her.

Annie cocks her head to the side in that Annie-like way. I take that as a negative.

She definitely has a unique way of expressing herself. Little by little, I will learn this Annie language. I totally misread her reaction in the car and came close to breaking down in tears. But Annie wasn't judging me. She was only being curious.

Annie puts her arm around Terra, blows me a kiss, and heads off toward home.

After tucking Finley into bed, I pick up a library book from her bedroom floor where it lies splayed open upside down. "Finley, what have I told you about using a bookmark, especially for hardcovers. Look how bent the spine is."

"Sorry," she says, pulling the cover up over her head. "But it's just a library book."

I'm too tired to argue, and bedtime is never the proper time to push life lessons. "Hmm." I look at the book cover. "*Slider* by Pete Hautman. What's it about?"

Finley uncovers her face and speaks so quickly my sluggish brain can make out only that it is about a kid who competes in food-eating contests. I open it to the first chapter and when I read the title, "Pizza," a memory torpedoes through the slurry. "Did you ever tell Terra how Daddy and I met?"

"What?"

"Did you ever say that I was Daddy's tutor in college?"

"I don't know, maybe." Finley kicks the blanket off and turns over. "Why do you even care?" she asks the wall.

I kiss the back of her head and walk toward the door. "No reason," I say, flicking off the light and closing the door.

KATE

The process of transferring the *ménage `a trois* from a couch in Denver to a king-sized bed in New York City is slow going. Matt's story was far more convoluted than usual and I've spent almost the entire morning twisting and turning and contorting Ruby and Macon and Audrey all over Audrey's sumptuous bedroom, and I still have yet to get control of the scene.

I take a drink of tea, then click to Goodreads. There are ten questions from readers and twelve new reviews—all but two with five stars. Someone named AnnTheAvidReader gave me three stars but didn't leave a comment. I hate that.

"At least tell me why you didn't love the book, you wench," I mutter.

Ann. Anne. Annie.

Tiny uncertainties claw at me like a kitten under the covers. I sink my face into my upturned palms and moan. Why am I still letting these silly ambiguities pester me, especially after we had so much fun the other night? Why can't I just *lean* into this relationship like I do with Heidi?

I close the laptop and pick up my phone.

"Kate! OMG, I'm so glad you called."

"Are you feeling any better, Heidi, or are you still on the rampage?"

She laughs. "You know me, Kate. I am *always* on the rampage, but yeah, I'm starting to get over it. I have to since I just took in a litter of puppies someone found in a dumpster."

"Heideee," I groan. "You really need to learn how to say no."

"I couldn't say no, Kate! You have to see them. They are the cutest things ever."

This from the woman who thought Ruby was the cutest thing ever.

"How are you, by the way?" she asks, switching gears. "Tell me what's happening in your life these days."

"Well." I called her for a reason and now I'm not so sure I want to share.

"Kate? You still there?"

I get up from the desk and move to the couch, lying down like Matt does. I stare at the ceiling for a few seconds before I decide to spit it out. "I made a new friend." There. Done.

"Who is she, he? Do I need to be jealous?"

I laugh. "As if anyone could ever take your place, Heidi. You and I are friends for life."

"You bet your sweet ass we are. So, who's my new competition?"

I breath in, collect my thoughts, and describe the woman whose daughter is Finley's best friend. I tell her about Annie's sarcasm and kookiness. Her Bible quotes. How she's really into healthy stuff and even makes medicinal teas. "We've gotten together a bunch of times, and it's always really fun."

I even told her two of my biggest secrets, I want to add. I don't.

"She sounds totally cool," says Heidi. "What *aren't* you saying?"

"I think she might be sleeping with Matt behind my back." I know I sound like a paranoid idiot, but it's out before I can stop it.

"What the hell!" Heidi screeches. I sit back up, quickly moving the phone away from my ear but can still hear her with it two inches away. "How is that even possible? You and Matt are, like, the most perfect couple I know! Why would he cheat on you? You're totally gorgeous and brilliant."

If only she knew the truth. "Aww, thank you. That's very sweet of you to say."

"Did you ask Matt if he was having an affair?"

"I did. He denied it." I gaze at my desk, trying to imagine how Matt sees me when he's sitting here sharing his exploits. Does he see the same woman he fell in love with all those years ago, or have I become nothing but a receptacle?

"Then where on earth did that come from?"

"Well, there's some freaky stuff I can't explain."

"Like?"

Sighing, I dig into the repository of bizarre coincidences, listing them off like a prosecutor introducing her case to the jurors. I describe Annie's allergies and the fact that Matt neglects to take Munch on runs with him. That he stopped wearing aftershave. I mention finding the pen. The weekend trip to Denver. Annie knowing I tutored Matt in college. As much as I want to win the trial, I have to withhold plenty of the more damning evidence. Nothing about GoodLove. No sex stories about women whose names begin with the letter A. Not a mention of hairy women either.

After the prosecution rests, Heidi observes, "It is kind of freaky, Kate."

"Right?"

"Yeah, freaky that you'd be friends with someone who's allergic to dogs."

"Ha-ha."

"My opinion is this. You should stop—" She's interrupted by loud barking from what sounds like twenty dogs. "Hold on," she says, throwing the phone down with a bang to my ear. I hear her open a door and yell, "Go out! Go play. Minx, you too, girl. Go!" before slamming it closed and picking up the phone again. "Where was I?" she asks.

"You were telling me to stop."

"Right. Stop worrying! You really like her, right?"

"Yep."

"So then just ask her straight out: Are you sleeping with my husband? When she says no, you can move on."

"What if she says yes?" I say wryly, followed by a jolt of fear slamming me in the solar plexus.

"Then we kill her," says Heidi.

"You're on quite a roll today, girlfriend."

After I hang up, I go into my desk, kick off my slippers, and reread the last few pages I've written. The scene is steamy, but it needs something beyond all the wet wanting flesh I have flying around. I left off as Macon is screwing Audrey doggy-style and I still cannot decide if he wants to go full throttle on the sex or if I should pause to thicken the plot. Have Macon thinking about Lizzie. I close my eyes and mind-meld with him, listening to all that's percolating inside his handsome head.

After a while I glance at the clock on the computer. It's four thirty! How have I lost track of the time? Where is Finley? She should have been home an hour ago. I stop and think where she could be. Matt doesn't have her: he woke up at sunrise and drove to Lyndonville to bike the sixty-nine-mile Glacial Lakes loop.

Is there an unscheduled soccer practice today? I text Coach

Eric, who texts back seconds later: NO PRACTICE TODAY BUT SEE YOU AT THE GAME ON SATURDAY!!

I put on my slippers and run outside. Where is Finley?

I call the school. Bonnie, the assistant principal, answers and, after an interminable hold, she perfunctorily informs me that Finley Parsons is nowhere to be found.

Where is Finley?

I call Matt. No answer.

I call Annie. No answer.

If Annie has her, surely she would let me know, right? Flushed with panic, I grab my keys, get into my car, and tear down Monroe, taking the left onto Forest too fast, almost side-swiping a kid on his bike. A quick right onto Dwyer Court, and darn!—the mailman is blocking Annie's driveway. I swerve in front of the truck and park against the curb.

Loud music is coming through Annie's front door so I have to knock hard. When no one answers, I try the doorknob—it's locked.

"Hello?" I scream, bashing my fist against the wood.

Then I remember I have a key to the house, but my hands are shaking so much I drop the whole set. The moment I bend down, the music stops. A second later, Annie opens the door.

"Hello, Kate Burke. Are you here to get Finley? I told her she could stay for dinner—"

"She's here? Finley *is* here?"

"Are you okay? You look like you've just seen a ghost. Nice slippers by the way. Very fashionable."

My heart is beating so strongly against my chest I can hardly breathe. I try to take in a full gulp of air, but it's as if my lungs erected a roadblock. "Why didn't you tell me she was coming here?"

Annie tilts her head sideways and looks surprised. "I told her to call you as soon as she got home. I take it, um, she did not?"

"No, she did not," I say, pushing past Annie into the foyer. "Finley Parsons!" I yell up the stairs. "Come here this instant!"

Finley appears at the top of the stairs. "Hi, Mommy."

"Finley, my love," says Annie. "Didn't I tell you to call your mother?"

Terra emerges by Finley's side. Finley looks at Terra, then back at the two mothers whose four hands are on our two hips. "Uh. I forgot?" says Finley.

"Do you have any idea how much you scared me?" I ask my daughter.

Why did Annie just refer to my daughter as *my love*?

"It's my fault, Kate," Annie says, touching my shoulder gently. "When I met Terra after school, Fin asked if she could come home with us and—"

"Why didn't you just text me when you were leaving school?"

Fin? No one calls her Fin.

"I left my phone charging at home. I'm so sorry," Annie replies, hugging me. "I am a bad, bad friend."

I hesitate, then put my arms around Annie, clutching her small body to mine. "No, you're not, Annie," I say, wondering why they didn't stop at the house. It's three houses from the corner and would have taken just five extra minutes. I let go of Annie, still unsure how angry I am. "Finley, get your stuff. We're going home."

"But, Mom, Annie invited me for dinner."

"I don't know. You didn't call—"

"I'm making my famous Glory Bowl tonight," Annie interrupts. "Kate, why don't you stay too?"

"Daddy's cooking," I tell Finley. "Would you rather eat burgers or tofu?" I ask, not doubting for a second who will win this clash of dinner plans.

Finley howls, "Tofu!" and before I can up the ante with ice

cream for dessert, Finley hustles Terra away, the two of them disappearing before my eyes.

Annie pumps her fist in the air. "Yes! Dwyer Court for the win! Soybeans, one. Dead cow, zero."

I want to laugh along, but I am not amused by what just happened. I should have insisted Finley go home with me. She and Matt haven't spent enough time together lately.

"Well, that was a surprise."

"What can I say?" she said, grinning. "I've got the magic touch."

I stand there, unsure what to do next.

"Come in, Kate. You need a glass of wine."

I have to go home and prepare the burgers before Matt gets to them. He can grill just fine, but he makes the patties too thick. I hate biting into raw meat.

"It's that merlot you had last time," she says, raising an eyebrow.

"What time is it?"

"No idea. For the sake of argument, let's say it's 5:01."

I laugh, my guard loosening enough to follow Annie into the kitchen. After she pours me a glass, I settle on a stool and watch as Annie piles veggies up onto the counter.

"Déjà vu," I remark.

"Yup. All over again."

"That was so much fun the other night. Thanks for going with me."

"Thank *you* for one of the best nights I've had since moving here. I mean that." She stops chopping and holds up her own glass of wine. "To my gloriously talented and fascinating friend, Kate Burke, who I am going to torture until she tells me the titles of her famous erotica books."

"Shhh!" I jam my finger against my lips.

"What? The girls are upstairs. They can't hear us."

"Drop it, okay?"

"What if I beg?"

"No."

"Whine?"

"You are not reading my books."

"Why? What have you got to hide?"

As I watch her slice a carrot, I mull over my answer, then say, "You might see me differently."

"You're right. I'll read your chapter about a man screwing a woman in an airplane bathroom and decide you're too depraved to be friends with." She cocks her head, grins, then continues slicing.

"One of my books has a sex scene in a canoe," I say, "but none on an airplane." I'm not sure Matt ever had the opportunity. "Have you had sex on a plane?"

"Of course." She glances at me with a raised eyebrow. "Want to hear about it and put it in your next book?"

"Maybe," I reply, tapping my fingernails on the glass. This is getting interesting. By and large, straight erotica books can be told from either a male or female perspective, or both. Because my stories come through Matt, it's only natural the books I've written are told from a male point of view. If I got the nitty gritty from Annie's sexual experiences with Steve—and whoever else— my next book could have a female POV. The thought excites me. When Annie opens the refrigerator, I ask, "You wouldn't feel weird telling me about your sex life?"

Annie takes a package of tofu to the sink and as she drains it, she looks at me over her shoulder and declares, "Girlfriend, I have stories that would blow your competition out of the water." Flopping the tofu onto the cutting board, she adds, "I'd be honored to contribute."

While she slices, I consider how such an arrangement might work. If I helped myself to her stories, she'd want to read them. For how long could I hold her off? "Let me think about it, okay?"

Annie refills my wine glass. "Whatever you say, doll."

"Hey, I never asked you about Denver," I say, putting a pin in the idea. "How was your trip?"

"It was unerringly beautiful there."

"Nice."

"On Sunday the ozone reading was in the green zone." She looks at me with a wide smile. Her skin has more color, more of a glow than the last time I saw her. "So, we went for a long hike on the Royal Arch Trail, and I didn't die doing it."

"Who'd you go with?" I ask casually.

For a second Annie's hand wavers over the tofu. "My friend Roxy."

"The friend who's drinking the GoodLove tea, right?" Roxy, the woman who is purportedly screwing like a rabbit while I languish in my coop, nibbling placidly on a lettuce leaf.

"Yup." Annie empties a bag of button mushrooms onto the cutting board and begins to slice them. They are covered in dirt, but I hold my tongue. "What's funny is that she's become such a sex fiend she actually asked me to have a threesome with her and Pete." She conveys this beguiling fact without the slightest modulation in her voice, as if she's just told me she found a pretty rock during her hike.

A minute ago, she bragged about having stories that will blow my competition away. Is she trying to tease me with this information? My brain is exploding with want. If I let her start now, will I ever be able to end it? "And?" I say, tentatively. "How, um, was it?"

"What?"

"The threesome?" An even better *ménage 'a trois* than the

one Matt had could be right here, two feet away from where I sit. From a female POV, to boot.

Annie ceases slicing. Narrowing her eyes, she points the knife in my direction. "Are you out of your mind? You think I'd ever do that? What if it killed"—as she says *killed* she stabs the knife into the board—"my relationship with Roxy? No orgasm, multiple or otherwise, is worth losing a friend over." From above comes a thundering crash. It sounds as if the girls are wrestling an elephant. The noise seems to snap Annie out of her tirade because she unsticks the knife and resumes slicing mushrooms.

Annie's admission astonishes me. Underneath that uninhibited free spirit of hers, there lurks a morally conscious human. Though I would have been willing to clean her filthy house in exchange for a juicy threesome, I'm happier having a friend who's honorable.

I'm about to tell her how much I admire her decision when her phone rings. After glancing at the caller ID, she says, "I gotta take this. Drink up." She goes outside.

I take another sip of wine and watch Annie walk in circles around the pool while she talks. One lap. Another. Her right hand gestures wildly at something. When she rounds the circle and is facing me, I can see from her facial expression that she's angry at someone or something. She stops circling and picks up a pair of swim goggles off the cement. She continues talking excitedly into the phone with her left hand while squeezing the goggles in her right. I feel guilty staring at her. Just before I turn away I watch her snap the goggles in two.

Unnerved a little by that, I find my phone and call Matt to see if he's home yet. It goes straight to voicemail, so I leave a message.

I'm dizzy. I should have eaten. Taking my glass to the sink, I clumsily miss the drain, and wine splashes up the sides and onto the counter. Annie's dish sponge is so disgustingly food-stained I don't want to touch it. Looking under the sink for a paper towel, I find a recycling bin. On top of a pile of torn, crumpled papers is a ticket stub from Denver's Clyfford Still Museum, one of Matt's favorite spots on the planet.

On our refrigerator, holding up one of Finley's drawings, is a Clyfford Still art magnet.

My nausea escalates just as Annie comes back inside.

"Kate, you're on my floor. Why are you on my floor?"

"I, uh." I stand but just barely, gripping the counter for balance.

"Are you okay, sweetheart? You're really pale."

Through the bilious haze of confusion and dizziness, I hear "sweetheart," and the term of endearment brings me back. "I spilled wine and needed a paper towel. Then I got really dizzy. That was weird."

"Did you eat anything today?"

"I forgot to. I was too busy writing."

"Too busy writing a book I'm not allowed to read?"

"Yup," I say, again not taking the bait, even though I'm flustered and embarrassed.

That Annie went to a famous museum in Denver means nothing. Ten minutes ago she said she'd never hurt Roxy. I know she would never hurt me either. "Everything okay with you?" I ask.

"Why wouldn't it be?" Annie says, apparently not wanting to share what it was about the phone call that made her destroy a perfectly good pair of goggles.

"No reason," I say. "I'm okay now. Thanks for the wine."

"Sure you won't stay for dinner?"

"I'd love to but I really want to eat a meal with my husband. I don't get to do that as much as I'd like."

"I hear you, sister. I hope you enjoy both the man and the meat," she says as we reach the door.

"I'll come back around seven or send Matt over. Is that good?"

"Most excellent. Bye, Kate," Annie says, closing the door.

Daughterless and still slightly off-kilter, I walk slowly down the driveway, glancing up the street toward Steve Hodges's house and see a woman at the front door, holding a car seat with a baby strapped inside. She's watching Steve remove a box from the trunk of his car. When he reaches the front porch, he leans down and kisses the baby, then the woman on the mouth. The three of them disappear into the house.

Just a few days ago Annie told me that she and Steve—how did she put it? Annie said she'd *tasted*, *touched*, and *smelled* him, and that he is, in fact, a bit *off*. From the looks of it, he appears to be a married man with a new baby. Had she lied to me?

I put aside my suspicions that my friend is a homewrecker and continue walking down the street to my car, parked right by Annie's mailbox, which was left open. I slam it shut as I pass by. Then, because something about the name showing through the little plastic window on the top letter caught my eye, I take two steps backward and open the lid.

Before reaching in, I look around. No one is mowing. No kids are out playing ball. I fold the envelope I grab in half, stuff it into my back pocket, and get in my car.

KATE

I'm waiting at the kitchen table when my husband arrives home.

"Hey, Matt, how was the ride?" I ask as he comes through the mudroom door.

"Hellacious. I don't think I'm going to walk normally again for a week." He sidles over and plants a dry kiss on my cheek. "Sorry I stink so much."

"You've got to be exhausted." My hands clench the crumpled paper in my lap.

"Yeah, it was a hard seventy miles," he says, pulling off his shirt and flashing me one of his pouty smiles. "Um, sweetie. Would you mind whipping me up a protein smoothie while I shower? I really need to down a lot of calories."

Making him a smoothie is not on my agenda. "You've been lying to me about Annie," I say.

He freezes before taking his next step toward the bathroom. He breathes in deeply, filling his lungs, as if getting ready to exhale more than just air. I watch his shoulder muscles tighten. As he slowly turns around to face me, the expression I expect to see on his face is a look of shock that he's been found out.

Instead he looks annoyed, as if I've just put him out.

"This again?" he says. "I'm too tired to deal with your para-noia, Kate. I'm gonna go shower."

"She was one of your recruiters in Denver, wasn't she?"

Again he turns to walk away and again his foot pauses mid-step. "Why would you say that?"

I hold up the invoice and attached check between my thumb and forefinger as if holding a stinking bag of dog crap. "It appears C and C Market Research in Denver *finally* got around to paying A. Roth Recruiting two thousand five hundred and fifty-five dollars, plus a two-hundred-and-thirty-dollar late fee for services rendered. That is, for *procuring* forty-two subjects for a Mercedes Benz focus group." Now I understand what Annie meant by *procurement* when I asked her what she does for a living. Annie is so clever.

Matt stares at the check, then at me. "But just because—"

"You knew her before," I state, dropping the paper onto the table. "She was one of *your* recruiters."

His brain is spinning, trying desperately to latch onto something to buttress his coming denials. I sit immobile, actually rooting for my husband; silently hoping, actually *praying* he might be able to convince me that this is yet one more freakish fluke. He will tell me he has never used Annie's services. Annie will remain the honest friend she purported to be a mere two hours ago: a friend who would never sleep with her friend's husband.

But when his face contorts into a painful grimace and his body deflates down to the floor, my world deflates alongside it. "I can't do this anymore. I'm sorry, Kate."

"How long have you been sleeping with her?"

"Just so you know, I've not been with her here in Rayburne. I swear to God, Kate!" He holds his hands out as if offering me a present.

"What do you mean? I'm confused."

He crosses his arms over his knees and drops his head on top. I wait.

When he raises his eyes to mine, there are tears in them. "I met Annie last April. You remember that contract in Denver for Alchemy Bicycles?"

I wade through my outrage, trying to recall who Matt *hooked up* with on that trip. "I remember the woman—Rachel—she wasn't one of your focus groupies. You said you met her at the hotel bar." They ordered every dessert on the room service menu and what they did with the food . . . I bequeathed the particulars of that ultra-lusty encounter to Macon and Phionna. That turned into one of the sexiest scenes I ever wrote.

"That was Annie. And yeah, she was the recruiter on the contract."

"Why did you lie about her? Why'd you change her name?" I ask matter-of-factly, as if questioning a sales clerk about a particular lawnmower. I need to keep my anger in check. I need to stay focused.

"Because it wasn't a one-off. I'm sorry, Kate."

"That was rule number two, Matt. Whose idea was it to make it an ongoing thing?"

When he doesn't respond, I demand, "Matt! Answer me!"

"The first time was like any other one-nighter, you know? We met up after a session, talked a little about work and stuff and just had this really great connection. Annie told me how her husband just died and maybe I felt a little sorry for her, I don't know. But anyway—yeah, we slept together. And it wasn't like I led her on or anything but she texted me the next day. I texted her back. I told her it wasn't going to go anywhere because I was happily married and—"

I snort.

"Annie said one more time won't matter and I, well, yeah—and the one more time turned into two, then three—"

"You saw her in other places? When? How?"

"You really don't want to hear this, Kate."

But I do. I need to gather it all up into a neat bundle of information I can cram down his throat and choke him with. My anger is becoming so extreme my face feels as if it is on fire. "Tell. Me. Everything."

Matt slides his legs out in front of him, then slams his head back against the wall—*Slam. Slam. Slam.*—before he speaks, "Annie met up with me every time I went away for business."

My mind does a backflip, then a forward somersault. It would have performed a cartwheel had I not put my hand out to stop it. "*All* the women you've been with since last April were—" It's impossible to wrap my already overwhelmed brain cells around what he is saying. "Audrey? Angela? Um—who am I missing?"

"Suki, Gretchen, Amelia," he says. "Oh, and Alyssa. I think that's all of 'em."

Curiosity shoves my shock out of the way. "If they were all Annie, how did you come up with those stories?" Matt's imagination is good, but not that good. No way.

"I told Annie about the rule that I can't be with the same woman more than once, and she totally got it," he says. "She figured out a way to make it so I didn't break the rule. Annie *became* all of those women. She'd . . . " He opens his legs wide and rubs his large hands across his face. I remember how he did that on our first date when I pushed him into admitting how much he liked sex. "She'd show up as *other* women."

"What?"

He closes his eyes, obviously going back in time. "Annie knew I was doing the beer study in Atlanta and she flew down for a night. She showed up at the hotel wearing a red wig and introduced herself as Audrey. See, she *pretended* she was this sophisticated older woman." The corner of his mouth swerves ever so slightly. "Everything I told you that happened between us was real. Crazy, right?" When Matt sees my look of disbelief, he says, "It's as if Annie"—he laughs—"as if she knew you were writing these books, and she was helping you out."

Annie seemed genuinely shocked at my confession the other night. Is she that good of an actress? My jaw is clenched so tightly I almost can't get it open enough to ask, "Did you *tell* Annie that I was writing erotica, Matt?"

"God, no Kate. I wouldn't do that."

Like a rat scurrying along electrified subway ties in search of another scrap, my mind skitters around the monstrous facts: the multiple meetups, wigs and false names. "Why didn't Annie meet you in Seattle?" I ask, remembering one of the few *dry* trips after which Matt brought home zilch for my story arsenal.

"She didn't want to miss Terra's spelling bee."

"Such a good mother," I say sarcastically, even though my heart isn't in it. There's no denying that Annie is a good mother. "Annie moved here from Denver to be closer to you?" I ask. What I don't ask: Is Annie a psychopath?

"Kate—I swear on Finley—I had no idea Annie was moving here. She had that asthma thing and had to leave Colorado, but—"

"You honestly didn't know?" The hairs on the back of my neck rise.

"You remember that day, the first day I met her on the playground? That was when I found out she'd moved here."

I leap back in time, recalling the afternoon when I saw the four of them talking at the corner. Finley ran home, twirling with excitement over the new girl whose name means *earth*.

"And you didn't think this hookup of yours moving to our neighborhood wasn't a wee bit creepy?"

"Shit, yeah. I was pissed, Kate. Actually, it kind of freaked me out."

"Then why didn't you do anything about it?"

"I tried. I looked around for other rentals for them, but you know Rayburne. There's nothing out there."

When it looks like I might halfway believe him, he continues, "As soon as I found out she was here, I made it clear she had to stay out of our lives."

Of all the gin joints in all the world . . . I'd laugh if I didn't feel so boiling-hot infuriated.

"So much for that plan, huh?"

"Everything spun out of control and before I knew it Finley and Terra were friends, and then you and Annie too. I didn't know how to stop it."

I walk over to the sink. Leaning against it, I fix my gaze on the man I've shared my life with all these years. The man who supposedly did not lie. Inside I feel like a burner on a stove is slowly being turned up, transforming simmering bubbles into spurting blasts. "I cannot believe you did this, Matt. After all the freedom I gave you. After all I let you do, you still broke the rule."

"If you want to get technical, I didn't really break the rule," he states almost defensively. "I mean you said I could have sex with other women. In my mind they *were* other women."

"If I want to get technical? Are you serious? The *rule*, Matt, is that you are not allowed to get involved, but you did. You got involved."

He peers up at the ceiling, saying nothing. I wait.

"Yeah. I guess," he finally says as if he has just listened to an oracle.

"You guess what?"

"I guess I fucked up."

In my heart I knew that one day this crazy compact we made would destroy us. It was inevitable. I just didn't know when it would happen. Or with whom.

"Do you love her?" I ask, immediately wishing I can retract the question, because if he is in love with Annie, I will die.

"No." He raises his eyes to mine.

A gust of relief—as if at the last second, I jerked my head away before the guillotine dropped—blows through me. "So it was because of the sex."

"Uh-huh."

"What exactly does she know about our marriage, Matt?" I ask with trepidation, like a blind person progressing along a corridor, slapping her hand against the wall in search of a door.

"I told her you don't like sex, and we have an open marriage. Just that."

So, Annie had already known I had no libido when I sat on her couch and confessed my vulnerabilities.

"The weird thing is, Annie is really jealous. She didn't want me screwing other women. But when I told her I wanted to have a threesome, she was open to it. She found a married friend of hers. Just so you know, Annie made that happen."

I knew it! Rory in the *ménage `a trois was* Annie's friend, Roxy. That demented hairy-legged cretin had actually pointed a knife in my face and *insisted* she would never sleep with her friend's husband.

I'll be sure to thank them in my acknowledgments when I finish the book.

Maybe when hell freezes over I will.

"This marriage is over," I say, forcing the words out of my mouth. I'm not certain this is true, but I want Matt to know how it feels to have everything you love threatened.

"No way! I love you, Kate," he exclaims, looking as if I'd just kicked him in the balls.

How can the man profess his love when he's been sneaking around, living two separate lives? "What do you love about me, Matt?" I ask, crossing my arms as if to shield myself from the possibility he might not say what I need to hear.

"What do I love about you, Kate?" he asks, stalling for what I hope are the right answers. "For one, you're the world's greatest mother. And, you and me, we're good together. We have fun, don't we?" he says, hope springing eternal as he stares at me with those beautiful eyes.

"Fun?" Not the answer I was anticipating.

"Come on, Kate. It's like what I said on our first date. I feel safe when I'm with you. You keep me sane."

Safe, sane, but unsatisfied.

"Does she want you to leave me for her?" I ask. Is that why she's boring a hole into our lives like an insidious wood beetle?

"What she wants doesn't matter," says Matt. "Kate, I do not want to get divorced." He pushes himself off the floor and limps over to me, grasping my hands. "I want to fix this. Please tell me what I need to do."

I was the mad scientist who created this monster. Now it's time I bolt him back onto the table and unscrew the cables I connected to his penis. "You need to make it clear to your whore that it's over," I say.

"Don't call her that, Kate."

"I'll call her whatever I want. You don't get to defend her."

"Come on. It's just as much my fault."

"I don't give a crap whose fault it is." Annie Meyers manipulated my husband into breaking our rules. She turned our solidly built arrangement into nothing more than flimsy scaffolding. But now game time is over; the bitch is going to have to pick up her silver pieces, put the box back on the shelf, and go far away. I am the wife here.

"Annie needs to leave town. Now."

"Don't make her uproot Terra again. It's not fair to her. I mean the little girl's father died, and she just started another school. Give the kid a break, Kate. Please."

True. It isn't the daughter's fault her mother is a conniving lying husband-stealing slut.

"Fine, but when school ends, Annie and company need to get the hell out of Rayburne. Make it happen."

I shoulder past my husband, the voice of Macon pulling me toward a place I prefer to be. Anywhere but with the weak man who just messed up my neat world.

"Terra has to quit the soccer team," I say before walking out of the room. "I don't want to see that kid's mother's face ever again."

ANNIE

When I open the door and see Matt, a frisson of arousal shoots through my big girl underpants. "Here for Finley?" I say, containing myself.

"Yup. And also—can I come in?"

"As if you need to ask?" I step back and as he passes, my body reverberates with want. The scent of him, the sight of him, his very presence, can bring me to my knees, which is precisely where I should be right now, but given that we made a pact never to fuck in the hood, there is no way he'll let me. "What's wrong? You want a drink?"

He glances upstairs. "They in Terra's room?"

"Yeah. You want me to get her?"

"No." He strides into the den like he owns the place, which is exactly how I expect him to act. He owns my body; no reason why he can't lay claim to all the territory around me.

"Kate knows about us," he says, sitting down on the faux-leather faux-Eames chair. He rubs his face a few times, digs an envelope out of his back pocket and tosses it onto the coffee table. "She found this in your mailbox."

"Snooping in my mailbox? That's not very polite."

"Whatever, Annie. It's over." He leans forward and for a second it looks like he might puke. "I couldn't keep lying to her. I just—I can't keep it up any more."

I almost laugh. No man can keep it up for half as long as Matt, but it is neither the time nor place to interject a pun.

"Bummer," I say. "I'm sorry. How's she taking it?"

"How the fuck do you think she's taking it? She's pissed off. She's talking divorce. She's . . . I screwed up and now I've gotta fix it." He stands and walks toward the stairs, but I catch him by the shirt.

"What do you mean *fix it*? Why not let it stay broken?"

He puts his arms around me and pulls me in close. I barely come up to his chest and can feel his heartbeat. Quietly, he says, "Annie, you know I adore you."

I nod into his shirt.

"But nothing's changed," he says. "I've told you from the beginning: I'll never leave Kate."

I try to yank myself free, but his arms hold me more forcefully. "Annie, I promised her I'd end it, and I also promised I'd ask you to move away at the end of the school year."

"Let me go," I say, straining against his grip.

"No." He is squeezing me so tight I fear I may get an asthma attack. "Not until you tell me you completely understand what I'm saying."

"Yeah, I get it," I utter sadly. "I hear you loud and clear."

He releases me but keeps his large hands clamped around my shoulders. "Do you, Annie?"

"But if she *wants* a divorce, why—?"

"Jesus!" He pushes me away—hard enough to throw me off balance—but then reaches out and steadies me before I topple over. "Sorry," he says as Finley appears at the top of the stairs.

"Hi, Daddy."

He straightens up and forces a smile onto his face. "Hey, kiddo."

"Do I have to go home now?"

"I've gotta talk to Annie about soccer," he says buoyantly. "I'll call you in a few." After she disappears down the hall, he marches into the kitchen and pours himself a glass of water. He drinks it down and wipes his hand across his mouth—the same gesture he does after spending an hour with his face between my legs.

"Matt, I'm sorry we got caught but it's good. I mean, maybe the three of us can sit down and—"

"Are you nuts? Just because she let me have sex with other women—not that that's going to happen anymore—doesn't mean she's going to let me continue seeing *you*. She wants you cut off completely."

"But you love me." I stay fixed to the spot, five feet away. I want to go to him but am afraid he'll try to smother me again.

"Annie, don't you get it? I love Kate. She's my wife."

"But maybe she'll leave you over this." If so inclined, any girl can wish upon a star.

"Kate will never leave me." He mumbles something I can't make out, then he looks me in the eye. "We're done here, Annie. There's nothing more to say."

"I have more to say."

"I'm sure you do, and I'm sorry I won't be coming around anymore to listen. Please—"

"*Are* you sorry, Matt?"

"You know I am." He shakes his head, and I am glad to see misery in his eyes. "I need you to stay away from us until school is out, okay? Just stay gone."

"Gone like the wind, my friend. But if you ever get a hankering for—"

"I won't, Annie. It's over." He steps into the hall and hollers up to Finley. I follow and stand next to him. As quietly as a mouse, I say, "I'm just saying if you ever get the need for a really good fuck, you know where to find me, Matt."

"Noted," he says, watching his child fly down the stairs.

KATE

Saturday morning blooms bright and sunny. I am eating a bowl of oatmeal, watching Finley race around the house hunting for cleats and shin guards, when Matt walks into the kitchen carrying his morning smoothie and sits down across from me.

"What?" I say when I take in the pained look on his face.

"They're going to the game. Annie just texted that Terra was crying and—"

"What?" I wait until I hear Finley slam the garage door. "When you picked Finley up on Thursday, you were supposed to make it clear you were cutting off *all* communications!" I throw my spoon into the bowl and get up. My neck burns and if I don't calm down, it will become ringed by angry red welts. Finley can't see me like this. I pace the tile floor. "You were never to speak to her again."

"I'm sorry, Kate. It won't happen again."

I twist the faucet on with so much force the knob almost comes loose. I watch the water fill the cereal bowls. "God, I hate you."

He pushes the chair back from the table, comes over, and

tosses his empty smoothie cup into the sink. It clatters against the porcelain with a bang. "I know you do, Kate." Without bothering to reach out a repentant hand, he walks away.

I never before said such a horrible thing to Matt. Do I actually hate him or do I love him with every square inch of my soul?

Either way, I need to make sure he is sorry enough that he'll sooner cut off his right hand than ever touch that sick woman again.

Annie is cheering from the opposing team's sideline, so at least I don't have to be near her. But I still have to see her.

I try to keep my eyes on Finley and the game, but my eyes keep wandering across the field to Annie in her baggy white shorts and hairy legs, her barefoot wildness and long braid. I really liked Annie.

What especially stinks is that I was psyching myself up to write a new book with a female POV.

But Annie moved to Vermont to be near my husband. She lied to me.

Christy Pell, Olivia's mother, drops her chair next to mine. "Hey there, Kate. Mind if I join you?"

"Not at all." Maybe small talk will extract me from the angry gorge I'm wallowing in.

"Things going well for Finley this year?"

"She's having a great year, thanks for asking. She loves Mr. Joplin."

"Things have gotten so bad with Max, we might have to ship him off to military school," she replies before I even get a chance to ask her how her kids are doing. So much for a gentle distraction. At the moment I have zero sympathy and no interest in listening to Christy harp about Max's rotten behavior in school. I'd rather hear about Christy's medical sales job—not about her annoying brat who threw a stick at Finley last year. Honestly, I'd prefer Christy go away, even if it means having to return to the brooding negative space of detesting the woman across the field.

"He's only in second grade, Christy. He'll grow out of it," I say, edging my words with politeness.

"That's what his therapist says." She takes a swig of water from a green plastic water bottle. "Maybe he needs to be medicated."

I ignore that and continue watching the game.

"Good thing I'm rocking my job. I mean, if we do have to send him to private school, it won't be so bad."

I say nothing.

"Wow!" Christy shouts. "Finley has really improved this year. And, whoa, look at that new kid. What's her name again? She is way aggressive."

"Terra," I reply flatly.

"What a bizarre name. That's her mom over there, the one in the white shorts, right? Why is she standing on the wrong side?"

I shrug. "No idea."

"I heard from Allison Conway she's a total weirdo. And kind of a bitch too."

"Is that so," I say." My curiosity is piqued. Maybe Annie's also sleeping with Allison's husband.

"Go, Olivia!" screams Christy. "Run, baby, run! You got this! Go, go, go!"

"Why does Allison think she's a bitch?" I ask.

"What? I don't know. I guess Allison tried to make conversation with her on the playground a while ago, and she was super rude. You'd think she'd want to reach out or maybe try to be friendly? And look at her. I mean, yikes, those legs." Christy dramatically fake-shivers. "Someone buy that woman a case of razors!"

"Do you know she's a widow?" I ask for no reason.

"She's a widow? Oh. That's sad."

"Sure it is."

"I had no idea you two were friends. I'm sorry."

"We're not friends, Christy."

Not anymore, we're not. Why did Annie befriend me in the first place? She could have stayed hidden over there on Dwyer Court, meeting up with Matt in Pennsylvania or Colorado, or wherever. Why did Annie push for that first playdate between our girls? Why did she make me feel as if I meant something to her? Was it all a lie?

Did Annie pretend to like me?

"Hey, it's halftime," I tell Christy. "I've gotta go get the girls their snacks. See you later."

After the Rayburne team wins by a score of 2-to-1 and Finley runs up to ask if she can go swimming at Terra's, Matt takes her by the hand. "How about instead we celebrate with a creemee at Rayburne Country Store?"

"Yes!" Finley, like most ten-year-olds, can be easily swayed by a cone filled with maple/vanilla soft serve. For now. What about tomorrow? Matt and I are going to have to figure out a way to explain to Finley that Annie hurt my feelings, and that we are no longer friends. And that means she won't be able to spend time at Terra's house anymore. I hate having to split them up, but my hatred for Annie takes precedence.

I tell Matt I'll meet them at home after I clean up and wander off in search of errant candy wrappers and forgotten hair ties.

As I'm reaching for an empty Dunkin' Donuts bag, I hear, "Hello, Kate."

"Go away, Annie. I don't want to talk to you."

"I'm sorry, Kate."

"I don't care what you are," I snarl. Behind us a few families are lingering, so I lower my voice and look Annie square in the face. "As far as I'm concerned, you're dead."

"This was never about hurting you, you know."

I scrunch the bag into a ball. "How sweet of you to say that. What the heck did you think I'd do when I found out? Do a happy dance? Tell you it's all good?"

"To be honest, I've just been taking it day by day. Seeing how things would play out between the three of us."

How typically Annie-like; how Be Here Now. "When I asked you about having a threesome with Roxy, you pointed a knife at me and said you'd *never* sleep with your friend's husband."

A quizzical expression cuts across her face. "What? No. That's not what I said, Kate. I said I'd never sleep with *Roxy*."

This throws me slightly, but not enough to detour me. She's a vicious cunning C-word. "Do you not know how disturbing it is that you moved to Vermont to be near my husband?"

"I really did need to get out of Denver because of my asthma, and Matt kept harping on and on about Rayburne being such a spectacular place to raise kids. And then I found the Waldorf school. I actually did not move here for Matt. You've got to believe me."

"I don't believe you, but I also don't care. You go live your life and I'll go live mine." My teeth are grinding together so tightly I fear one of my crowns might crack. "Terra is no longer Finley's friend. School is almost over, and when it is I want you to move away from here. I want you gone, Annie." It is as if I am channeling one of my characters; I cannot believe the words flying out of my mouth. My face is probably bright red at the moment and I pray none of the other parents are paying us any attention. Across the field I spot Terra sitting on the ground waiting for her mother.

"I'm going now," I tell Annie. "Are you done lying to me?"

"Think what you will, Kate, and if you want to end the girls' friendship, I'll honor that."

"Oh, you'll honor that? That's so beautiful, Annie. I'm so glad. But tell me one thing before we never talk to one another again. Tell me why you gave me that tea."

She comes closer, sticks her hands in her pockets, and sighs. "I gave you the tea for the same reason I gave it to Roxy. Because you're my friend and I want all my friends to be able to experience the joys of a healthy, fulfilled sex life."

I again look around to make sure no one is within ten feet of earshot. "Why would you care about me if you want to be with Matt?"

"Maybe because I'm fucked up in the head? I mean, I love you, Kate. I didn't expect to but I do. Don't look so surprised."

"You don't *love* me, Annie. You used my daughter to get close to me so—" I have no idea where I am going. She's manipulating me again, twisting my logic into curlicues.

"Come on, Kate. You really don't believe I dig the shit out of you? You're so cool. I totally get why Matt married you."

"Screw you, and do *not* talk about my husband. Why'd you give me the tea, Annie?" I ask again.

"I figured if Matt was happy with you, like you two were having sex again, he wouldn't need to sleep with other women." Annie half-smiles at me. "Believe it or not, I'm the jealous type."

"But you'd keep seeing him behind my back," I state, incredulous.

"Sure. I mean I want to keep hanging out with both of you."

"And you assumed Matt would still—?" She actually thinks that Matt would continue seeing her even if *we* started having sex again? The woman is cracked beyond repair. How *dare* she believe she possesses something Matt can't live without. "Annie, that would never happen. Matt loves me and he's not going to be with you ever again." My heart pounds so forcefully I feel it pulsing up through my throat.

"I hear you, Kate," she says with a smile so insidiously angelic I want to slam her to the ground. "I only hope someday you'll be able to forgive me."

"Forgive you?" I laugh, sounding more like a witch than a soccer mom. "I gotta go, Annie," I say, moving away from her. "I've got some garbage to throw out. Have a nice life."

KATE

Macon unstuck the white plastic lid and took a swig of the lukewarm latte. Audrey wandered the store, touching each and every item as if she wanted to leave her scent on the goods she owned. She walked back over to him and ran her finger down the small of Macon's back. "You still haven't thanked me for your present."

Macon bent into the cheese case and rearranged a couple of blocks so they faced the right direction. After he stood up, he grinned, remembering their threesome adventure.

"Thank you, Audrey, for one of the best nights of my life."

"You mean it?"

"I do."

"You're welcome. But, Macon, don't expect that to ever happen again."

"I won't."

"Good. Because I like it better when I have you all to myself." The greedy tone in her voice pushed against Macon's chest, making him feel like he was suffocating.

"So, listen, darling," she said, wandering to the front

of the store. "I hope you weren't expecting me to stay and help because I have a thousand things I want to get done before Harland lands."

"No," he said, relieved. "I'm good."

"May I please have a kiss goodbye?" she asked, giving him a playful pout.

"Sure." He came around the counter and wrapped his arms around her, planting a hard closed-lipped kiss on her red mouth. Through the thick scent of coffee, he tasted peppermint on her breath.

The moment he released his lips from Audrey's, he saw Lizzie Wilder standing on the sidewalk in front of the shop, her mouth agape and eyes wide.

Before he could reach out for the handle, she took off running. He opened the door, glanced back at Audrey, and chased after her.

When he catches up to Lizzie, I'll have Macon push her into Ferrara's. The warm comfort of the bakery will seep into the space between them. Or—shoot! I can't have them in a pastry shop. I already used that setting in the last book. I growl then continue typing.

(PLACEHOLDER: Where do they have this conversation?) "I've been looking for you for weeks, Lizzie," Macon said. "Where have you been? Why didn't you answer my emails?"

Lizzie kept her eyes on her hands, responding without meeting his eyes. She spoke quietly. "When I said I was *close*, Macon, I meant it. I've been working over at Murray's Cheese Shop."

"Are you kidding me? It's just around the corner!" She looked even better than he remembered. She put on a little weight around her hips, and her face seemed to exude more character, more maturity, as if her time in New York had filled in the hollow college graduate she was when he'd first met her. Her lusciously plump lips were still as enticing and erotic as he'd been dreaming they were.

"When Miles and Arthur bought the store," Macon said, "I jumped because I knew I'd be closer to you."

"You never said that in your emails," she said, puzzled. "You just said you were coming to New York to open a cheese shop. You—"

"A man can't lay all his cards on the table, can he? I figured I'd, you know, run into you and see how you reacted."

"Well, you saw how I reacted. Not so good," she said, grinning, then changed her expression. "So you're with someone else now, huh?"

I stop typing and sit back. Macon must tell Lizzie the truth about Audrey. If they're not honest, their relationship won't be worth fighting for.

Maybe it's not worth fighting for.

"What are you doing, Kate?" I say out loud. "*Sheesh*. Just decide already."

Either way, Lizzie must believe Macon still wants her. She will invite him to stay in her apartment. But Macon will have to tread carefully before letting Audrey go for good. She's got an evil selfish streak, and he is desperate to hold onto the cheese shop.

I rotate Adam's arms so the bendable man is hugging himself and take a sip of tea. Obviously, they are going to have scorching sex once they're at Lizzie's place. What kind of sex? Since I cut Matt off from other women—all women—my notepad has remained blank.

As has my bed.

While I haven't felt an ounce of guilt over giving Matt the silent treatment or making him sleep in his office, this morning I pulled his pillow to me and held it close, breathing in his scent. I miss him. Us. Maybe it's time to move on, though I can't imagine ever getting back what we had.

All because of a woman named Annie Meyers. No; actually her name is Annie Roth, and she is, according to what I read online, one of the best focus group recruiters west of the Mississippi.

As important as my marriage is, it's my writing that will take the biggest hit. This new book was going to be my best, but it won't be if I can't come up with something fresh and hot for Lizzie and Macon's reunion.

I swivel back and forth in my chair. Matt broke the rule. But if we can cement our trust again, maybe I can let his leash out a little.

An email from the Park County Coroner's Office suddenly appears in my inbox. I open the attached PDF and wade my way through myriad indecipherable bits until I get to the important stuff:

EVIDENCE OF INJURY: The incised wound of the thigh is gaping and exposes femur.

ADDITIONAL: Signs of cardiomegaly, pulmonary edema and congestion. Postmortem specimens of heart and femoral blood, bile, stomach contents and vitreous fluid were collected and submitted for toxicological analysis.

TOXICOLOGY ANALYSIS: 20 mg/L of 4-hydroxy-N, N-dimethyltryptamine (*Psilocin*) detected, as were trace amounts of *Pausinystalia johimbe* and *Epimedium*.

CONCLUSION: In consideration of the circumstances surrounding the untimely death of Clayton Meyers, a 37-year-old
white male, after examination of the body, and toxicology
analysis, it is my opinion that the probable cause of the death
is the result of drowning and traumatic injuries, possibly but
not absolutely sustained due to ingestion of high levels of a
psychedelic compound, which may have rendered the victim
incapacitated and/or confused. Speculative causation due
to the accumulation of excess fluid in victim's lungs derived
from cardiogenic pulmonary edema.

I Google *Psilocin* and *Epimedium*. *Psilocin* is the scientific name
for magic mushrooms, the kind of "shrooms" that can cause euphoria, sensory distortions, even hallucinations. *Epimedium*, I
discover, is the yin yang huo herb—also known as horny goat
weed, commonly used in Chinese medicine to boost libido.

Why would Clayton take magic mushrooms before going
whitewater kayaking? Annie called Clayton an adrenaline junkie.
If that was true, wasn't the adrenaline enough of a high?

As for the yohimbe and yin yang huo, I am even more
confused. Did Clayton have a problem with *his* libido? And
what about his heart? I remember Annie asking me if I took
any blood pressure medications, and if I did, I couldn't drink
the tea. Was Clayton drinking so much of the stuff that it was
damaging his heart?

I look at the mug of GoodLove tea on my desk. It doesn't
seem to be helping my libido but I really like the taste. Still, I
resist taking another sip.

Maybe Clayton didn't know what he was drinking.

KATE

I'm having trouble concentrating on the novel I'm reading so I toss it onto the night table. Next to me, Matt sits propped against the wall, making notes on a report. I've let him back into our bed—not that it's enough to keep him fulfilled.

I close my eyes and begin to will myself into arousal, picturing Macon and Lizzie having sex, but that only makes me want to get out of bed and write. I let go of the image and pull the turquoise Proem Marketing pen out of Matt's mouth—willfully ignoring the tiny shock of anger that races across my heart—and say, "Make love to me, please."

He whips his attention toward me, his eyes wide with delight. "Really? You want to?"

"I do," I lie. I want to bring him closer to me again, to make certain he knows what an amazing wife I am. It's a charade I am willing to perform.

Matt throws the papers onto the floor and wraps my body into his muscular arms. He kisses me softly, his eyes open. I close mine and concentrate. When he puts his hand on my breast, I don't freeze. I relax into the new sensation, an almost perceptible pulse running down my chest into places below.

"I love you so much, Kate," he whispers hoarsely into my neck. I push my fingers through his thick hair. He caresses my breasts, kneading the flesh. He moves his mouth down to my belly and places his large hand on the band of my underwear. Within seconds we are at the bottom of the same familiar staircase we've climbed together hundreds of times before. I know before he lifts his foot where it will land.

"Yes, that feels good," I say, compelling the words out of my mouth.

I feel nothing. His mouth should be a match firing up my kindling, but once again I am nothing but a pile of cold sticks on a forest floor.

As he moves in and out of me, I imagine a camera on the ceiling filming our half-passionate act and I pretend to be an actress in a porn movie. Mechanically faking it for an audience. I use every inch of my willpower to urge him on until, finally, he collapses on top of me.

"Thank you for that, Kate," he says, breathing hard with his face turned away. "I thought for sure I was going to shrivel up and die if I didn't have sex again."

"You're welcome," I reply, knowing full well we are never again going to make love.

With Matt asleep, I head to my office, turn on the computer, and remembering that term Annie used all those weeks ago, I type "Sex-Repulsed" into Google.

I read a few magazine articles and meander my way through myriad conversations on various sexuality forums. What I pick up on almost immediately is that there is a distinct difference between "sex-repulsed" people and those who consider themselves "sex-averse."

> *While sex-repulsion is a general feeling of disgust, distress, or discomfort about sex, sex-aversion is a more personalized experience, such as a strong dislike of the idea of actually having sex. In other words, whereas sex-repulsed people may feel disgusted by other experiences relating to sex, such as talking about sex or seeing characters having sex in books, on TV, and in the movies, sex-averse people may not find the idea of sex gross or disgusting. They just don't want to engage in it.*

I make a living *depicting* sex? Of course I don't find it disgusting!

I keep reading.

> *Successful mixed relationships do exist. Some of these relationships are sexless; in others, the partner might be open to compromise and have sex occasionally . . .*

I did compromise. For years.

> *You may be tempted to hold back on accepting your sex-aversion but you might feel more confident if you accept who you are now as a whole completely valid person . . .*

Nodding, I repeat the words out loud, "I am a whole completely valid person." I am about to click on another website when the bulb in my desk lamp flickers once then dies.

I sit there in the silent dark, thinking.

Up until he cheated, my marriage to Matt was a well-oiled

—well-lubricated—machine. Matt and I found what worked for both of us: we were devoted to one another. It took effort on both our parts, sure, but once we reached an understanding and agreed on the rules, we turned our unconventional arrangement into a thing of beauty and balance. The give and take between us was fair: Matt was compensated with abundant sex. And, in return, my stories steamed. Now, though? The image of Annie gurgles up into my throat. I gag it back.

What I need to do now is own up to my sexual aversion. But what do I do in the meantime? I don't want to pretend again.

I have no interest in writing nonsexual books. I have no interest in having sex. Life is not playing fairly with me. I tried the tea. Tried to be the perfect wife. Where is my consolation prize?

I am screwed if I screw and screwed if I don't screw.

I close the computer and dislodge the dead bulb, tossing it in the trash. I feel alone and more vulnerable than ever. It is as if I am floating in a canoe in the middle of a lake watching my only paddle sink slowly toward the darkness below.

I wish it were Annie's dead body sinking instead.

KATE

After walking Finley to school the next morning Matt comes into my office and throws himself onto the couch. "That was fun last night. Can we do it again tonight?"

"I thought you were flying to Portland today."

"Nope. I'm there tomorrow till Tuesday."

"Oh."

"How's Macon these days? I haven't heard much about him lately."

"He's fine," I say, relieved he wants to talk shop and not sex. "He reunited with Lizzie, the intern, but Audrey isn't going to let him go so easily," I reveal, swiveling back and forth in my chair.

"What do you mean? She's the married woman who owns the cheese shop, right?"

"She's obsessed with Macon," I say, still not sure if transforming Audrey into a villainess is the right decision.

"How so?"

"Macon tries to break it off with her, but she goes crazy and tells him she won't let him. He's torn; he doesn't want to leave the cheese shop. So he's juggling all these balls being thrown

at him and ends up sleeping with Audrey when she comes to
New York again, to keep her happy—which means he has to
lie to Lizzie, which kills him. But the sex between Audrey and
Macon is different, like he's clearly less into it, which makes
Audrey suspicious. When she gets back to Burlington, she hires
this shifty private eye—Gabriel—to follow Macon and report
back. That's how she finds out he's with Lizzie."

"Uh-oh."

"So Audrey threatens her."

"Threatens her how?"

Talking with Matt about my plot feels like being a kid in
a candy shop. Sure, sometimes I bounce ideas around with my
editor Kimberlee, but she has just one goal: sell more books.
Matt actually cares about the story and characters. I love it
when he asks questions, or throws out suggestions—even if I
rarely use them. "Audrey sends Gabriel into Murray's Cheese
Shop—where Lizzie works—to buy cheese and when the PI
hands Lizzie the money for his purchase he also gives her a note
that says she should always remember to look both ways when
crossing the street."

"Wait. So that's a threat. What does Lizzie do?"

"She tells Macon, and right away he guesses it's Audrey
making them. He texts her and demands she leave Lizzie alone
or he'll tell Harland—her husband—everything.

"Audrey texts back that she doesn't give a damn. She can't
stop thinking about Macon and refuses to let him go. She's
flying down to New York the next day."

"Macon tells her to go screw herself, right?" asks Matt.

"I'm not sure yet. He has to decide whether to continue
lying to Lizzie so he can keep the cheese shop—he's put his
heart and soul into it—or break it off with Audrey and be with
Lizzie, but—"

"But what?"

"I'm still not sure what's going to happen." When I began the book, Audrey was meant to be merely a minor distraction, the formulaic barrier between the two lovers who will get their Happily Ever After. But Audrey isn't letting me get rid of her so easily. She's holding on for dear life, demanding I give her a happy ending too.

"Why don't you make it easy on him and kill off one of the women?" Matt stands up and jams a pen through Adam's wire stomach. "You know, the last one standing gets the prize?"

"This is erotica." I need to add more sex, and far less confusion to the book. What about Gabriel? I could make him sexy. I could even use him in the next book. Start a series about a roguish private investigator who—

"Kate?"

"Sorry. I was thinking."

"I could tell," he says, laughing.

"I'll figure it out. And I'll do it without resorting to murder."

"I have no doubt you will, because you, Daphne Moore," he says, pointing dead Adam at me, "are the woman with the golden fingers. I'm going to take a bike ride out to Hinesburg. See you later."

"Matt, wait," I say before he is completely out the door. "You should, um . . ."

"I should, what?"

I sense his impatience filling the space in the room so I quickly speak through it. "You should go back to sleeping with other women. Starting tomorrow in Portland, if you meet a woman you're attracted to, I mean." There. I said it. It's out there. I can add fresh intimacies to my book, and he can go back to his sexcapades. It makes total sense.

I wait for him to blow me a kiss, or come over and ruffle my hair. He just stands there, blinking.

"What?" I say. "I want to go back to what we were like before."

"You mean before I met Annie?"

"Before you—yes, before you met Annie."

I was expecting a look of gratitude to materialize on Matt's face, but when a glaze of anguish appears there instead, it frightens me. "I don't want to be with other women anymore. I only want to be with you."

"But I'm . . . I'm pretty sure I'm sex-averse, Matt. It means that even though I love you I'd prefer not to, you know . . ." Do I really need to get into specifics?

"What about last night? You seemed pretty into it."

If I lie I'll be no better than he is, having lied about sleeping with Annie for so long. "I wasn't into it," I say meekly. "I just wanted to make you happy." Below my office the washing machine switches to the spin cycle and the floor begins to vibrate. Usually it annoys me, but at the moment I welcome the rumbling beneath my bare feet.

"Well, that sucks."

"I'm sorry I haven't changed, Matt. I really want to be"—I almost say *normal*, but fight against it. I will no longer think of myself as abnormal. After what I read last night I have every right to feel as normal as anyone. "I would love to be into sex, but it is what it is."

"It is what it is. Yup." He runs his hands through his hair and cracks his neck.

"You and I both know you need sex, Matt, so why not go back to your one-night stands?"

"What do you want from me, Kate? It's like you're asking me to light myself on fire so you can be warm, is that it?"

"No, I mean yes, I—" His metaphor throws me. "I'm not just talking about my writing, Matt. You are never going to be able to live without having sex. Remember what it was like before? You were miserable."

"God, Kate. This is so fucked-up."

"It doesn't have to be. It was so good before. We were a team, remember? You did your thing and I did mine." The spinning stops, and the room goes still. Through the open window behind the closed curtains comes such a rowdy chorus of cawing; I assume there's a mob of crows attacking a defenseless creature. "What the heck?" I say, getting up to check. Munch is staring up at our large oak in a scene that looks like it's from *The Birds*. There must be fifty black crows screaming down at him. I turn back to Matt. "I don't understand. Why should anything have to change?"

"Because the only *other* woman I'd want to have sex with is Annie, and since that's not gonna happen . . . I guess I'm done having sex with other women."

"You're *done*? What are you saying, Matt? Are you that obsessed with her?"

"Obsessed is a big word, Kaybee." He props his large body against the door frame and crosses his arms. "I wouldn't go that far. But it's like I tasted something different with her. Something I never knew existed."

I think about the sex scenes I wrote over the last year and a half—the entire time he was cheating on me with Annie. Those scenes were the hottest ones I ever created. The sex he had with Annie gave my stories the hard-boiled edges they needed to go beyond the average straight erotica romance book. I am a popular author because of them.

What am I willing to give up to keep Daphne Moore on the bestsellers' list?

ANNIE

It is too nice a day to spend inside adding newt eyes, frog toes, and owlet wings to the cauldron that is my anger. Macbeth's witch friends have nothing on the way I am feeling.

Double, double, toil and trouble, indeed.

I pack a tempeh wrap, drive east, and park my car at the Mossy Glenn trailhead. Not another car is in the lot, which fills me with gladness.

As I walk along the flat shaded trail I try not to get worked up over my present predicament. Why did Kate have to stick that scarred nose of hers into my mailbox? I kick a rock and watch it smack against a tree, then fall into the middle of the trail. Catching up to it, I kick it again, trying to keep it on the path. Five more times it does what I want it to do, staying inside the border of the narrow trail where I can get to it. But a sixth kick sends it into the damp undergrowth. Driven by the need to force it forward, I dig the toe of my hiking boot into the muck and flick it back onto the trail.

That's when I catch sight of the clump of morel mushrooms sticking up from the ground.

"Holy shit," I say, reaching down to inspect them. I cannot believe my eyes. Morels? I am madly in love with morels and every single spring in Colorado I foraged for them along the banks of the South Platte. That is, other than last year when I was too busy pretending to grieve for my dead husband. I resented him for making me miss what turned out to be a bumper season. Morels' strong, earthy, almost woodsy flavor is ambrosial. They taste like three-orgasms-in-a-row sex.

I had no idea they also grow in Vermont. Obviously because of how far north the state is, they are appearing so much later here than I am used to. I look around for something sharp to use to cut through the base of the stem. There are those experts who say it's bad etiquette to pluck the entire morel because it pulls all the mycelium out of the ground with it, while others insist cutting will inhibit regrowth.

"Ah, screw it." I dig my hand in and retract the fungus out from the earth in all its glory. I hold it up, admiring its dark gray honey-combed cap. I brush dirt from the smooth white stem. I smell it. Visions of morels sautéed in a splash of olive oil with just a touch of Himalayan sea salt dance in my head.

Pushing further into the rangy forest, I root around the ground with my hands and feet, and sure enough, an abundance of fungal bursts are scattered about. In Colorado I'd bring along a basket when going mushroom hunting. That allowed the spores to fall through its weave, allowing for a politically correct, sustainable hunt. I have nothing on me but wax paper, and a metal water bottle. Neither will work. Without a second thought, I flip off my T-shirt and tie the arms and lower half together, creating a satchel. And then I get to picking.

A half-full cotton bag later, I am squatting over a newly discovered clump of deliciousness when I hear someone clear their throat. I jump up.

"Hi there." It is a man-being. In his sixties, maybe. Holding a walking stick. "Mushroom hunting?"

"That I am."

"You know there are lots of false morels up here. You want to be careful." It doesn't seem to faze him that I'm topless and I respect him all the more for staring not at my breasts but rather at the improvised bag in my hand.

"Can I take a look at what you've got?" he asks.

"Dr. Mushroom, I presume?" I say in a whirly British accent.

He laughs. "No. Carl Miner. I walk here just about every day. First time I ever spotted a mushroom nymph though," he says sweetly. "I'm guessing you forgot to bring a bucket?"

A good man, to be sure. I grin and hand him my tied-up T-shirt. He rummages around and pulls out a shroom. Again, his eyes meet mine, not my nipples. "See the color on this cap? It's completely different. Purplish. It's also wavier-looking and a bit more squashed than the others."

I'm aware that false morels exist, but I've never come across any in Colorado. I move in closer. "Yeah."

"And here," he says, flipping it over. "The cap looks like it's just sitting on top of the stem, rather than attached to it."

"Mm-hmm." I am starting to get a little cold.

"It's a false morel."

"A lying morel?"

"Yup. An ersatz asshole of a morel."

I want Carl the mushroom man to fuck me against that tree over there, but I have to get home before the school bell rings. "And I'd be wise not to eat this asshole, am I correct, Carl?"

"Wise indeed, my dear," he replies back in a terrible British accent. "It's highly poisonous."

"Meaning I'd die if I ate it?"

"A strong possibility, yes."

I look in my T-shirt bag. There are a few more assholes mixed in among the delights. "Good to know," I say as I gently remove the mushroom from his age-spotted hand and toss it back in.

"But, aren't you—"

"Have a lovely walk, Carl," I say. With the bag swaying at my side and the cool breeze goose-bumping my naked skin, I recite, "'For a charm of powerful trouble, like a hell-broth boil and bubble,'" while skipping back to my car.

KATE

I am in the middle of typing a sentence when Matt opens my door and announces he is going for a short run through Mekins Cove. He always tries to get in a couple miles before getting on a cross-country flight, and this afternoon's trip to Oregon will be a long one.

As much as I want to keep writing, I am worried enough that Matt might run into Annie that I offer to grab Munch and tag along to the trailhead.

As we stroll together down Forest, the early morning sun warm on our backs, Matt takes my hand in his. When we stop at the end of the street, he turns his head ever so slightly to the right, glancing down Dwyer Court.

"You miss her, don't you?"

"Nope." He kneels down and makes a show of retying his shoelaces.

I wait for him to stand again so I can see his face.

"Seriously, Kate," he says, straightening up. "You've been so good to me. I mean, what you've let me do all these years—it's crazy."

"I did it for us, you know. Not just you."

"And now because of me you're going to have to quit writing."

"No, I'm not!" I say, the assertion detonating from the base of my throat. "I will never stop writing." He might well have suggested I stop breathing.

"Of course. Calm down."

"Why would you say that? I still have plenty of stories to tell." Although if I want to keep telling sex-laced boy meets girl/boy screws girl/boy marries girl stories, that may not be true.

"Of course you do," says Matt. "I mean, you can always go back to writing other stuff, like murder books without the sex," he says with a chuckle, trying to be helpful.

Munch eyes a squirrel and tugs at the leash. I almost let go so he can chase it down and kill it. Watching something get torn to pieces sounds oddly tantalizing.

Matt is looking at me, waiting for me to nod or get enthusiastic about writing in a new genre. But I don't want to write literary novels or historical fiction. I want to continue writing sexy romances.

Why?

Why *do* I love writing about Matt's sex with other women?

Up until that very moment, I've convinced myself it was because I'm so successful at it—in both the literary and financial sense. But now I wonder if, in some distorted way, I do it in lieu of having sex *with* Matt. Have all those other women been my sexual surrogates?

I'm still pondering this realization when Matt kisses me on the cheek so lightly I barely register the contact, then runs off.

I stand, watching him hurl his tall powerful body down the path.

Instead of going back home I roam to the end of Dwyer

Court, slowing as I pass Annie's house. I picture her wandering that box-filled chaos, pining for Matt.

I want her to be pining for me as well.

After turning onto Monroe Street, I unhook Munch's leash and let him bound the rest of the way home unfettered.

"Hello there!" Widower Bob calls from the top of his driveway, where he's tinkering with his car engine. "Say, how's your computer doing?"

I laugh nervously, still humiliated over what Bob most likely saw on my hard drive. My very hard drive. "It's fine. Working perfectly. Thanks again, Bob. I really appreciate your help."

"Anytime, Kate. I hope you remembered to change that password of yours."

"Oh, I forgot. I'll go do it right now. Bye, Bob." I turn to leave and see Matt round the corner holding his right elbow in his left hand, grimacing in pain.

"Oh no, Matt!" I run to him. "What happened?" I can already see the swelling in his wrist before he opens his mouth to speak.

"Fucking assholes. They came tearing out of the woods on their bikes and I tried to get out of their way and I tripped over a tree root."

"Who? What?"

"That stoner kid Eli and his buddies. I'm pretty sure it's broken, Kate. You gotta take me to the ER."

"Shouldn't we at least put ice—?"

"No, Kate. Let's go now."

I lock Munch in the backyard and grab my keys. As I back down the driveway, I see Bob staring our way, concerned, unable this time to do a thing to help.

Three hours later I delicately position Matt on the living room couch, tucking a pillow under his arm to keep his wrist raised above his heart. When I go to the kitchen to get an icepack from the freezer, Matt yells, "Hon, bring me my phone please. I've got to cancel the Portland trip."

"Oh, shoot, I forgot all about Portland."

"I didn't. This is going to screw up a lot of people's plans."

After he studied the X-rays, the ER doctor at Fletcher Allen Hospital reported that Matt suffered a Grade 2 moderate wrist sprain. Although the bone isn't fractured, he has partially torn ligaments. For forty-eight hours Matt has to keep it elevated and compressed, icing it every two hours for twenty minutes at a time. To keep the wrist immobile, he'll also have to wear a splint for at least the next week. Carefully placing the ice on Matt's swollen wrist, I ask him, "What time did that nurse give you the ibuprofen?"

"Like I paid any attention?"

While Matt makes business calls, I go back into the kitchen and blend up a soymilk, peanut butter, blueberry, and banana smoothie. I add agave to sweeten it even more and pour the thick liquid into a glass for Matt. He's still on the phone, so I decide to clear up the toys and books that Finley left scattered around. Then I sit down at the end of the couch and wait until he ends his last call.

"Where did this little doll come from?" I ask, holding out a plush handmade doll in a red cotton dress. It's a Waldorf doll. "Did Terra leave it here?"

"No, Terra gave it to Finley."

"When? Why?"

"Terra brought it to school last week and told Finley if she ever gets lonely she should pretend the doll is her. Finley made me promise not to tell you because she thought you'd get mad at her."

"She thought I'd get mad at her?" I repeat incredulously. I look into the doll's expressionless face. Its eyes are two small blue dots. The mouth is a half-inch line of red thread and its hair is a tangle of black woolen strands. The doll bears a striking resemblance to Terra. "Those two really love each other," I say sadly.

"Yeah," Matt says, looking at his injured wrist as if it wasn't attached to his body.

I get up and throw the doll into the basket.

"Too bad you screwed her mother," I say, walking back into the kitchen.

KATE

A pall settles over 68 Monroe Street. For seven days straight Matt does little more than sit on the couch playing computer games and watching television. He snaps at me every time I try to ice him or rewrap his splint, as if it's my fault he isn't healing more quickly. He whines about having to use his left hand when he uses the bathroom, brushes his teeth, and eats. He scolds Finley for not cleaning up her toys. He yells when Munch tries to jump on the couch, fearful the dog will bump his wrist.

I'm determined to finish Macon's story, even if it means having to reconfigure old scenes into new ones. I refuse to let Annie disable my writing, although Matt's doing a pretty good job of it himself. Like so many men, he's a needy patient. It seems as if every time I'm deep in the middle of a scene, he needs me.

Make him a smoothie.

Bring him the paper.

It's not like his legs are broken.

So far today it's been quiet, and I'm exploring all the possible scenarios with my trio of protagonists. I want all three of them to be happy but know it's impossible; someone will end up getting crushed.

My thoughts are interrupted by the clatter of something breaking.

"Dear lord, what now?" I say to the computer screen. In the living room, I find the television remote on the floor, its back case open; its batteries on the carpet next to it.

"Matt, what can I do for you?" I ask, picking up the wreckage. "Can I make you tea? How about I make you another smoothie. I have frozen raspberries—"

"That fucking doctor lied. He said I'd be able to move my wrist after a week and it's been a week."

"That's not what he said." My patience is draining from me like air from a punctured inner tube. "He said everyone heals differently. He said he was *hopeful* you'd be able to use it after a week."

"I'm dying, Kate. I can't run. I can't bike."

"I'm sorry."

"If I can't work, I'm going to start losing accounts."

I sit on the beige easy chair next to the fireplace. If it were winter, I could stoke a roaring flame for him to stare into. It'd be easier for Matt to be trapped inside when it was negative-five outside. But it's a dry and sunny June day.

"Why don't you take a walk?" I say.

"Hand me the remote so I can fix it, would you please?" he says, ignoring the suggestion.

"Come on, Matt. It'll be good to get out of the house. You haven't been out since Finley's soccer game."

There's a knock on the front door. I can only hope it's someone who can distract Matt so I can get back to writing. At this point, I'd be happy to see Heidi with a three-legged dog.

But when I open it, the only person in the entire world I'm

not pleased to see is standing on the top step, holding a large canvas bag.

"I told you I never wanted to speak to you again."

Annie pulls a pile of index cards out of her back pocket and hands me the one on top. On it is written: *I KNOW YOU NEVER WANT TO SPEAK TO ME AGAIN.*

"So then why are you here?"

Another card. *I CAME OVER TO HELP FIX MATT'S WRIST.*

I stiffen. "How'd you know Matt hurt his wrist?"

Annie shuffles through the stack of cards. *I SAW THE SPLINT ON HIS WRIST AT THE SOCCER GAME. HE WAS CLEARLY IN GREAT PAIN.*

Another card. *AND LAST NIGHT TERRA TOLD ME THAT FINLEY SAID HER DAD BROKE HIS WRIST AND IT WASN'T GETTING BETTER.*

"It's not broken. Just really badly sprained."

Annie smiles.

"What; no card for that? Hey, thanks and goodbye." I go to close the door but she promptly holds up another. *I BROUGHT COMFREY. IT WILL HEAL HIS WRIST. I PROMISE.*

"Enough of the cards already, Annie. Give it to me and maybe I'll try it. Thanks," I say, putting my hand out.

"Can I at least give you the card with all the instructions on it?"

"Sure."

Annie slides out a card from the bottom of the deck. What other questions had she anticipated? "Here. But you need to be precise. Follow the directions exactly or it'll be useless."

I turn and look at Matt. He's too far away to see or hear who I'm speaking to. With the TV remote balanced on his lap, he's attempting to jam batteries into it with his left hand. The look of frustration on his face is pathetic.

I face Annie again, weighing my hatred of her against the persistent annoyance sitting on the couch.

"Just come in," I say.

After putting Munch outside and locking the dog door, I lean against the refrigerator with my arms crossed, watching Annie put a handful of large green comfrey leaves into our blender. She adds water and whirls it into a gloppy consistency. She has on a pair of cutoff denim shorts and a pink T-shirt that reads NEVER TRUST AN ATOM. THEY MAKE UP EVERYTHING. "You don't want this too soupy," she says, pouring the mixture into a bowl. "To make it hold together, we'll need to add some flour."

"I have plenty of flour," I bark.

"I brought organic flour." She pulls out a baggie of flour and a pint jar of muddy-looking brown liquid. She flips through the index cards from her pocket and places one next to the jar. *CREAM OF MUSHROOM SOUP*, it reads.

"Matt and Finley hate mushrooms, but thanks anyway."

"Oh, sorry. I didn't know that."

"Yes, you did."

"I guess I forgot. May I continue?"

"Sure."

Annie sprinkles flour into the bowl and massages it into the wet leaves. "Add enough so it looks like this." I peer over her shoulder and as I do, I inhale Annie's familiar herbal aroma wafting off her body. "Add hot water from the tap at the last second so the poultice is warm on his skin."

"Can't I just microwave it?"

Annie cocks her head sideways like she always does when I exasperate her. "Please do it my way."

"Fine."

She waits for the tap water to turn hot, pours in a third

of a cup, mashes it up, and spreads out the green sludge on a piece of triple-folded cheesecloth. "Okay, grab the PVC and come with me."

I look at the counter. "The what?"

"The plastic wrap."

On the living room couch I can see from Matt's shifting facial expressions that he has no clue how he's supposed to react. He's obviously shocked that I allowed Annie into our house. He tries not to look at her and is fighting to keep his attention on the poultice as Annie methodically places the fabric side over his bruised wrist.

Seeing how hard it is for him to keep his eyes off her stings my skin.

"Kate, you see it's kind of wet, right?" she says, not making eye contact with Matt. "You want it to be wet. Otherwise it won't seep into the skin." She lets out a raspy cough, then stretches a layer of plastic around Matt's hand and wrist to keep the poultice in place. As she presses on it, she coughs again, more hoarsely. The couch is covered in dog hair.

"You're sitting in Munch's spot," Matt says apologetically.

"I can tell," Annie coughs the words more than speaks them. "Kate," she says, trying to take in a breath but having trouble, "you see how tight this is? How I pressed it down?"

I nod.

After rising from the couch, Annie starts wheezing so hard, she doubles over, resting her hands on her knees.

I look at Matt who is staring wide-eyed. I sense how desperately he wants to reach out to her. "Hey, thanks, Annie. You should probably go now," he utters with such despair I almost feel sorry for him.

Gasping for air, Annie straightens up. "Kate," she says, "leave it on for an hour. After taking it off, let the residue air-dry on his skin." She looks directly at Matt before lightly touching her forefinger to his cheek. I imagine I can see an electric current running between them.

"Hurry up and tell me the rest," I insist, "so you can get out of here."

"Do this exact same thing two more times today and three times tomorrow and the next day," Annie instructs as she moves away without a backward glance at Matt. When she gets to the kitchen, she strains to take deep breaths, each one getting caught halfway in. "I . . . brought you enough supplies for eight more treatments," she says, reaching into her bag.

She's barely able to keep herself erect, and I don't understand why she's still standing in our kitchen or why she is not at least using her inhaler. Asthma has a full grip on her lungs now, with coughs spasming out of her chest in heaving bursts.

"Thanks, Annie. I can get the rest of it. Leave the bag and I'll return it to you," I say, moving over to the front door. I open it.

"Leave, Annie," I say, but she's struggling with the stupid bag.

"I brought you more tea," she says, pulling out a huge jar of GoodLove.

"Fine. Okay," I say. "Please. Go."

"I'm leaving." She balls up the empty bag and strides out of the kitchen, pausing on the top step to cough. Then, before closing the door on her, I see Annie take the index cards from her pocket. She sifts through the stack and hands me one before walking away.

I MISS YOU, it says.

ANNIE

Terra runs into my room and flings herself onto the bed.

"I'm bored," she says, stretching her legs upward while rolling back and forth on the duvet. She looks like a dog trying to scratch its rump.

"Only boring people get bored." I toss the electrophoretic display of lexemes—more commonly known as a Kindle—aside and tickle her belly with my feet until she giggles. As she inches away—screaming, "Stop! Stop!"—I slide closer, kneading her spasming body until she falls to the floor, laughing deliriously. It takes every inch of reserve I have to keep from laughing along with her. After that last near-fatal asthma attack during which I stupidly left my inhaler at home, I am keeping my emotions in check.

"Let's go for a walk." I push off the bed and go into the bathroom to pee. When I come out, Terra is staring at the Kindle. Her jaw hangs loose and her eyes balloon out. When she realizes I caught her, she jumps back as if she's been stung. "Which part did you read?" I ask my blushing child.

"A man was licking cream from a girl's vagina," she replies uncomfortably. "That's gross."

I sit down next to her on the bed and take her hand. "Sex is not gross, Terra. When people care about each other, they show it in lots of different ways. Like when they kiss."

She nods. "Duh."

"Or they might do other things just for fun." My list of *other* things is long enough to wrap around the planet. "Even silly stuff like eating whipped cream."

"Okay, but I want to go to Stockwell Farms Camp when school's done," she says, detouring toward a less mystifying subject. As much as I want my daughter to appreciate how beautiful and natural sex is, shoving the subject into her face or down her throat before she is ready is not a tactic often found in parenting manuals. "You know I hate summer camps," I tell her. "Camp is where the children of entitled Caucasians spend their summers."

"Finley goes every summer," she says.

"Ah." I can't blame the kid for wanting to hang with her friend. She still doesn't understand why they are being kept asunder and I can offer little remediation regarding the outlandish excuse Finley's parents used. A liar was I, they said. Enough of one, they deemed it necessary the children shall suffer the fall. "What's this camp again?" I ask, my curiosity piqued.

"Finley goes to the one with farm animals so—"

"Sorry. No."

"Stop interrupting me, Annie!" She flops back on the bed and when her hand accidentally brushes against the offensive Kindle its gooey contents pop back up. "There's another one at the same time with just gardens and hiking and stuff, but all the kids get to eat lunch together and swim and stuff."

"Let me think about it." There is a distinct possibility that Kate might not like it if I enroll Terra in Fin's camp. Given the rocky boat on which my daughter and I are presently drifting, I certainly don't wish to displace what little ballast we have.

Since delivering the comfrey, I've been hoping my graphic display of compassion might cause Kate to reconsider banishing us from Rayburne, a town I have, surprisingly, come to consider home. Healthy food is readily available, as is clean air, good friends, and a neighbor who would lick my lady parts all day long if I let him.

Now that both Terra and I found what we've been searching for when we left Colorado, I only have to convince Kate that keeping me close is a win-win. I eye the Kindle. After I perused the stack of mail on their kitchen counter while grinding comfrey leaves for Matt's wrist, it was easy enough afterward to track down Kate's nom de plume as well as her books. Clue one: an envelope with Amatory Press in the return address. Clue two: I recalled Kate mentioning a sex scene in a canoe. How many books written by Amatory's authors include a canoe? The "Search Inside" tool on Amazon produced two possibilities. I downloaded both and began with *Slow Burn* by R.J. Cameron. It wasn't half bad. I particularly enjoyed the orgy scene inside a firehouse. If this was Kate's writing, I was impressed. Then I started *Strong Lust: Crossing Borders* by Daphne Moore. There were no orgies but to my astonishment many of the book's sex acts seemed precisely drawn from Matt's and my vast sexual repertoire. By the time I reached the scene where Macon covers Phionna's vulva with pastry cream, I was 99 percent certain Matt had shared our intimacies with his wife. When Phionna requested Macon use his tongue to spell out the entire alphabet against her clitoris, the last 1 percent of doubt fell out of the sky.

Matt and I had made brilliant use of a can of whipped cream when we fucked in Minneapolis.

So much for her amazing imagination. Kate Burke—AKA

Daphne Moore—is a plagiarist, a weak sexually useless fake who is using my life for her profit.

"On second thought, going to camp is an excellent idea," I say, giving Terra a kiss on the cheek, lest she forget affection shouldn't need to come with cream on top.

KATE

By Sunday, Matt's swelling is completely gone. On Monday, when I come out of my office, I find him in the living room squeezing a rubber ball in his right hand while typing on his laptop with his left.

"Check this out, Kate!" he shouts as he proudly shows off his new range of motion up and down, side to side.

"Should you be doing that so soon?"

He picks up a can of black beans and bends his wrist upward, holds it for a second, then lowers it. "This is a strengthening exercise from that list the doctor gave you. I do it ten times up, then down."

"It's only your first day, Matt," I say before going into the kitchen and opening the refrigerator. I twist off the top of Annie's mushroom soup and give it a sniff, frowning when the smell of soymilk hits my nose. I was planning to eat it for lunch, but instead I'll be dumping it down the drain. I hate soymilk. The only person in the house who doesn't is Matt, who puts it in his smoothies.

I make myself a cup of Earl Grey and turn to watch him twirling his hand. "Don't overdo it," I say.

"Are you kidding? This is amazing."

Annie's poultices have proven miraculous. With his wrist almost back to normal Matt should be able to at least go for a run without pain. And hopefully, go back to work.

"Do you think you can use it to write?" I ask.

Matt reaches into Finley's art box and pulls out a purple marker and sketchpad, slowly drawing a heart with his right hand. "Close but no cigar. It's not like it hurts. It feels weak, sort of spongy. No way I'd be able to write for four hours at a stretch."

"I'm sure it will be completely better soon enough," I say, trying to sound optimistic.

I need him to get out of the house.

To stop interrupting me.

I need to persuade him to have sex with other women again.

Since Matt's stories stopped coming, so have my characters. I still haven't filled in all the placeholder sex scenes. Every time I try to rework an already played-out tryst, my fingers stall on the keyboard. I must scare up new words, new sensations, new moves. If I can't get my husband interested in one-night stands in hotel rooms, I might actually have to switch genres.

"Maybe someone else can do the writing while you do the questioning?" I offer.

He grabs the rubber ball again and squeezes it. "You know I hate to share the glory."

"Matt, but—"

"I'm pulling your leg, Kate. I just got off the phone with Dave Egan. He's got a multilevel restaurant music study coming up in Dallas, and he asked me to do a joint contract with him."

"That's great, sweetheart. You'll be so much happier working again."

"Don't I know it."

I hesitate before taking the shot. "And maybe while you're there you'll meet someone . . ." I hold my breath.

"Kate, we've been through this. I said no. I'm done having one-offs."

"You mean if they're not with Annie, you're done."

He stares at the ball in his hand and after a few seconds, says, "We should do something for her, you know."

"I'll be sure to send flowers," I reply flatly.

"Kate, she came here to help and almost died. You saw what she did for me."

"And your cup runneth over with gratitude, is that it, Matt?" I bring my mug of tea into the living room and sit down. "Would having sex with her again be thanks enough?"

"What?"

I have no idea why I just allowed such a preposterous suggestion to tumble from my mouth. But I recognize that if I let Matt have sex with Annie, I could kill more than a few birds with one vagina. I won't have to be the one to satisfy him, sexually speaking. I've been letting strangers take my place in Matt's bed for years. Would it be so different to let Annie be my surrogate lover?

Perhaps I can even get past the lies and deceit, and she and I can be friends again. I truly miss being "Miss Kate, mother of Finley."

And . . . if we became friends again, I'd ask her to share her stories. My next series could be told from a powerful woman's point of view, a woman who picks and chooses who to love, and who to leave behind.

"Tell me again that you're not in love with her and that it's only about the sex," I say to my husband, revved up, trying now to convince myself this could work.

Matt lets go of the rubber ball, and we both watch it roll across the carpet. Munch jumps off his bed and grabs it in his mouth.

"Drop it, Munchie," Matt commands. "Good boy," he says before looking up at me. "I'm still not sure what you're suggesting here, Kaybee."

"I want you to go back to Annie, as long as it's just for sex and nothing more."

"But . . . you wouldn't want me to tell you after I saw her or—"

I put down the mug and kneel in front of him. "I *do* want you to tell me about it. I want to keep writing about Macon, and I can't do it without your help."

"Have you really thought this through? The last thing I want is to come home after being with Annie and have you plunge a knife through my heart."

"Matt, I just need to be certain you're not, you know, going anywhere."

As Matt rubs Munch's ear with his left hand, he speaks slowly, methodically. "Kaybee, you're my home base, but . . ." I watch his eyes dart back and forth, back and forth. He is strategizing. Trying to decide where to step next. "I mean, yeah, I want to be with Annie again; we have this intense chemistry. When we're together, she takes me to this world I've never—" He stops speaking when he sees the look on my face.

"You're right. You can't be with her again." What possessed me to think I'll want to hear Matt talk about screwing Annie? As Annie. Not as Angela or Suki or the rest of those personas Annie so brilliantly played. Do I really think I'll be able to sit calmly at my desk lapping up the details like a tigress licking blood from a freshly killed gazelle?

I cannot, will not, ever get over the naked fact that Annie stabbed me in the back. Real friends do not do that.

So what if Annie, the vegetal Florence Nightingale that she is, fixed Matt's wrist? So what if she made me laugh? She also trampled all over my marriage. I can't allow her back into our lives, no matter how much it means giving up. "You're right. You can't be with her again."

"What? You just changed your mind? Like just this second?"

"Yeah. I did. Just this second."

Matt stares at me, a gray glaze of shock washing across his eyes. "Are you serious?"

"I'm sorry, Matt. I don't know what I was thinking." I put the can of black beans into his right hand and get up. "For a moment there I had my priorities confused. I want to go write," I say, heading to my office.

"You're insane!" he shouts at my back.

"Call me if you need anything," I answer.

ANNIE

"Matt. What are you doing here?"

"Look!" he says, twisting his wrist around in tiny circles. "You're amazing."

"You could've texted me that. Won't Kate skin you alive if she finds out you're here?"

"I'm only gonna stay a minute. I'm out for a run."

"I can see that," I say amiably.

"I really am going for a run, but I had to thank you in person. Honestly, Annie, you saved my life." He says this with so much admiration in his eyes I believe I may swoon.

"I just saved your wrist, my man, but sure, I'll accept the life achievement award."

He has on tight black running shorts, his bulge pressing against the fabric. Even without an erection, Matt has quite the package.

"How's the divorce going?" I ask.

He shakes his head. "I told you: not gonna happen." He crosses his arms. "But you know what's funny? Wait a sec." He moves a few inches inside and shuts the door behind him. One small step for man. One giant leap for Annie-kind. "Kate almost let me go back to seeing you."

"What do you mean *almost*?"

"On Monday I was showing her how my wrist was so much better and I said maybe we should, you know, do something nice for you and she—what'd she say?—she was saying that it wasn't good for me to go without sex and that I should find someone new on my trip to Dallas."

So she can use it in her next book. "When are you going to Dallas?"

"Tomorrow morning."

Clayton's family lives in Dallas. What a coincidence, I think, and am already planning ahead when I realize Matt is trying to explain something. "What did you say?" I ask. The sexual tension between us is alive, a third presence glowing like an orb with rays of light spreading out and filling the space separating us.

"I told Kate I didn't want to sleep with anyone other than you."

That's my boy. "And she said have at it?" Daphne Moore needs a pussy to write about, and she obviously wants the best one.

"Yeah, but like a minute later she changed her mind."

"Why?" I cross my arms in front of me. "Did you express too much euphoria over the prospect?" The dude had us in the palm of his large hand, then let us drop. Men are hopeless. They need to learn how to strategize better.

"I guess, yeah, I did. I don't know. I mean if I were her I wouldn't—" He sits down on the bottom stair and stretches his arms over his head. Now that his hair-kissed stomach is in full view, I can't control myself.

I drop to my knees and open my mouth. Matt doesn't move a muscle.

KATE

I close the curtains, slide off my slippers, and type:

It was still dark outside when Macon crawled onto the bed and gave Lizzie a soft kiss on her mouth.

"What are you doing, Macon? It's four-thirty in the morning. Why are you dressed?"

"Bread delivery at five. Gotta meet the truck."

"Oh," she said, running her fingers through his hair. "I forgot you're the only person working there."

"Do you have any idea how hot you are?"

"I can feel a very hard cock pressed against my thigh, so yes, I have an idea."

"I'm never letting you run away from me again. Do you understand?"

Lizzie took her hand away and stared up at the ceiling. "Well, I'm not so sure about that, Macon."

Panic shot through his muscles, rippling over his belly and down into his thighs. He put his hand on her chin and made her look into his eyes. "I thought we were on the same page here, Lizzie."

"And what story are you reading, Macon? *Romeo and Juliet* or *Sleeping Beauty*? Will someone have to die or will your kisses bring me back to life?"

Before he could answer, his cell phone rang. Audrey Mansfield's name flashed on the caller ID.

Why can't I get rid of Audrey and leave these two to their love? I massage my temples. All week I've been having penetrating headaches. Tension headaches. Ever since I dangled Annie in front of Matt's face, then snatched her away, my husband's been acting like a bratty kid who got nothing but socks for Christmas. And even though his wrist is almost completely healed and the Dallas project was handed to him on a silver platter, he's been irritable and distant. I should resolve this before he leaves for Texas tomorrow.

After searching the house and finding it empty, I figure he's out on a run. Since Munch is in the yard, he must have gone to Mekins Cove. I pull on a pair of leggings, a sports bra, and T-shirt, and tie up my running shoes. A run and fresh air will help my headache. I'll meet up with Matt and walk back with him so we can talk. Enough of this festering doubt and anger. We need to get back to some version of normal.

I stroll to the end of Monroe, turn left, and jog down the middle of Forest. Within seconds both my knees start throbbing. "What the heck," I say, bending over to massage them. I reconsider the run, walking instead to loosen them. As I reach the corner of Dwyer Court, Suzanne Madden's car appears. She brakes and lowers her window.

"Hi, Kate," she says, smiling. Her dark hair is tied back in a tight ponytail and she's wearing a pair of tortoiseshell sunglasses so large they take up half her face.

"Hey, Suzanne. What's up?"

"I was trying to garden but my neighbor hasn't stopped blasting her rock music all morning. It's really annoying so I figured I'd scoot over to Garden World and pick up more annuals."

"Which neighbor?"

She pushes her sunglasses up onto her head and peers over her left shoulder. I follow her gaze. "The couple with the little girl renting the Hendersons' house next door to me. I don't know their names. I waved to the wife a few times, but if you ask me she's kind of a b-i-t-c-h," she says, spelling the word.

"There's just one parent, and her name is Annie Meyers."

"Oh, gosh, I'm sorry. I didn't realize you knew her." She puts her hand on her chest. "I'm so embarrassed."

"Don't be," I say, reaching in and patting Suzanne's arm. "Our kids play together sometimes, but it's not like we're friends. I mean, you're right, she's a total bitch."

Suzanne appears relieved. God forbid she not love her neighbor. "She's really loud. She and a man are over there having a pool party."

"A man—? Hey Suzanne, I've got to get going, okay?"

"Sure. Have a great run. And thanks for not thinking I'm a meanie, Kate."

"You, Suzanne? Never." I wink, and before she drives away, I hurriedly ask, "Suzanne, is Eli working at the market today?"

"Yeah, he's there now, why?"

"Just checking. He's the best deli slicer there. Never too thick. Never too thin."

"I'll tell him you said so. Bye!" she yells, driving off.

I run into the woods and stop behind a tree wide enough to hide behind. I wait until I am certain I can no longer be seen in Suzanne's rearview mirror, then walk back to Forest and turn down Dwyer Court.

At Suzanne's house, I unlatch the side gate and duck around back. She really does have a lovely garden. It's clean and organized with numerous raised beds surrounding a pretty fountain. Crossing the large backyard, I hear music coming from Annie's backyard. It isn't loud enough to be truly irksome, but everyone has their own acoustic limit.

The privacy hedge between the two properties is a thick maze of tight shrubbery and thorny blackberry bushes. I'll need a weed whacker to see into Annie's backyard. I survey the grounds, hoping to locate some clippers but find nothing useful. So I just stand and listen.

Music. Splashing. I don't hear Annie or Terra. Suzanne probably heard a man's voice on the stereo.

If that's what I believe, why can't I stop the quickening in my chest? Again with the palpitations. I'll go see a doctor about them soon. Maybe when Matt goes to Dallas I'll—Matt? Is that Matt's voice?

Without thinking, I ram my body through the bramble, barely noticing the branches and thorns scratching and clawing at my skin. I make my way to the fence line, wiping away a smear of blood from my upper arm and peering through a small opening.

I can barely see them through the brush but I see enough to know that my husband and former friend are lying cheating pigs.

Even in my state of hysterical fury, I won't confront them here. I push back through the serrating bushes, protecting my face as best I can, and run next door to Annie's, letting myself in with the spare key. I step over Matt's running shoes. Matt's black shorts have been tossed on the bottom step of the stairs. From the kitchen window I witness them, large as life.

Matt's behind Annie, thrusting his body against hers while

she holds onto the pool ladder. They are screwing with such fe-
rocity I gasp. Rage shoots through me. My hands clench as my
heart punches at my ribs.

Matt lied to me again.

Again he betrayed me.

I step toward the back door but stop, both repulsed and
mesmerized by what I'm witnessing. I've never before actually
watched Matt having sex with another woman. When he relives
his affairs in my office, I simply translate his words into my
writer's imagination. Matt's sexual encounters are nothing more
than colors on a palette that I use to paint a story, like an artist
dipping a brush into a glop of cerulean blue. The colors only
exist in my mind. I never *feel* anything about them in my heart.

Now I feel the color, and that color is black. Ugly inky black.
What am I waiting for? I need to go out there and—

I pace the kitchen. It's over with Matt. I will never forgive
him. He is deceitful and he deserves to lose me. When I look
out again, they're in the shallow end of the pool with their arms
around one another. Matt is staring at Annie as if no one else in
the world exists. Not me. Not Finley. Only Annie.

I screech into a parking space, put a quarter into the meter on
Cherry Street, and run up the steps of the Judge Edward J.
Costello Courthouse. After my body is scanned for concealed
weapons, I grab my keys out of the gray bin, race up to the Family
Court Office on the second floor, and stride up to the counter.
It is quiet and clean, the opposite of what I'm feeling inside.

I am a little taken aback when a woman walks toward me
looking upset.

"Is everything okay?" she asks me. "Do you need help?"

"What?" I look around to see if she is addressing someone else.

"Were you in a fight? Did someone hurt you?"

"Did someone hurt—?" I glance at my body. Scratch marks and dried blood run up and down my arms and hands. I look as if I've gotten into a fight with an army of feral cats. Thank goodness I wore leggings instead of shorts or I might have bled to death. "No . . . no," I say, lightly laughing it off. "I was gardening and fell headfirst into a blackberry bush. That's all."

"That must have been some blackberry bush," the woman says before clearing her throat. "What can I do for you?" she asks as professionally as possible.

"What do I need to do if I want a divorce?" As I say this, I feel a fiery blush cross my face.

The woman raises her eyebrows so subtly that if I hadn't been staring at her I would have missed it.

"With or without a minor child?" she asks, pretending not to be alarmed by the deranged woman standing in front of her.

Finley. What will this do to her? I stare at my feet. "With," I answer.

"Certainly." The woman walks away, returning with a stack of papers held together by an enormous paper clip. "Fill these out, bring them back, and pay the fee. It's pretty easy."

Easy? Letting go of a lifetime of love: *easy*? After thanking her, I make for the exit and run down the stairs. When I reach the first floor I notice out of the corner of my eye a large metal sculpture behind the staircase. As eager as I am to get home and start filling out the papers, I walk over to take a closer look.

Two dancers, abstract bodies, arms around one another. It's beautiful, fluid and evocative. The placard reads, "*Pas de Deux*, Hy Suchman, 1995." A Dance For Two. How fitting.

Past the statue I watch the progression of people walking through the X-ray machine. One after the other, lost in their own thoughts, wants, worries. How many of them will bother to notice this balletic gem as they make their way up the stairs? Probably none. If it wasn't for Matt, I wouldn't have noticed it either. Or have appreciated its presence. Matt, the lover of art, who introduced me to the world of abstract expression. Who taught me how to see beyond the colors.

Slowly I reach out and touch the tip of my finger to the face of the male dancer, remembering how Annie had done the same thing to Matt's cheek the day she came over with the comfrey leaves. I anticipate a spark of electricity to pass between me and the dancer, like it had between them, but I feel only cold metal.

When I close the front door, Matt calls from his office, "Is that you, Kate? Where were you?"

"I was up in Burlington!" I reply loudly enough for him to hear me.

"I'm finishing stuff for Dallas. I'll be out in a sec."

"No hurry."

I am cleaning the last of my scrapes and cuts when Matt comes into the bathroom. "Holy shit! What the hell happened to you?"

"I had a run-in with a blackberry bush," I say calmly.

"Here. Let me see." He lifts my right arm and inspects it, turning it toward the light as if looking for a scratch on a record album. I breathe in the smell of him, surprised by the whiff of aftershave. Guessing he doused himself to cover the chlorine, my anger magnifies to the point I worry the hairs on my arms will catch fire. "Man, you really got your neck, too, but it's all pretty superficial." He ruffles my hair. "I think you're gonna live."

"Yeah. I think so," I say limply. Although the writer in me wants to jump ahead to the final scene of our tragic love story, I decide it is prudent to wait until he's back from Dallas. For

Finley's sake, and because I really want to have the papers filled out completely.

I realize that keeping my hatred inside also makes me feel kind of empowered. And to be perfectly honest, a little turned on. "How was your run today?" I ask, following him into the bedroom.

"Excellent. Boy, I really needed that run."

"I bet."

"And my wrist was totally fine," he says, hoisting his suitcase out from under the bed. He unzips it and opens his dresser drawer. "What are you doing, Kate?"

"Just hanging with my husband. Is that okay?" I say, sitting down.

"Of course." He laughs. "I just know when you get close to finishing one of your books you're like a machine."

"Yeah. A machine." That I married a man capable of such duplicity horrifies me. How could I have fallen for someone who lies without breaking a sweat? As I watch him stuff his socks and underwear into the zipper compartment, I wonder if I've been seeing him through a distorted lens all these years. Has he always been an inherently deceitful person, or had Annie brought about this change in his character?

I debate this for a few moments and decide that Matt's always been this way—basically a fifteen-year-old from New Hampshire who lives for sex. A man who puts his own desires above all else. All this time I thought I was the defective one in this relationship. What a fool I've been. Here I was trying to change, to make myself a more perfect wife, when all this time he's stayed exactly the same.

"You know how you always say I make you feel safe?" I ask.

"You do," he says with a smile. "You're my home base."

I stifle the snicker. It's been this sense of entitlement that's allowed him to take chances.

"Why'd you ask that? What's up, Kaybee?"

"Nothing, sweetheart."

"Tell me what's happening with your book. Are you going to kill off Audrey?" He puts an imaginary gun to his head and pulls the trigger. "Puh-kew!"

I roll my eyes. "You're hysterical, Matt."

"Right that." He blows the smoke from his finger gun and stuffs it into the front of his pants before walking over to the closet.

"I'm still not sure," I say to his back. "Do you think I should kill her?"

"Audrey shouldn't have to die just because she's obsessed with the guy. She can't help herself, right?" he says, taking out his blue Armani suit.

She shouldn't have to die just because she's obsessed with the guy?

"I'm not so sure you're right about that," I say, standing up.

ANNIE

I am transferring a freshly-grown Kombucha SCOBY into a mason jar of tea when Matt's text arrives.

MATT: That was truly amazing,
but it should NOT have happened.
That was the last time.

ME: Really? You're breaking up
with me through text? 😑

MATT: We already are broken up.

ME: I feel like Bendrix,
after the bomb fell.

MATT: Wtf?

ME: The End of the Affair.

MATT: ?

ME: Graham Greene. I thought
you read 📚

MATT: Whatever. I gotta go get
ready for tomorrow's trip.

ME: Where are you going? Are
you leaving Kate? 😂 😍 🙏

MATT: Stop it. I told you. Dallas.

ME: Are you doing that Musak
study?

MATT: How'd you know about that?

ME: I'll meet you there and we
can fuck with cowboy hats on.

MATT: No.

ME: What does Kate give you
that I can't?

MATT: She's the mother of my child.
Plus I love her.

ME: But you love me too. Or do
you just love my vagina?

MATT: I'm signing off.

ME: What if there was no Kate?

MATT: No Kate? Not happening.
She'd be lost without me. I'm her
world .

ME: Would you and I be together?

ME: Matt?

ME: Hello?

ME: Matt?

KATE

Now that Matt is in Texas and I have the privacy I need, I reach into the bottom drawer of my desk and take out the stack of divorce papers. Form 800. Form 802. Form 849. Real estate holdings. Life insurance policies. Child support order. Self-Employment attachment.

Easy? It will take hours.

I'm barely four pages in when I hear Finley's voice ring through the house.

"Mom! I'm home!"

I shut the computer, stash the papers away, and walk out to greet my daughter. "Hi, kiddo. How was camp?"

"Good. We got to collect the eggs today. I found the most."

"That's exciting."

"Sage's mom said she can't bring me home on Friday."

"Okay. I'll get you."

"Can I have food? I'm starving."

I kiss the top of her head and retrieve a bevy of snacks from the pantry. Finley unwraps a pack of seaweed strips and stuffs one into her mouth, causing flecks of green to fly all over the table. As I scoop the dust into my palm Finley asks, "How long is Daddy gonna be in Texas?"

"He'll be home next week," I reply, picturing the divorce papers in my drawer.

"Hey, Terra's going to Texas too."

"What? How do you know?"

"I don't know." She makes a show of tearing the seaweed into perfectly parallel strips.

"Finley?"

"Um."

"Finley, you can tell me. I promise I won't be mad."

"I know about it because Terra goes to my camp. Well, not my camp—'cause I do the animal stuff, but Terra goes to the other one, the one where you plant stuff and do real farming. I didn't want to go to that one, remember, because you said I'd like the one with the animals and Terra, she . . . " Finley continues describing in rich detail the differences between the two camps, while I, fuming inside, consider all the implications.

". . . and today she told me she's not gonna be in camp again till next week because she's going to Texas to see her cousins—I forget their names—but they have horses and she gets to wear a cowboy hat when she's there. She promised to buy me one too." Finley lowers her eyes to the table. "Is that okay, or should I have told her not to?"

Annie put her child in camp with my child. And now she will be in Texas with Matt. My pulse accelerates. My face is probably as red as the strawberry rollup Finley is unsticking from its paper. "That's fine if Terra buys you a hat, sweetheart."

"Thanks, Mommy."

"You really like Terra, don't you?"

Finley strokes her chin as if she's an adult deep in thought and murmurs, "Will you be mad at me if I say I do? You and her mom don't like each other anymore so maybe it's better I say I don't?" The sadness in her voice seeps through the cracks in my already broken heart. Finley has lots of friends, but she's never bonded with another child the way she did with Terra.

I almost feel guilty for keeping them separated. Almost.

I pull her out of the chair and onto my lap, squeezing her into a tight hug. "I could never be mad at you, Finley. I love you with all my heart." I hold her by the shoulders and move her curled hair off her face. "You can like Terra as much as you want."

"Thanks, Mom." She jumps off me and runs into the living room. "Can I watch a video please?"

I laugh. If only adults were able to tame our emotions as easily as children do. "Sure, sweetie. I've got work to do anyway."

With Finley installed in front of the television, I yank open the drawer and again toss the papers onto the desk. I am about to slam the drawer closed but stop when a white card catches my eye.

I MISS YOU

It's that stupid index card Annie handed me right before she left our house, coughing so much I thought she might die before making it home.

"I kind of wish you had died that day, Annie," I say before ripping it to pieces.

I sit back and pick at one of the many scabs lining my arms. If I go through with the divorce, will Matt move in with Annie? What if they get married and that psycho becomes Finley's stepmother? I choke on the thought. I pick up Adam and force his arms and legs backward. He looks as uncomfortable as I feel. I throw him onto the couch. He bounces once and falls to the floor.

I glower at the papers and they scowl back, challenging me to a duel, daring me to thrust my pen onto their waiting blankness. I finger a turquoise pen.

Click-click.

Click-click.

I reach for my mug and after taking a small sip, I fill in my name and address, then slam my hand down on the desk. Annie is unhinged. She doesn't deserve to have Matt, and I cannot let her be a part of Finley's life. I eye the computer screen, the words blurring across the page.

I need to do what makes me feel good: write. Be with my other family for a little while.

Closing my eyes, I try to clear the anger out of my head. I have to finish this darn book already, meaning that Macon needs to decide once and for all who he is going to live Happily Ever After with. Audrey is rich. Beautiful. Smart. But he can never have children with her. Lizzie is everything and more.

Maybe I do have to kill Audrey. I can have her try to physically hurt Lizzie, and Macon will—or is that too much like *Fatal Attraction*? Is there such a thing as an original idea anymore? Of course, I'd have to steer clear of dead rabbits.

I shove aside the divorce papers and type a possible scenario:

Macon knew Audrey would eagerly agree to meet him up at Smiling Girl Farm. With Miles and Arthur down in the city, he told her they'd have the place to themselves. As he sat on the couple's porch sipping expensive bourbon on the rocks, he watched her BMW appear over the horizon and wind down the dirt road.

She wore a tight pair of jeans and a black blouse sheer enough to show off a lacy black bra beneath. He felt himself getting hard.

"Hey there, stranger," she remarked as she walked up onto the porch and took a seat beside him. "God, it's hot. You have another one of those?" she said, nodding at his glass.

Macon handed her his glass. "Finish this. I was thinking we should go for a swim."

"A swim?" She moved her hair off her face with a graceful swipe of her hand. "You know I can't get my hair wet, darling."

Macon stood up and pulled off his shirt. Then he unbuckled his belt and slid his jeans and boxer shorts down. She stared at his hard-on with a gleam in her eyes bright enough to light up her whole face.

"You don't have to dunk your head under," he said. "I just want to fuck you in the water."

"Well, if you put it like that." Audrey drank down the rest of the bourbon and started to unbutton her blouse. "I'd love to take a dip."

PLACEHOLDER (Macon and Audrey have sex in the pond)

Why did I just type PLACEHOLDER? The scene is ready to go. What I witnessed in Annie's pool is too good; too hot, not to include.

I sit back, reach up to touch my nose, but halt midway. I stare at the couch. Then I close my eyes and allow visions of Matt and Annie's ferocious watery coitus entrée into my head. The way their bodies moved together was a thing of beauty.

I sit forward, touch the keyboard. Stop.

"Come on, Kate. Don't be such a chicken." Why should it be so difficult to transpose Matt and Annie into Macon and Audrey? Is it because I watched the act with my own eyes? That it was Annie and not a stranger described to me by Matt? Or maybe it's due to my having such a strong image of Audrey in my mind, that it's impossible to morph Annie into her. What-ever the reason, I am not ready. Not yet.

PLACEHOLDER (Macon and Audrey have sex in the pond)
Macon stared down at Audrey's naked body spread out on the grass. Her eyes were fixed on him with such intensity he wondered if she could read his mind. Did she know he was planning to kill her?

This is supposed to be a book of erotica. Why am I letting it devolve into a tale of anger and murder? How is Macon supposed to get Audrey, the possessive bitch, out of the picture so he can get on with his life and be with the woman he truly loves? He has no choice but to kill her if he wants a Happily Ever After, right?

More importantly: How am I going to live Happily Ever After if Annie stays in *my* picture?

I stare at the screen.

Macon kneels down and kisses Audrey hard on the mouth, his hand around her throat. He—

But—

I don't really want to kill Audrey, do I? I want to—oh!

As if a masked man has just strolled into my office and slapped me hard across the face, it dawns on me that I've been channeling my own rage through Macon. Poor handsome Macon. He has become my emotional doppelgänger, my alter ego. My proxy.

Why should he have all the fun?

I am about to take a drink but stop. With the back of my hand, I hurl the mug off the desk. It crashes against the wall and shatters into a million shards. I stare at the long dark trails of coffee dripping down the white plaster.

"Screw you, Annie," I say, standing up. My fists are clenched so tightly I can feel the rage burn through to my biceps. Before going out to the living room I give my hands a quick shake as though air-drying them. "Finley," I say, feigning a smile. "I'm going to take Munch for a walk. Will you be okay without me for a little bit?"

She's so engrossed in her movie she doesn't even look over at me. "Sure, Mommy," she replies, pushing Munch off her lap.

ANNIE

When I asked Terra if she was into going to Texas, she screamed loudly enough to wake the dead. She loves her cousins Seth and Sadie, maybe nearly as much as I miss touching Matt in far-away places. Never before had the thought of Texas filled me with such delight.

Although once we arrive at my sister-in-law's house, I regret using up so many frequent flyer miles. I forgot how much I abhor Gayle, an ungainly whiny woman who, when she isn't grilling steaks or frying chicken wings, blathers on about how devastated she is about the passing of my former husband, her little brother Clay. She neglects to acknowledge the fact that Clayton despised her and her husband and their flamboyant consumerism. In all the time we were together, he rarely made us visit his side of the family, much to my relief. Our last sojourn south was two years ago, for Seth's bar mitzvah when Terra fell head over heels in love with her big cousins and their big house and their big horses. The scene was like a western amusement park to Terra, and she's been begging to go back ever since.

I've been biding my time now that we're here, nodding and

commiserating, even going so far as to eat iceberg lettuce and canned asparagus. When evening rolls around and I'm sure Matt is finished with his sessions, I make my excuses.

"Hey y'all. I'm going out for a little while," I state to the bloated lot of them lying across their leather sectional, staring at the oversized television. Terra waves to me without taking her eyes off the screen. The rest of the kinfolk offer nary a jowly chin wag in acknowledgment.

I arrive at the Hilton as a cowgirl named Felicity. Felicity is eighteen, give or take. She has on a pair of tight denim shorts, a red-checkered blouse unbuttoned low enough to show off the white lace push-up bra she has on beneath. Her hair's in pigtails. Her boots are shit-kicking gorgeous.

The girl is ready for a rodeo. *Yee-haw.*

But when Matt opens his hotel door, he looks disappointed, which pretty much guts me. I spent a minor fortune on this outfit and thought for sure, given our previous hotel theatrics, he'd be up for some riding and rolling.

"What are you doing here, Annie?" he asks bleakly.

"Felicity. Mind if I come in?" I say with a zesty twang. I look past him. The television's on mute, and a half-eaten burger and his ever-present black smoothie cup are on the coffee table.

"No, Annie."

"How about I just come in and sit a spell? You know, keep you company for a little?"

He looks over his shoulder as if someone else is in the room and he's waiting for their response. "Sure," he says in a resigned voice. "But just to talk."

"Got it," I say, gliding in and taking a seat in a chair situated a respectable distance from the bed. "How'd it go today?"

"I killed it," he says, perking up. He then goes on to tell me about the three groups of white middle-aged Republicans he spent the day with, questioning them about the kinds of background music they prefer to listen to while slicing through slabs of prime rib. It's almost as if I never left Gayle's house.

When he finishes speaking, I pull out the strap-on I brought along, waving it slowly in front of him like a hypnotist. *You're getting horny, Matt. So horny.*

"No, Annie." I hear the rattle and clinking of a room service cart making its way down the hallway.

"Felicity."

"Stop."

"I can't."

"You should go, Annie."

"Why?"

"I thought I made it crystal clear. Kate said no more."

"You mean no more *Annie.*"

He shakes his head, looking so sad I have a hankering to hug him, but I stay fixed to the distance between us. "I thought she also said she wants you to fuck other women. Can't we just keep pretending like before?"

"Annie—"

"Come on. You know you want to get pegged, dude." I drop the dildo onto the rug and pluck a cold french fry off his plate.

He shifts his gaze to the silicone schlong splayed out on the floor. He says nothing, but I can tell there's a United Nations-sized debate raging inside both his brain and balls. "No, I don't," he says finally. "It was a nice thought, though."

"Plenty more where that came from."

"You've gotta go, Annie. I'm sorry you flew here just for—"

"I didn't come for you, Matt. Clay's sister lives here, and Terra wanted to visit her cousins." I don't want him thinking my life decisions revolve around him, even though they do.

Nodding, as if my familial excuse makes perfect sense, he

walks over to the large rain-stained window that looks out across the flat Texan cityscape and pulls the curtains closed. "I'm gonna take a shower and hit the sack. We've got three groups tomorrow. I don't know if it's the burger or what, but I'm not feeling that hot."

I retrieve the toy and stuff it back in my bag. "So, this is it then?"

"Yup."

"Friends?" I say, extending my hand.

Ignoring my hand he yanks my cowgirl body to him, hugging me close. "This has been one crazy fucking ride, Annie."

"True dat," I say, breathing in his sweat, his pheromones. The smell of grease.

"If there was a way to keep everyone happy—I don't know, I'd . . . yeah."

"You'd uh, what?"

He leans his forehead down to mine. "You're an amazing woman and I'm going to miss you." Then Matt kisses me gently—like he's never kissed me before. "Now do me a favor, Felicity, and mosey home."

I get out but know I am not done.

When I arrive back at the compound and tell Terra we're heading out, she begs me to let her stay for a few more days. I ponder the notion and decide it's actually a splendid idea. If I am going to bring my plan to completion, it is best I do it sans child.

With Matt's words echoing through all four chambers of my heart, I get online and book a flight for tomorrow morning. Matt needs to figure out his life, and it is high time I clear away any confusion.

KATE

Heidi pulls her smelly van into our driveway and shuts off the engine. I lower the window all the way so I don't have to continue breathing in the stink of wet fur.

"You have no idea how much I needed that. Thank you for listening," I say, resting my elbow out the window. Behind me a herd of filthy dogs is scattered across the passenger seats, panting from exhaustion. Two of them, including Munch, are sound asleep.

I spent the entire walk this afternoon telling Heidi about what's been going on between Matt and Annie. Or most of what happened. It was enough to get her so riled up she didn't even holler at her dogs for rolling in mud puddles.

"Nothing like a long pack walk to clear the head," Heidi says as I gather my stuff to leave. "I'll tell you though, Kate, I'm worried about you." She pats me on my thigh.

"Don't be. I'll be fine," I try, hoping that by saying the words, they'll be true.

"Kate, I'm afraid this is going to—" Heidi turns in her seat and yells, "Stop licking your dick, Angus! Dude, that's disgusting!" Angus looks up at Heidi for a beat, then goes back to licking. "Seriously, Kate, this is gonna get ugly."

"You're probably right."

"What are we going to do about that bitch?"

"I have no idea. What I do know is that I won't let her raise Finley."

"Like I said before, get yourself a good lawyer."

"I need Annie Meyers gone is what I need, but it's not like I can run her out of town."

"Why don't you just shoot her? I'll let you borrow my gun," Heidi states without an ounce of sarcasm.

I pout. "I wish I had it in me."

"Bullshit, Kate. You absolutely have it in you!" She stares at me expectantly as if waiting for me to agree that I am capable of deliberately hurting someone. I gaze at my house, picturing Annie on our doorstep, holding mason jars filled with Good-Love tea. "I told you she makes these herbal teas, right?"

Heidi nods.

"Well, they taste really strong, like dirt."

"Yeah?"

"She always puts agave in hers, to sweeten it."

"What are you getting at?"

"You said antifreeze is sweet."

Heidi shouts, "That's brilliant!" while applauding.

At the sound of her clapping, a few of the dogs wake up and start barking.

"Except, um, how exactly are you going to spike it without her knowing? Do you plan to invite her over for a tea party?"

I glance down and check my watch. Finley should be getting dropped off any minute.

"Wait! Oh no!" I scream. "It's Friday. I was supposed to get Finley from camp!" I push open the door and run out, stop on the front lawn, go back, pull my purse off the front seat, reach in and find my phone. My hands are shaking as I dial the camp. "How could I be so stupid" As it rings, I tell myself to calm down. Finley is probably still waiting for me. Why didn't the camp call?

"Hello? Hi. This is Kate Burke, Finley Parsons's mom. I'm so sorry I completely forgot to pick her up—what? She—*who*? But I didn't have her listed as—never mind. Thank you."

I jump back in the van, slam the door, and lock eyes with Heidi.

"Annie has her," I say. "Let's go."

"It's the red house. Pull into the driveway."

"I don't get it," Heidi says as she puts the van in park. "I thought she was in Texas with Matt."

Ignoring her, I rush to the front door and turn the handle. It's locked. I knock twice. Ring the bell. Coming up beside me on the porch, Heidi says, "Maybe they made a mistake and it wasn't Annie who got her."

I run back to the van and grab my purse with all my keys. "Finley's here, I can feel it."

Opening the door, I race in, Heidi following close behind.

They are playing in the pool together, with Finley perched upon Annie's shoulders, wobbling and laughing as she tries to balance herself. A second later she tumbles into the water.

"Stay here, Heidi!" I insist, rushing out the back door.

When Finley surfaces and sees me, she hollers, "Mommy!"

I am furious but do not wish to scare my child. "Finley, what are you doing here?"

"Hello, Kate." Annie bobs up and down in the water and greets me with a friendly wave. Her long hair is plastered to her head, framing her tanned face. She's wearing a navy blue speedo suit that shows off her strong shoulder muscles. She's the picture of health and I hate her all the more for it.

"Why didn't you wait for me to come get you, Finley?" I look around, confused. "Where's Terra?"

"She's in Texas," replies Annie.

The last time I saw Annie in this pool she was getting pounded by my husband. At least now she is wearing a bathing suit. Dressed or not, she's screwing with my whole family.

"Who gave you permission to—?"

"The camp lady called you, Mommy!" Finley shouts as she splashes water this way and that. "But you didn't answer. Then she called Daddy, and *he* didn't answer so I told them to call Annie because I forgot she was in Texas, but then she wasn't—so please don't be mad because I didn't want to wait there anymore."

Annie shrugs. "You forgot her."

"I did *not* forget you, Finley!" I say, lying to my child. "I was on a walk where there was no cell service and—never mind. Finley, get out of the pool. Let's go."

"I did swing by your house, Kate, but no one was home, so I figured we'd go for a quick swim." Annie speaks to me as if nothing weird is happening. "What's the problem?"

You're the problem, Annie.

"Finley. I said let's go! Now!" Before she makes it to the top of the ladder, I squeeze her arm and jerk her the rest of the way out of the water.

"Ouch. You pinched me."

"I'm sorry. Wait for me inside. Heidi's in there." When she's out of earshot, I grasp the ladder, arching my trembling body over the water. "Annie, stay away from my child."

She stares at me confused, as if I just spoke to her in Farsi. "I was only trying to help, Kate. I don't know what you're so upset about."

I'm upset that you want to steal my family from me. That's what I'm upset about. "Finley is not your child, Annie, and she never will be. Am I making myself perfectly clear?"

Annie shrugs again. "Crystal. Except what I don't get," she says, dunking under and coming up again, "is why you're so angry. Although I've gotta admit you're incredibly beautiful when you're angry."

"Why I'm—" I have no idea where to start. "You put Terra in camp with Finley when I expressly asked—"

"It's not the same camp—not technically."

"You pretended not to know Matt. You're a liar, Annie. You're evil."

Annie's face drops. "Granted, I slept with your husband, but you let him sleep with other women all the time, Kate. Why are you singling me out as the evil one?"

"I know what you're up to, Annie. I'm not blind." I come close to telling Annie about seeing her and Matt having sex in this very pool, but I'm saving that big reveal for the divorce papers. "You pretended you wanted to be my friend just to—"

"I didn't need to be your friend to keep seeing Matt. I wanted to be your friend, Kate. I still want to."

What I want to do is jump into the pool and hold Annie underwater until the bubbles stop rising. "Just . . . just stay away from us," I say, running back inside.

ANNIE

I spend the entirety of the flight from Dallas to Burlington raging over Matt's repudiation. So much so that at one point a red-headed flight attendant named Marcia kneels down next to my seat and whispers a stern, "I need you to stop raising your voice. You're upsetting the other passengers."

Minutes after my plane skids to a halt on the tarmac, I turn on my phone and get a distress signal from Finley's camp. Kate forgot to pick up her own kid, they tell me, and could I please come retrieve her?

I grab my car from the parking garage and head south. Mandy, one of the counselors, smiles when she sees me stroll up the lawn to the front office.

"Hi, Ms. Meyers!" She waves a chipper hand toward me. "Why are you here? Terra wasn't at camp today."

"Someone from the camp called, said Finley Parsons needed a ride home." I put my hand out to open the screen door when Mandy's voice stops me.

"I can't let you take her. You're not on the list," she says in a voice less genial than one would expect from a twentysomething maker of merry.

"Why not?"

"Ms. Burke said under no circumstances are we to let Finley go home with you. I'm sorry," she adds with no contrition.

I hear the gears of Mandy's brain grinding as she attempts to decipher just why Kate has christened me persona non grata. "Okay. Well, apparently, Ms. Burke is unreachable at the moment. Hold on."

I text Matt: *Emergency here in Rayburne. Need you to call me ASAP.* I figure this will get his attention, and I am not incorrect.

"What's wrong?" he asks after I answer.

"Your wife forgot to get Finley from camp so I came to get her but they won't let me because I'm not on the list of approved pick-her-uppers."

Matt says nothing for a beat then, "Hold on. You're in Vermont?" he asks, sounding wildly puzzled. "But you were just here—why are you back? Where's Kate?" I half expect him to add, "What have you done with her?"

I don't bother answering his questions. "Can you just do me a favor and tell the counselor who I am standing next to that I have your permission to take Finley home?"

"Yeah, sure. Let me talk to her."

I hand Mandy the phone and watch as her expression changes from disarray to relief. She hangs up, gives me back the phone, and goes to find Finley.

Seeing as I now have a child with me, I change my plans once we hit Rayburne and tell Finley she's coming home with me. She doesn't bat a small eye. After we go into the house, I tell her to grab one of Terra's suits and meet me in the back-yard. I feel hot, annoyed, and dirty. I figure a few laps in a basin of disinfectant should do the trick. I drop my suitcase by the steps, pull out my own bathing suit, and head outside for a quick swim with the kid.

Our fun lasts all of twenty minutes, after which time Kate shows up to chastise me for doing a good deed.

After the berating and her subsequent departure, I swim laps, then go inside to nap. I strip naked and crawl under my covers, whereupon I soon start gasping.

Even after sucking on my inhaler, I cannot breathe.

I barely have enough strength to hit 911, and by the time the ambulance arrives at the hospital, I am in respiratory failure. Thank God the doctors there know their shit. In the ER, they give me oxygen, hook me up to corticosteroids, and after what seems like an eternity, the steady stream of anxious faces recedes, and my lungs calm down.

Once I am stabilized, I call SERVPRO, a biohazard cleaning company, and pay them a king's ransom to sterilize my house. I tell them to treat it as if it'd been hit by a nuclear bomb. I even pay extra for them to flush the air ducts. As I do not wish to freak Terra out while having the time of her life with her raucous cousins, I share nothing with the Texans.

After an Uber picks me up from the hospital and drops me on Dwyer Court I enter my house hesitantly, taking small gulps of air. I roam from room to room, inhaling more deeply with every step. The house is as hygienic as a tattoo parlor after three code violations.

I walk into the kitchen and see that SERVPRO has left me a detailed report on the kitchen counter. When the details reveal that I came close to dying because a canine bacchanalia had taken place in every room of my home, I become more determined than ever to instigate some restorative justice.

KATE

I'm at the supermarket picking up a few things, lost in my turbulent thoughts in the produce section when a voice behind me yells, "Kate Burke!"

Startled, I drop an overly ripe tomato onto the floor, where it explodes, spraying red juice everywhere. I look up.

"Suzanne. You scared me," I say.

"All I did was say your name, silly."

I laugh nervously. "Look what a mess I made." I fumble through my purse and find a packet of tissues. "I'm so sorry," I say, offering Suzanne the pack.

Suzanne plucks out two tissues and hands the pack back to me. "Don't worry about it." As if in a trance I watch her wipe tomato pulp from her ankles. When she stands back up Suzanne gestures downward. "It's all over you too, you know."

"What?" I laugh again. "Silly me," I utter. I lean over and start to wipe the juice off my lower leg, but all I see is spattered blood. I straighten and prop my elbow against the cart. I smile, hoping Suzanne doesn't notice.

"Are you all right, Kate?" She's staring at me, concerned. "You're really pale. Maybe you have the flu?"

"Maybe I do." I touch my forehead as if I am feeling feverish. She doesn't need to know my world is spinning out of control and I am holding on for dear life.

"Something bad is going around. You heard about my neighbor, right?"

"The loud one who was having the pool party?"

"Yeah, her."

"No. What happened?" I try to sound only mildly interested, but inside my chest my heartbeat accelerates.

"I'm not sure, but she—" A voice jumps on the PA system and announces a phone call for the seafood department. Suzanne takes a breath and is about to continue when Michelle Ryan, another tedious Rayburnite, slows her cart to a stop next to ours. Dressed in skin-hugging workout attire and holding a giant bottle of bright orange liquid, she obviously is just coming from a fitness class. Her skin glistens with sweat but her makeup remains perfect. How do I live in this world? Are these women my friends?

"Hey, you two," says Michelle with a cutesy nose wrinkle. "How's it going?"

"Hi, Michelle," I mumble.

"Did you just do yoga?" Suzanne asks.

"Not hardly. I'm into Barre now. Have you tried it?"

Suzanne shakes her head. "I was just telling Kate about my next-door neighbor being hauled away in an ambulance last night."

"Is she okay?" *Or did I kill her?*

"I have no idea. I was putting my recycling out and a fire truck pulled up, then an ambulance came, and they all rushed into her house. I don't know, maybe ten minutes later, they brought her out on a stretcher."

"She's going to survive," Michelle states.

Suzanne and I both look at her.

"How do you—" Before I finish my question, the answer comes to me: Michelle's husband is an ER doctor. Michelle clasps her hands, wriggles her shoulders, and glances around. "I'm not supposed to say anything because of, you know, HIPAA and all . . . " She raises her left hand and waves us closer to her like she's the Queen allowing us entry into her realm. I move in, transfixed by the alarmingly large diamond on her finger. I can smell her sweat. It smells like clean money. I make a mental note to add that to my description of Audrey, then focus back on Michelle who says, "Marc was on call last night. Annie Meyers was brought in with—shoot—what did he say?"

"Respiratory distress?" I let slip.

They stare at me. "That's it. How'd you know?" Michelle raises a leery eyebrow as Suzanne adds, "You just said you didn't know what happened."

"She has terrible asthma. She told me she's been hospitalized because of it before. I'm just guessing, you know . . ."

They both nod. "Oh. So, anyway," Michelle continues, "Marc said it was pretty serious. Her lungs were completely . . ." I listen long enough to know Annie is lucky to be alive.

For now, she is.

KATE

"Time for bed," I say, removing the book from Finley's hands.

Finley grabs it back. "Oh come on. All I have is camp tomorrow. Let me keep reading."

"It's late," I say, flopping on the couch and putting her feet on my lap. "How about I give you until 8:30?"

Finley grunts her acceptance and continues reading while I rub her feet and stare at nothing. Munch comes through the dog door and jumps onto the couch, paws it once, then curls into a ball, his body heat rippling through my left hip. This is what our future will look like. No more marathon rounds of UNO with Matt doing his crazy "I won!" dance around the living room. No more nights cuddled in front of a Disney movie, our daughter stretched between us.

Is it better to have a lying husband and father than no husband and father?

Until recently the idea of Matt being gone from our lives would have killed me, but I feel differently now. I don't have to be tied to a marriage that isn't what I thought it was.

I think back to the night not so long ago when I scolded

Finley for saying how lucky Terra was to have only one parent bossing her around. I was appalled when she insisted Annie and Terra said they were better off without Clayton because now they could be as free as birds. Now I get it. If only I could figure out a way to continue being a bestselling writer without Matt.

Finley yawns, and I shift away from these self-absorbed thoughts. "I thought you decided to read all the Harry Potter books this summer," I say, noting the book cover. "What happened?"

"I'm still on the third one, but it's in my backpack," she says, her face hidden by the cover of Philip Pullman's *The Golden Compass.*

"And you're too lazy to get up and get it?" I laugh.

"I left it at Annie's."

I stop laughing.

"Don't worry, Mommy. When Terra comes home from Texas, she can bring it to camp." The way she speaks makes it clear she's thought this through. She is protecting her mother.

Thinking of my daughter's belongings in that house incenses me.

I slide her legs off me and am about to get up to make myself tea when Matt comes out of his office. He was supposed to have stayed in Dallas for another two days, but flew back today because he felt like he was coming down with something. Now he's both pale and flushed.

"Finley, don't go near Daddy," I demand. "I don't want you catching whatever he has."

Finley looks up from her book and pouts. "Are you really sick, Daddy?"

"I'm doing fine, kiddo," he says, flashing her a bright smile. He walks into the kitchen, puts his smoothie cup down, and slumps forward onto the counter. "I don't know what's wrong.

Jeez." He keeps his voice low, out of Finley's hearing range. "I feel lousy, Kate, really nauseous."

"Did you take your temperature?"

"Yeah. 98.6," he says, dragging himself over to the kitchen table. He flops down onto a chair so laboriously it's as if he's just returned from a long run. "Think maybe you can whip me up a health smoothie? I'm hurting."

I can see that he's hurting, though he has no idea how much I'm hurting too—stung by his lies and deception. He is unaware of the resentful rage building within me. I was hoping to have the papers filled out and filed before he came home. I wanted them signed and sealed before I delivered the coup de grace. Matt's early return from Dallas means I'll have to make nice for a little while longer. I'll bide my time, be merciful, and not kick him while he's down.

"I'll add ginger," I tell him, "to help with the nausea."

"Thanks, babe. You're the best." He pushes himself up. "I'm gonna go hide out in my office and see if I can get some work done."

"You do that," I say, smiling. I take the NutriBullet off the shelf and start throwing in as many healthy ingredients as I can find. I insert the cup into the power base and watch the sharp metal blades pulverize the solids into liquid. I pour it into Matt's smoothie cup and twist it closed.

See this, Annie? I think as I carry it over to Matt's office. *You're not the only one who knows how to brew magical elixirs.*

KATE

Early the next morning Matt flings open my office door, comes over to my desk, and slams his hand down with a bang. "I don't know what you've been putting in my smoothies, Kaybee, but holy shit, I feel great!"

He wears a pair of green running shorts and a black San Francisco Museum of Modern Art T-shirt. He's almost glowing.

"You know, a little of this, a little of that." I grin.

"Yeah, well, whatever it was, keep 'em coming. My body is on fire. I have so much energy, I feel like I can run a marathon!"

"Is that your plan right now?"

He laughs. "No."

"Hey, you know what? You should run the Rayburne Loop." The Rayburne Loop, at just over eight very hilly miles, skirts the entire town.

"I haven't run that far in ages."

"But you were just bragging that you have tons of energy. But yeah," I say, frowning. "I guess that run is probably too hard."

I watch him contemplate it. "You're right. I can run it. I know I can."

That's my husband; always up for a challenge.

Matt aims his dazzling smile my way. "So, if you don't need anything from me, *Daphne*, I'm going to get going while the going is good."

I lean back in my chair and our eyes connect. He has no idea how generous I'm being, allowing him to experience such unfettered joy before I snatch it away.

"I do want something from you, Matthew. Now that you're no longer sick, I would very much like a kiss." I beam a wide toothy smile his way. "You owe me one, darling."

He whips around the desk, pushes his hand into my hair, and pulls my head back. Staring into my eyes, he says, "Gladly, Kaybee," before leaning down and kissing me passionately. As his tongue moves around my mouth I hear my brain tell me to sink into his love and desire.

Ultimately, it's my body that makes the final decision. "Thank you for that," I say tenderly pushing him off.

Matt is unaware of the significance of that kiss. He walks over to the door and is about to leave when I make one last inquiry, "Did you, um, happen to get together with anyone in Dallas? Before you got sick?" I'm positive Annie showed up there, probably as someone named Alicia or Ainsley or who knows. I need a new sex scene.

"Sorry, Kate. I'm done being your lab rat. See you later," he says, closing the door behind him.

So be it.

ANNIE

I'm at home, filling in the vacuum of cleanliness with my own mess by whipping up a fresh batch of hummus when someone knocks on the door. I open it and see Kate. She's wearing her customary pair of baggy jeans that hides her hot ass and an oversized University of Vermont sweatshirt. It's a shame the woman never lets her body out in public.

"Hello Miss Kate, mother of Finley. What a pleasant surprise." It's obvious my joy throws her a little because she flinches as if I'd spit on her.

"Finley left her backpack here last week," she says accusingly, as if it's my fault her child was too busy getting yanked out of my pool to remember she'd brought over a backpack.

"She did?" I ask, feigning surprise. "Bummer."

"Can I please have it?"

"Sure you can, but I just had the house sanitized, so I have no idea where it is," I say, though I clearly remember stashing it in the hall closet under a pile of Terra's shoes. "Why don't you come in and help me look for it?"

She hesitates for a second then waltzes past my extended

arm, strides into the kitchen, and props herself against the granite island.

Being as I was raised by a woman who wouldn't let me eat
dinner until I wrote thank you cards to every fifth grader who
attended my birthday party, I ask, "Can I get you something
to drink?"

"No, thank you," she replies, but then I see her wipe her
hand across her brow. "Actually, I'd love some water."

"I have something even better," I say, opening the refrigerator. "It's a new blend I made. It's kind of sweet, but I think
you'll like it."

I pour some for each of us. "Cheers."

She looks at the tea, then at me. Only after I take a small
swig does she take a sip of hers. "This is delicious. It tastes kind
of floral. Totally different than GoodLove. What do you call
this one?"

"TerraTea."

"Cute." She takes another sip. "I, uh, heard from your neighbor you were in the hospital," she says innocently enough.

"Yup. I was."

"Was it because of your asthma?"

"Yeah. Crazy thing, huh? One minute I'm swimming laps,
and the next thing I know it feels like someone's got a pillow
over my face and they're smothering me to death."

"That must have been pretty scary."

"Oh yeah," I say, "but, honestly, the food they served was
the scariest part."

Kate lets loose a weak laugh.

"I gotta say, Kate, that was pretty fucked up of you," I state,
getting the ball rolling, "but given all I've put you through, I'm
totally willing to forgive and forget."

"I don't know what you're talking about."

"Really?" I hoist myself up onto the counter and grin. "Hey, the house got washed. My lungs are working again. It's all good."

Then I bark.

"You know?" Kate asks. Shock and guilt swarm her face like a frenzied hive of bees.

"Yes, Kate. I know that you let that mutt of yours dry hump every square inch of my house." And then because I like the sound of my own voice, I recite, "'Thus says she, if you refuse to let my husband go, behold, I will smite your territory with dogs.'"

A blank stare.

"Exodus? The ten plagues?"

Still nothing.

"Never mind," I reply. It's a wonder more people don't read the Bible.

Kate moves over to the window and stares out. "I'm sorry about what happened."

I jump down and stand next to her. The moment I look outside, a bluebird lands on the metal pool ladder and that last excellent fuck Matt and I had in the water flashes before my eyes. Before I allow myself to get too lost in the memory, I tell Kate that I forgive her and, to drive the point home—and also because I am such a fan of irony—I add, "Remember what Buddha said: 'Holding onto anger is like drinking poison and expecting the other person to die.'"

"What?"

"I forgive you," I repeat, gently placing an arm around my friend Kate's shoulder.

"Don't," she says, shaking it off as if I were contaminated. "Just go find Finley's pack so I can get out of here."

"Aye, Captain Burke," I reply like Scotty in *Star Trek*, waiting a beat to see if she gets the reference. She does not (too bad because it's a damn good one). I shrug, then saunter into the living room and pour the contents of my glass into the potted palm before kneeling down on the floor, pretending to look under the coffee table. Kate appears a second later holding her almost-empty glass and leans against the French door, watching me. I can hear her respiration start to pick up.

TerraTea is working its magic.

"I think I need to lie down on your couch for a minute," she says. "I don't feel so well."

"What you need is fresh air," I say, jumping up and taking her by the arm. "I think the cleaners sprayed too many chemicals or something, because I'm feeling a little dizzy myself. Let's go out back."

"No. That's okay. Maybe I should—" She attempts to move toward the front door, but I catch her hand and lead her outside, where she flops down on the grass like a rag doll.

"What's wrong, Kate?" I ask with as much sympathy as I can muster.

"I don't know," she says feebly. "I'm suddenly getting these weird head rushes."

I sit down next to her and peer into her face. "Take a few deep breaths. Good. Another one. There you go."

She opens her eyes to look at me. "What was in that tea, Annie?"

"Herbs, my friend. Nothing but herbs. Take a few more deep breaths for me."

"What kind of herbs?"

"Um, let's see. There's yohimbe bark, of course. A couple of other things. Oh, and I threw in some shrooms."

"In Terra's tea? You put shrooms in—?"

"Terra's tea. Yeah, right." I snicker. "I wouldn't let Terra get within ten millimeters of that stuff."

"You know you're sick in the head, Annie. You're a sick evil mon—" Before she has the chance to tell me what else I am the pool pump starts to screech. The pool guy said the bearings are shot and I should replace them ASAP, but hey, we've all got priorities. I walk over to the shed and open it. I'm sure there's some on/off switch somewhere, but it's just as easy (and far more exhilarating) to bash the timer in with a rock.

Once I achieve silence again I turn back to see Kate on her all-fours, futilely trying to stand up. When I see how much she's struggling to catch her breath, I almost utter, "See? Now you know what you put me through," but I hold back because why kick a gift horse in her mouth?

Plenty of folks take yohimbe to improve their sex lives. But most people ingest it only once or twice, not every day for two months! That's way too dangerous. That much yohimbe is apt to cause super high blood pressure and liver damage, along with numerous other small but potentially deadly side effects.

If a person—Kate, for example—happens to have a whole lot of yohimbe flowing through their system, they should at all costs avoid consuming *other* substances that might cause rapid heart rate and acute hypertension. Consuming such substances might lead to, who knows—stroke? fainting? sudden death? It doesn't matter which, because any of them would prove satisfactory.

"I'm leaving Matt." Kate can hardly get the words past her lips. "You. Can. Have. Him."

"But I already do have him, Kate!" I cry. "I knew he was going to be mine after the second time we *hooked up*. The first time, *whoa*, I mean that husband of yours sure can fuck, you know? Oh, I'm sorry—" I squat down and lift her chin so she can see my face. "You *don't* know, do you?"

I go over to the pool ladder and balance my body on the metal bars. "You know, it's too bad Matt never told you about the time we fucked in this pool," I remark while playfully swinging my legs back and forth. "That scene alone would have won you a Pulitzer, *Daphne Moore.*"

"Our marriage is over," she says, now panting like a dog.

"Sorry," I say, sadly, "but it ain't over till the skinny bitch is dead."

Kate urges one of her feet under her. "You're insane, and I hope you rot in hell for what you've done." And then, just like that, she pushes up to vertical.

It's common knowledge that when one gets up as quickly as she does, gravity will pull about a quarter of the body's blood supply into the lower body, forcing the heart to respond with enough pressure to keep blood pumping to the brain. If said heart is way too speeded up—perhaps because one has *also* just drunk down a concentrated dose of licorice, bitter orange, country mallow, and a little psilocybin thrown in for good measure—one would, at the very least, faint. Which Kate does the moment she stands up. I stroll over and roll her into the pool.

All that swinging and berating and killing have completely tuckered me out so I go inside and head upstairs for a nap. I strip down naked and collapse onto the bed, but before I drift off I decide my victory deserves a celebratory orgasm. With what toy, I wonder, opening my night table drawer. My eyes roam across the myriad colors and shapes and vibratory offerings until they alight on a 7-inch purple dildo. I pull it out and hold it up to the ceiling, picturing Kate's body bumping up against the purple pool noodle Terra likes to hang on.

I place the dong between my legs and close my eyes.

I wake to the sound of a faraway ringtone. Pushing through the confusion from a most chimerical sleep, I sit up and try to get my bearings. I see that I'm naked.

Isn't there something I'm supposed to do?

Oh yeah, Kate. At some point I'll need to pull Kate out and pretend to perform CPR so the paramedics and cops don't get suspicious when I call them in hysterics over finding my friend floating in my pool. I roll off the bed, throw on my underwear, and go downstairs. My phone is again ringing. I find it, of all places, under the coffee table.

I grab it and say, "Hello?"

"Hi, Annie. It's Kate."

"Who?" I run into the kitchen and look out the back window. Isn't that Kate's body out there, floating?

"Hey, so two policemen were waiting for me when I got home. Matt collapsed while he was out on a run."

"What? I—" Am I still asleep? Am I having another episode? I squeeze my eyes shut then open them. Kate's body is not there. It's just the fucking purple pool noodle.

What is happening? Where is Kate?

Oh, yeah, she's on the phone. And she's saying something about Matt . . . Matt running . . . Matt collapsing . . . . The police . . . I try to absorb what she's saying, try to focus.

"Is he okay?" I ask.

"No, Annie. He had a heart attack. He's dead."

This can't be right. Kate is dead. Matt is mine.

"We're all so shocked. But listen, the medical examiner said he's willing to perform a more thorough forensic autopsy if I want him to. Do you think I should let him?"

"What medical examiner? What are you asking me?" Which Kate is fucking with my brain: Dead Kate or Live Kate? I can't tell them apart.

"If they test his blood, Annie, they'll discover Matt's system has dangerously high levels of yohimbe and maybe even some other lethal herbs, who knows?" she says, gentle as a lamb.

"Obviously I'll have to tell them about your tea." She laughs a strange laugh, an empty laugh. It doesn't sound like any Kate I've heard before. "I bet the police would be interested to learn about Clayton's autopsy results too. What a weird coincidence: I mean *two* perfectly healthy men dying from cardiac edema. Both of whom drank your tea."

As Kate coos these words, I imagine myself melting, mutating into a measly spit bug. I am afraid to look up because I know I will see a monster-sized blond-haired woman with a fuzzy slipper raised above my head, ready to squash me into eternity.

KATE

I've been sitting in the world's most uncomfortable folding chair on and off now for over four hours. When Heidi called last month to ask if we wanted to volunteer at the "Make A Dog's Day Fest" at Stockwell Farms, I'd said, "Of course. What do you need us to do?"

This morning started out chilly and overcast, but now the skies are clear and the early autumn sun is warm enough that most of the people strolling around the large field next to the cheesemaking barn have their jackets and sweatshirts tied around their waists.

A young couple approaches the caged enclosure next to Heidi's booth. Heidi has more than twenty dogs at her house that she needs to find homes for, but since she couldn't bring all of them to the festival, she chose six long-termers.

We watch as the woman points to Jake, a large shepherd mix, then says something to her friend. Heidi stays sitting, patiently waiting until, finally, the woman makes eye contact with her.

A second later Heidi's up. "Are you interested in Jake?" she asks enthusiastically. "You should take him for a walk, get to know him. Here, let me get you a leash."

I've already lost count of how many people have stopped by her booth to meet the dogs, and, more importantly, to fill out the "I Want To Adopt" form. I smile, thrilled that Heidi's Haven is getting so much attention.

It might have something to do with the fact that adopting a dog from Heidi is not only free, but also comes with a lifetime supply of dog food and medical care, paid for by me. That, plus the enormous visually-stunning metal sign I commissioned a local design firm to make. It definitely is the classiest sign at the fest and it sure beats the hand-painted cardboard poster Heidi planned to use. When Heidi first saw it, her jaw dropped.

"This must have cost a fortune!" she exclaimed through her excitement.

It did, but these days I have more than enough to spare—courtesy of the last novel I wrote.

I began writing it after finally finishing *Strong Lust: The Taste of Her*. I barely managed to fill in my PLACEHOLDER scenes, modifying Matt's less tantalizing anecdotes, but I did manage to plow through, determined as I was to give Lizzie and Macon their Happily Ever After. Once Miles and Arthur got wind of Audrey's villainy, they bought out her share and handed over full control of Smiling Girl Cheese Shop to Macon. Naturally, Lizzie became the store's manager.

I reshaped PI Gabriel into a sexier character for Audrey's benefit. When, at the end of the book, Harland Mansfield goes missing under suspicious circumstances, Audrey and Gabriel join forces to track him down.

Two days after I sent the finished manuscript off to Amatory Press, I was ready to write the book I was destined to write: *The Widow on Dwyer Court*, a domestic thriller about the friendship between Greta Sorenson, a sex-averse erotica writer who uses her sex-loving husband Jeffrey as her muse; and Bea Holt, a sociopathic herbalist who moves to their neighborhood and threatens Greta's livelihood—and her life. In my novel, Bea dies.

Not only did the debut novel written by "Kate Burke" make the *New York Times* bestseller list, Netflix bought the film rights and is adapting it into a series. Like I said to Matt long ago, murder stories *are* sexy.

Finley is standing next to a boy by the Lucky Paws Dog Rescue booth. She's got one hand in her pocket and the other is holding the leash of Billy, a pit bull mix Heidi asked her to walk.

When I was in sixth grade, like she is now, I was more interested in books than boys but Finley is already bubbling with adolescent longings. She must have inherited her father's amorous genes. She definitely wants boys to be aware of her, to see her. But she's not quite sure what to make of them, or what they are good for.

There will come a time in the not-too-distant future when I will have to help her answer those questions.

It's taken time, but at last I've embraced who I am and how I am, sexually speaking. I believe we humans are born with specific genetic codes, and however much society, social media, or friends try to push us in any one direction, we are already pre-programmed. We don't *choose* what turns us on. We have no idea who or what is going to move us, but there it is.

Writing turns me on. This much I know.

In the last two years, I've developed a stronger sense of self and will do my best to model self-empowerment for my daughter. She will see that just because you love someone, you must not let them shape who you are or who you might be.

I will teach Finley to hold tight to her truth, and to be proud of her own authentic self.

I look at my phone and yell over to my friend. "Heidi, I've got to get to an appointment."

"Fine," she says, a little disappointed. "Are you taking the girls with you?"

Terra walks up to Finley and hands her an ice cream cone. Finley hugs her and then blushes as she introduces her to the boy she's talking to. "No. They should stay and help you pack everything up. Do you mind dropping them off?"

Heidi throws a dog biscuit at me. "As if. God, Kate. I would do anything for you."

After I take a hot shower and wash the dog off me, I realize I still have time to kill so I go into my office. I pick up the hardcover version of my novel from my desk and rub my hand across its smooth surface. I smell it.

I open the cover and turn to the dedication page.

For Matthew. I miss you every day.

It didn't take my being a biology major to figure out that the botanicals in the tea Annie continued to ply me with were the same ones she'd used to murder her husband Clayton. Once I saw the coroner's report I realized Annie was also trying to kill me, so I stopped drinking it. I only pretended to drink her "TerraTea" the day I went over to get Finley's backpack. As soon as Annie left the room, I spilled most of it down the drain.

Truly, I hadn't planned to mess with Annie, but after that first odd-tasting sip, something in me snapped: I thought, *I'm going to have some fun fucking with her. See what she tries to do to me.* What a blast I had, making believe I was so dizzy I could hardly move. And oh dear, was I ever having trouble breathing!

After I feigned passing out, she dragged me to the edge of the pool. For my own amusement I tried to be as heavy and cumbersome as possible. After she finally managed to roll me into the water, I stayed inert, holding my breath for quite a while, a skill I learned from all my years as a swimmer. When I couldn't hold it any longer, I made tiny turns with my head, catching a quick breath and checking to see if she was in sight.

I gave it another five full minutes before getting out and driving myself home.

Two police officers were waiting for me on my front lawn, talking into their radios. They'd tried calling me, they said, to tell me that my husband had been found by a runner on the Rayburne Trail.

I motioned to my dripping wet self. "My phone fell in a pool," I'd replied, working hard to stifle my grin.

The best part of all this was letting Annie think she'd won; that she'd taken everything from me—my life, my husband, my child—and then ripping it all away from her.

Not since giving birth to Finley had I ever known such joy.

When Annie first gave me the GoodLove tea to help my libido, she'd warned me not to drink it if I had high blood pressure. Oddly enough, Matt had only that very week been diagnosed with hereditary hypertension and handed a prescription for beta blockers: tiny white pills he more often than not forgot to take. It was a beautiful coincidence.

Which is why I kept that last jar of tea Annie brought over. Just in case.

Just in case Matthew Parsons, the pathetic, sex-obsessed, narcissistic, two-faced dirtbag of a human being lied to me one more time.

Don't get me wrong. I'm thankful for all my husband did to help me find my writer's voice. To make my initial mark in the erotica market.

I am even more grateful that I no longer need him.

I shut the book and drop it onto the desk.

GoodLove, indeed.

I grab my keys and head out. I park in front of the house and walk up to the door. I knock. She opens the door.

"Kate, I wasn't expecting you until tomorrow. I literally just got home."

"I'm aware." I walk past her into the living room and sit on the couch. "I tracked your flight."

"Can I get you something to drink? You want tea?" Annie asks, grinning ever so slightly.

"No. Just come here. Sit down. How was Phoenix?"

I can see she's tired, but Daphne Moore doesn't give a fuck. Annie does as I ask, sitting in the chair across from the couch. "Phoenix was great," she says with a sly smile.

"Did you meet anyone?"

She raises her eyebrows. "I met a smoking hot insurance salesman named Garrett."

"Awesome," I say, pulling a notebook and pen out of my purse. "Tell me everything."

ACKNOWLEDGMENTS

I began writing *The Widow on Dwyer Court* back in 2017, but, as is so often the case, some not-so-trivial life circumstances kept me from seeing the novel through to the end page. I'm thrilled that now, at last, Kate and Annie—who've been talking to me nonstop for all these years—are finally getting to share their stories with you, most precious reader.

Making sure this book saw the light of day required a writer of one, supported by a crew of many. First and foremost, I want to thank my tenacious agent Stacey Donaghy whose unbridled enthusiasm and long-distance camaraderie kept my creative fires burning through the dark winter days and nights. There was never so much as a twinkle of doubt in Stacey's eye. As a writer who often questions everything and everyone, I am forever grateful for Stacey's belief in me.

During much of the time my characters took up residence in my head and home, I could not help but talk to friends and family about the developing tale. It's what writers do when they perchance stand up from their desks and walk out into the real world. To these folks I want to say, "Thank you for listening.

For reading early drafts, later drafts, and even later drafts. Thank you for the probing questions and the not-so-subtle criticisms. Thank you for filling in the blanks about subjects I didn't know enough about. Your help was invaluable." In no particular order, thank you, Rebecca Ramos, Amy Luoma Duganne, David Rensin, Karin Roberts, Debbie Hodapp, Margot Harrison, Janet Cohen, Lela Emad, Sherie Maddox, Marc Kusel, Debora Llontop, Susannah Kerest, Priya Doraswamy, Nancy Bercaw, Susan Nance, Sheila Matheson Kerr, Kim Dauerman, Anne Page McClard, Victor Prussack, Jamie Sumner, Darien Gee, Candice Sawchuk, Tawnya Pell, Andrea Hope, Ariel Lewis, Jenny Mary Brown, and Loy Prussack.

Thank you, Dana Isaacson, for your editing prowess: sure, we fought a bit, but, in the end, you are the reason this book shines. Thank you for your sensitivities and sensibilities, and for making sure all the pieces fit together just so.

If I was up to making the six-hour car journey, I'd drive down to New York City and hand a huge bouquet of flowers to Marilyn Kretzer and every other person on the marketing, publicity, and publishing teams at Blackstone Publishing. Thank you, one and all, for helping to make this book a reality and being an absolute pleasure to work with.

I'd like to give a huge shout-out to everyone and anyone who buys, borrows, steals (as in the case of my uncle), checks out, downloads, listens to, reads, reviews, and posts about all things books.

And finally, I am grateful to the person who pushed me out into the world and who never, ever stopped thinking I was a miracle. I so, so wish you could have read the final draft, Mom. I miss you.